FREE RALPH!

An Evolutionary Fable

Stephen Wing

*Wind
Eagle
Press*

FREE RALPH!
An Evolutionary Fable

ISBN-13: 978-0-9793907-0-8
ISBN-10: 0-9793907-0-2

Wind Eagle Press
P.O. Box 5379
Atlanta GA 31107
www.WindEaglePress.com

Attention Corporations, Universities, Colleges,
Professional and Nonprofit Organizations:
Quantity discounts are available on bulk purchases of this book
for educational and gift purposes, or as premiums for membership
or subscription renewals. Special books or book excerpts can also
be created to fit specific needs. For information, contact
Wind Eagle Press at the address above.

PRINTED ON 30% POST-CONSUMER RECYCLED PAPER

Comments from Advance Readers . . .

"**FREE RALPH!** asks us adults to indulge what every child knows: there is a simple and authentic wisdom in animals that we all could learn from. With childlike pleasure I turned each page and didn't want the book to end. I salute Wing for opening such a creative angle and look forward to the sequel *and* the movie. Great work!"

—*Melanie Carlone, MPT, physical therapist*

"A fun adventure novel sure to appeal to action, animal and nature lovers of all ages. Wing's moving story about Ralph expresses sophisticated environmental concepts with a light, experienced touch and showcases the delightful possibility of rediscovering our human relationship with nature."

—*Glenn Carroll, artist & activist*

"I love **FREE RALPH!**— staying up past my bedtime to finish it, which is most unusual for me and a tribute to you for creating a really delightful, fresh, entertaining, and yet very thought-provoking book. . . . I became emotionally and philosophically titillated by the story and impressed by how smoothly you wove it."

—*Sharon Williams, teacher*

"An excellent story which I thoroughly enjoyed . . . The author is adept at weaving several seemingly disparate narratives together in support of what is, in my opinion, the central message of the book— that we are all, humans, non-humans and in-humans, connected through the original world wide web, that of the biosphere itself!"

—*Bill Fleming, guitarist & geographer*

"**FREE RALPH!** moves smoothly and develops dramatic tension well . . . A touching and deep story with profound implications about how we live our lives here on this Earth."

—*David Wheeler, writer & environmentalist*

"As fate, faith, family, and loyalty entwine and tug at each other, the lives of all involved take turns they could have never imagined, and we are all drawn toward a world of new possibilities. I look forward to the further adventures of Ralph and his friends!"

—*Tom Yelle, driver & flower processor*

FREE RALPH!
An Evolutionary Fable

Author's Foreword

This book was a gift of my adventure with cancer— along with a new and deeper appreciation of my life and loved ones, and a new and curlier head of hair.

Late one night as I lay in the hospital, suffering a rare toxic reaction to one of my chemo drugs, running a high fever and unable to eat or sleep, the opening scene began to unfold in my head. I followed the words to see where they led. When I came home to recuperate and then resume my treatment, the story kept coming, scene after scene after scene.

It did not come out of nowhere. *Free Ralph!* is the culmination of my bachelor's degree in Fiction Writing, 30 years of writing in several genres, 15 years of professional editing experience, and a lifetime of novel-reading. It also draws on my longstanding love and concern for the natural world.

The depiction of our biological cousins the chimpanzees that emerged from my fever is not a "realistic" one, however. In the midst of writing it, I discovered in my bookcase Jane Goodall's first book, *In the Shadow of Man*, which I must have brought home from a yard sale for my animal-loving wife, Dawn. Reading Dr. Goodall's account of her pioneering work helped me re-shape the daily habits and activities of my chimps to outwardly resemble "reality." But realism is not the point of this particular story. Nor is it exactly a fantasy. Calling it a "Fable" seems to sum it up best.

Like all fables, the story came with a message. I believe the timeliness of this message is one reason I "lived to tell the tale." One who has lived through the ordeal of cancer dares not question its gifts. But writing *Free Ralph!* was the most fun I ever had, and I have no doubt that this played an equal role in my recovery.

Among the many authors to whom the story owes a literary debt, I am particularly thankful to Edgar Rice Burroughs, author of the *Tarzan* novels— one of my earliest passions as a reader— and to Daniel Quinn, author of the *Ishmael* novels. I hope you'll find *Free Ralph!* worthy of my debt to them.

But if not, don't blame me. Blame it on my fever.

On to the next adventure! Blessings,

Stephen Wing

to my parents,

Douglas and Carol Wingeier,

with love and gratitude

Chapter 1

A Monkey Without a Tail

*

TRAPEZE ARTIST REPLACES HUMAN PARTNER
WITH CHIMPANZEE NAMED RALPH

by Maxwell Martin
Dade County Entertainer
Miami, Florida

Mexican immigrants have already claimed most of the backbreaking minimum-wage jobs in south Florida. Underpaid Chinese factory workers underbid us on everything from crayons to computers. Customer service calls are now answered by cheap labor in India, and even cheaper labor in minimum security prisons.

But could a chimpanzee steal your job? If you are a trapeze performer in the circus, the answer could be yes.

The credit for this new milestone in primate history goes to Dale Hardy, a trapeze star or "aerial artist" with the Rufus Barnabas Circus Spectacular, which winters here in Dade County and starts each annual spring tour with a special hometown show.

After the tragic death of his wife and trapeze partner Tess Michaels during a performance in Oakland, California, almost a decade ago, Hardy stopped performing for a while and disappeared completely from the circus scene. Last year he announced his return to the heights under the Big Top. But prudently, perhaps, he chose as his second wife not a trapeze performer but an animal trainer with the circus, Peg Tyler.

At a press conference yesterday, the couple proudly unveiled a stunning breakthrough in interspecies cooperation, and its name is Ralph— a seven-year-old, three-and-a-half-foot immigrant from the African jungle.

"He's the smartest chimp I've ever trained," Tyler says. "I can't sneak anything past him."

"Ralph catches on so quick that sometimes it seems like we're inventing our routine together," adds Hardy with a chuckle. "Pretty darn good for a monkey without a tail!"

Chimpanzees share 98% of the human genetic blueprint, and are known for their delight in climbing and swinging through the giant trees of their native Africa. So it was probably only a matter of time before they cracked the south Florida aerial-artist labor market.

Still, it's clear that for the Hardy-Tylers, who are childless, training Ralph as Dale's new partner has been a labor of love. Not only is Ralph the first non-human primate ever to be teamed with a human on the high trapeze, Tyler has pioneered a revolutionary new style of animal training which involved giving Ralph his own bedroom in the Hardy-Tylers' circus trailer and raising him like a human child.

"I've just about got him toilet-trained," says Tyler, smiling. "He only has to wear his diaper at night now."

The Hardy-Tylers' project is so unusual that when the Dade County Animal Services department caught wind of it, they came sniffing around the circus grounds for evidence of animal endangerment. To avoid any potential legal problems, the Hardy-Tylers have agreed to use a safety net for all performances in this first season, as they do during training and practice sessions.

The entire world waits breathlessly to see the daring and dynamic duo in action on the flying trapeze. But Dade County gets to see it first! "Dale & Ralph," as the new act bills itself, will be one of the star attractions in the annual hometown exhibition of the Rufus Barnabas Circus Spectacular, Saturday, April 1— your chance to witness evolution unfolding before your eyes!

Ralph? said Guma, studying the large color photograph that accompanied the article. Grandmother Min had been staring over his shoulder as they read together, trembling from head to foot. Guma's brother, Uncle Noko, held the mud-stained newspaper open for them, braced on the knuckles of one front paw.

The picture showed a short, muscular, square-chinned human male and an even shorter male chimpanzee with wide, gentle eyes. The man leaned to the left, the chimp to the right, each gripping one end of a shiny metal bar and flinging a hairy arm out toward the edge of the picture. Both wore identical red and blue oufits that showed off the hair on their chests, and both were grinning broad foolish grins.

The resemblance is unmistakable, Noko murmured to his brother. *Otherwise I never would have brought you this piece of journalistic trash. But who could forget that crooked little grin?*

It— it looks like my little Kumbu— all grown up! said Min, and fainted to the forest floor.

Dar looked over from a group who were feeding at a termite mound and hurried across the clearing. Her companions continued to take turns threading a long stem of grass into the tiny hole at the top of the mound, drawing it out again and licking off the juicy termites.

Around them the other chimps browsed among the ferns, chattering soundlessly across the silence and the slant of afternoon sun. One by one they looked around and saw Grandmother Min lying among the ferns. Soon the clan had gathered around their fallen elder, stroking her fur and glancing curiously up at Guma and Noko.

The two brothers looked somberly at one another for a long moment.

Perhaps I should have shown it to you privately first, said Uncle Noko.

It wouldn't have mattered, Guma replied. *She knows her baby. Her reaction would have been the same. But where in the world did you get it?*

Litter, snorted Noko. *I told you it was trash, didn't I? Another expedition of tourists with guns. I couldn't believe what I was reading. What a load of dung!*

I don't think it's serious, Guma said. *Just some clever advertising disguised as journalism.*

Sure it is. And they looked nearly stupid enough to believe it!

The two powerful full-grown males gazed down at Min as she lay breathing gently, surrounded by the clucks and murmurs of her closest loved ones, peacefully asleep.

Sometimes I wish we chimps were not so damned intelligent, said Uncle Noko. *Picking up their mental noise as they traipse through the forest is polluting our minds. It's not what Life gave us the Gift for.*

Well, it does help when they're coming after one of us, said Guma. *I mean,* to know just a little about that alien dimension they come from.

It didn't help little Kumbu, Noko growled.

Guma glanced up through the sun-speckled canopy of leaves. Then Noko realized his eyes were closed. A tear was glistening in a beam of sunlight.

Sorry. Uncle Noko began to groom his brother's thick black fur, searching for tasty insects. *I'm forgetting Kumbu was your little one, too.*

That was six years ago, Guma went on, returning from somewhere deep inside. *We didn't know who we were dealing with then. We were still hiding out in the hills, waiting for them to go away, as some of the other clans still do.*

We learned, said Uncle Noko, wrinkling his nose. *They don't go away. We've got to deal with them on their own terms.*

And simultaneously on ours. It's the only way we can possibly survive.

Then maybe picking up their mental pollution is what Life gave us the Gift for after all! Uncle Noko was teasing now.

It's what all our gifts are for, said Guma. *You know that. To survive, so we can reproduce, so we can evolve. We can outlast them, I'm sure of it— our poor, dumb, wayward cousins. I have a feeling it won't be long now.*

I know, chuckled Noko. *I read a few of the other stories in that paper.*

Still, Guma said. *Kumbu was so young. His Gift was barely beginning to develop. It's been hard for poor Min, casting her Gift out in search of him again and again, waiting for him to reach the stage where he can respond.*

At least now we know where he is, Noko said. *I'm sure he's just as brilliant as his papa, even over there in Dade County Florida. That could explain why this couple, these surrogate parents, are so convinced they've trained him.*

Because he's been training them, you mean.

Precisely. I guarantee you, most chimps that get hijacked out of here end up living sad, boring, frustrated lives. Kumbu is going to be a star!

A star named Ralph?

Guma and Noko thought for a moment, looking down at Ralph's ridiculous grin.

No, said Noko, shaking his head. *I guess showing off for the humans is no substitute for a quiet life in the forest among your family. Even if you're a star. Besides, how can a young chimpanzee's Gift develop properly among humans? It takes teachers who understand the Gift and the world and the Giver. Teachers like we had when we were young, remember?*

I guess you're right. But don't underestimate the Gift, or the Giver.

The two brothers meandered off, leaving the newspaper where it had fallen. Dar reached for it, drawn by the brightly colored picture and the oddly grinning chimpanzee in the clown suit. Suddenly she gasped, eyes widening. The other chimps who had gathered to comfort Grandmother Min clustered around the younger female as she held her open palm just above the newspaper's columns of print and began to read.

∗

Dr. Jane Keller, BA, MS, PhD, narrowed her eyes and read it again. All of it, flaring her nostrils when she reached the part about Dade County Animal Services. Then she folded the page along the margins of the article and tore it precisely out of the *Entertainer* without losing a single word.

She wasn't a regular reader of the *Entertainer* by any means; it had surfaced in a stack of newspapers donated by a neighbor. She had been spreading out sheets of newsprint to line the bottom of Coo and Caw's luxurious birdcage when the young chimp's lopsided grin and obscene circus costume had caught her eye.

The clipping decorated her refrigerator for a little over six minutes before she snatched it off, scattering little magnets across the gleaming finish of her kitchen floor. She slipped it into a fresh manila folder, which she marked *CIRCUS* in square, neat capitals and slid into the file drawer in her desk. She didn't bother to file it under *C*.

"This one goes right in front!" she exclaimed aloud. "The things wild creatures have to put up with . . ." She was muttering now, and uncomfortably aware that no one was listening except her two African parrots. Coo and Caw looked at one another and did not reply.

The parrots had grown up in human custody and sadly no longer qualified as wild. That was only one more example, one she'd lived with every day since she had rescued them— the only survivors of an entire colony of escaped pet African parrots that had nested in her apartment complex until management called in the exterminators.

The really obscene thing was that the gorgeous, garrulous birds were still being captured every day in the African jungle and shipped out to pet stores around the world.

If Jane Keller were only the household word it *deserved* to be, came the next thought, startling her— if that other Jane had not had the uncanny luck to be *first*—

But that was unjust. Jane Goodall deserved every bit of her fame, had earned it with stellar devotion to her chimps and had never compromised it in any way. Jane Goodall and her chimps, Dian Fossey and her gorillas, Birute Galdikas and her orangutans: they had done more to keep the primate kingdom wild and free than anyone else she could name.

It was Jane Keller's uncanny bad luck that she too had fallen in love with a band of African chimps, a few years after Dr. Goodall and in another country, and that Goodall had published her research first. If Jane had only chosen baboons, or gibbons, or mangabeys, she too might have joined the pantheon of primate saviors, and perhaps the baboons or gibbons or mangabeys would be a little more wild and free today.

She might have been featured in her own Hollywood movie, like Dian Fossey.

She might have been shot down by poachers in the jungle, like Dian Fossey.

But it was the chimpanzees who had chosen her, after all. So she'd had no choice but to join the chorus of voices praising Goodall, Fossey and Galdikas, present papers citing their pioneering work, testify at hearings and appear on television panels when they were not available, do her bit to preserve precious African habitat.

Nearing retirement age, long since divorced and denied tenure once more at Miami State University, her latest book turned down by yet another publisher, Jane's trips to Africa were no longer as frequent. None of the chimps she had fallen in love with so long ago could possibly have survived this long; her heart had broken all over again each time she went back and discovered another familiar face missing from the little mountain valley.

It hadn't helped when after her divorce she had legally reclaimed her maiden name, breaking her long string of published academic papers in two and forever confusing the record of her accomplishments.

"Keep quiet, you two, I'm working!" Coo called out, mocking her.

"Why don't you both get jobs and buy your *own* crackers?" Caw chimed in, never content to let Coo have the last word.

Staring across her tidy living room from the study, the file drawer still open beside her, Jane let her eyes feast on the bright feathers of her companions in exile. And gradually began to smile. Dr. Jane Keller, BA, MS, PhD, might be washed up academically. But if a chimpanzee needed help, especially right here in Dade County, she was ready.

Duty calls.

She would have to move quickly, however. The newspaper story was already several days old; April first was just over two weeks away. She flicked open her cell phone and began to scroll through her large collection of contacts.

Every time she closed her eyes the garish photo of little Ralph was still there, imprinted on her memory, superimposed on the unforgettable faces of the chimps she had named Hamlet, Ophelia, Desdemona, Romeo. The little fellow's clownish grin still bothered her. But gradually, as she dialed number after number and refined her call to action, her own smile was spreading just as wide. Perhaps wider.

Min lay face down in the gentle, fragrant ferns, dreaming of Kumbu. Her favorite. Was it because he was her last-born, child of her last fertile season? Or was it because she'd lost him so early, never watched him grow and learn and develop his Gift, like her six other sons and daughters? Or was he truly different from the others, as she had sometimes suspected?

She'd lost a few the other way. The mothers always got over that. It was their silent understanding with Life: *Send another.* Another bright little face to love, lips to suckle, another sacred living sprout to feed and teach and protect until the little boy chimp or little girl chimp grew big enough to browse among the clan and join the mating dance. And then: *Life, send another.* Her sacred duty: to reproduce, in order to evolve.

But Kumbu. She had missed him so. Snatched so suddenly away from her, and still so young. Was it only her imagination, her feverish memories of him, that sealed him in a secret vacuum inside her heart?

She saw there his innocent, undemanding smile, awakening the morning after the birth. His amazement at the wide beams of sunlight coming down through the forest, all at the same broad, smiling angle.

She saw his wide gentle eyes discovering each new thing, just as fresh and surprising to him as to every newborn chimpanzee before him. A lizard. An orchid. A spiderweb.

She saw his tender little face upturned to hers in helpless, hopeful questioning. His Gift was stirring. He saw the adults communicating with looks, grunts, gestures, and she could watch day by day as he began to sense the silent, simultaneous higher levels of syntax. Just like all the others at his age. But somehow . . . different.

And now, just as suddenly, Kumbu had returned. Just a picture of him, dressed up as a clown named Ralph, but it was Kumbu all the same. Suddenly she knew where he had gone and what had become of him there— adopted by humans, forced to perform in a circus, and to judge by the look on his face, thrilled about it.

She wondered if he loved this human couple who had adopted him. Of course he did; Kumbu was always filled to overflowing with love for everyone around him, and never shy about spilling it.

But did they love Kumbu in return, this man and this woman? They spoke of him affectionately, but as a lower being: an animal they had trained. The man was almost as hairy as a chimpanzee himself. But what about the woman? The newspaper had shown no picture of her, so Min had to reach far into the fog of space and time, stretching her Gift, seeking clarity.

All she received was an impression of deep attachment, strong love, holding steady across the species barrier. Still, something she felt out there troubled her. Something that was coming, something yet to be. Trouble between the chimpanzee and the two humans.

Her Kumbu was loved.

But . . . *Ralph?*

Min slept.

In Min's dream, Kumbu and the man in the photograph wore their red and blue circus costumes, but they had changed places. The man now stood no higher than Kumbu's waist. Towering above him, Kumbu held a cluster of vines in each fist: one vine attached to the top of the little man's head, one to each of his hands, one to each elbow and knee. Kumbu raised the two clusters of vines and the man danced an awkward, grinning, elbow-flapping dance.

Kumbu was grinning too, but it was a sly, proud grin— a little like the grins of the paleskinned humans Min had seen, posing over the lifeless heaps of flesh they had speared with their noisy metal weapons. She wasn't sure she liked that grin on her precious Kumbu's kind and gentle face.

But the little man danced on, unaware of the looming chimpanzee who held him upright and moved his elbows and feet. His clumsy dancing seemed to be growing more skillful, but Min saw that in fact it was Kumbu whose skill at manipulating the vines was gradually improving.

Now Min began to hear the drumming: a complicated rhythm, steady and powerful, the kind of drumming the villagers by the river used to dance to when Min was young. That was before they had all acquired radios and begun to listen to simpler rhythms from across the sea— crude, noisy music from that hellish netherworld where the humans had taken little Kumbu to make him a star.

But Kumbu had grown up now, twice as tall as any human. He raised the vines high above his head and began swinging the little man back and forth in wide arcs. Deftly he dropped one arm and the man crouched in mid-air, flipped upside down, then somersaulted and straightened again, still grinning that silly grin.

The look on Kumbu's face had changed, she noticed: still proud, but lovingly protective, as if the little man were a responsibility Kumbu cared about. It was like a mother's look when she huddled with the other females in the grooming circle, glancing away every so often to check on her little one. As the little one grew, the glances were less frequent and less anxious, yet the feeling of responsibility took a long time to fade. The mothers only gradually let go of the urge to look around and search the faces of the browsing clan for their special one. And then: *Life, send another.*

Now Kumbu was carefully lowering the little man's feet to the ground, where a little woman waited, exactly the same size. Kumbu had somehow gathered all the little man's vines in one hand, and in the other he now held a second set of vines that were attached to the little woman. The drumming slowed and grew quieter. Kumbu swung the two faces carefully together and they touched. Then he lifted the two sets of vines and the little couple danced, swaying gently.

Min could see that they loved each other, this couple. Kumbu loved them both. And they loved Kumbu. The clown suit, the circus act, the grotesque photograph, the sleazy newspaper article— none of that mattered if her Kumbu was loved.

Min slept a while and woke up feeling comforted. Dar, her spirit-daughter, smiled anxiously down. Her eldest son, Tunga, her sister Shan and several younger ones sat around her feet. Guma squatted beside her holding a ripe, perfect mango.

Kumbu was loved.

✳

Wilbur Trimble stood up and stretched, staring down into the red-hot intensity of the campfire. Then he turned, nearly tripping over the camp chair he'd been sitting on, and shivered. The night wasn't cold, really, but it was astonishing how dark everything became as soon as he turned his back on the fire.

Regaining his balance, he stepped away from the warmth and light and the laughing voices in search of a little privacy, and started into the forest.

Was it his imagination, or was the African night blacker than the nights back home in Indiana? Instinctively he looked up, but saw no stars. They were hidden, of course, by the arching canopy of branches he had admired before the sun went down. The safari's base camp stood just under the trees at the edge of a vast forest. But still . . . Indiana had forests, too, and Wilbur had never seen a night so dark.

He stopped, sensing a treetrunk directly in front of him. Glancing back, he saw a burning matchstick that had to be the campfire. He'd wandered farther than he thought. He unzipped his safari pants and aimed into the blackness, his thoughts drifting away on the dark.

It was hard to believe he was really here. Coming to Africa had been his lifelong dream. How had it started? All those Tarzan books he'd read as a kid, he supposed. Then the movies and the TV shows. The actor playing Tarzan had changed from time to time, but the same steamy, overgrown jungle or wide savannah filled the background of every scene, the same supporting cast of wild, exotic animals.

Now he was here, surrounded by the scenery he remembered. It still looked the same, in a way, but somehow . . . especially at night . . . Wilbur shivered again. Then he zipped up his safari pants and turned back toward the fire.

It had been over there, hadn't it? Or maybe that way? Surely they hadn't put it out and gone to bed. Not yet. Not without noticing one member of the safari party was missing— surely not! Not after the sizeable chunk of his savings he'd handed over to Great White Hunter Adventure Tours—

But whichever way he looked he saw the same black starless shadow of African night. The more he tried to recall which direction he had wandered from to stand in front of this particular tree, the more directionless the night around him became.

And here he was. Lost. With nothing to defend himself with except the Swiss Army knife in his pocket. Which, he remembered suddenly, his father had given him for graduating from the Cub Scouts, almost half a century ago.

Suddenly Wilbur laughed out loud. It was too ridiculous to take so seriously. All he had to do was take a couple of steps directly away from the tree he'd just watered, and the fire would appear again from behind whichever other tree was momentarily obstructing his view.

Still he hesitated, breathing deeply, waiting for his heart to stop pounding so loudly against the dark. Then he took three resolute steps in a direction that felt right. Something moved under his foot. He felt his safari pants rip at the crotch as his feet went in opposite directions, and with a frightened yelp he fell.

In an instant he was up again, calling at the top of his voice, begging for a noise, any noise, to help him locate the camp.

Something laughed, much too loudly, from somewhere directly overhead. It wasn't human laughter, though, and with another terrified yelp Wilbur turned and ran. Tripped, rolled, leapt to his feet, and ran again. Caught a low-hanging vine across his throat, twisted free, collided with an invisible treetrunk, and ran again. All directions were the same in the black, quietly breathing African night.

Kumbu woke up without opening his eyes. He'd been dreaming about the forest. His mother must have been thinking about him again. He couldn't recall her face, but he remembered how she felt. He lay curled around himself for a minute, stroking his fur, remembering. Her soft touch. Her soft murmur. Her soft, fragrant breathing. Her strong arms lifting him to her breast, and the taste of her milk as he held on and sucked.

The milk his human parents poured over his cornflakes every morning didn't taste nearly as good as this favorite memory. His human mother treated him kindly, gave him plenty of good things to eat and drink, but she had never offered him her breast. He knew she had them, just like his first mother— two of them, hidden under her blouse and her bra. Even at the swimming pool she wore a bright yellow bra that covered her breasts without actually hiding them.

Kumbu had seen her without her bra only once: that night years ago when she'd brought home his human father for the first time.

The milk they gave him came in plastic bottles from the supermarket. Still, it was as close as he could get, so he had sucked it greedily from his rubber-nippled bottle, and later from each spoonful of cornflakes, remembering home.

It was the games his human Mommy played with him that he'd always liked best, ever since she had brought him home to the little circus trailer. When his Daddy had come to live with them, the games had grown even more interesting. Soon Kumbu had found his strange life with the humans becoming a challenge: something he had to work at, not just to please Mommy and Daddy but to satisfy himself.

And yes, he'd found, over and over: he could do it! He could master the swinging bar that started low and gradually moved up, higher and higher every week. He could learn the games his Mommy and Daddy taught him, each one more complicated than the last. Lying there in his crib with his eyes closed he went over the moves he'd learned in order, one by one. He loved the excitement of swinging, letting go, flying across space, catching hold of another bar— or even better, catching his Daddy's wrists or ankles— and swinging on through the familiar routine.

Most of all he loved the feeling that his Mommy and Daddy were pleased when he learned a new thing. They loved him, he knew, but they loved him most when he performed the right move at the right time, exactly the way they wanted. It made him feel almost as if he were back in the forest with his mother again, learning to answer the sounds she made with sounds of his own.

And when he made a mistake, missed his grab and hit the safety net below with a squeal and a roll, he could feel their hearts falling with him, and he knew they loved him then, too. But the flying love felt so much better than the falling love that he tried hard not to fall.

He lay holding himself in his crib, remembering everything.

When he opened his eyes, the light came slanting low through the slats of the blind, striping the wall with light and dark. It reminded him of the sun coming through the trees when he was a tiny furry ball clinging to his mother. For a long moment, the memory held him as he held himself. He let his fingers wander through his stomach-fur and down into his diaper to scratch his balls. He loved the tickling sensation.

"Good morning, Ralph! How's Mommy's little baby?"

The cheery voice was his Mommy's, but for another moment Kumbu lay staring up at the stripes of light on the wall, scratching his balls and remembering.

"No no no, mustn't scratch there, no!" Mommy tugged the cord that raised the blind, and the dark stripes between the light ones fled up the wall and vanished. "That's your private place. We can't let people see us scratching there, not even Mommy, no no!"

She was smiling as she scolded him, but Kumbu recognized the gentle pressure that slowly, day after day, pushed and molded him into the Kumbu she wanted. He couldn't understand why it mattered when no strangers were watching. But he didn't mind, because he'd also noticed that slowly, day after day, his life with his human mother and father grew more and more interesting and exciting—until now, every single day he was swinging high in the air, dangling from his Daddy's wrists and ankles. What could be more wonderful?

He knew the answer to that: tomorrow. Every day, it seemed, something came along that was even more wonderful than the day before. He could hardly wait for each new day to begin.

"Ready for your cereal, Ralph?"

Kumbu was always ready for cornflakes. Mommy opened the bedroom door and led him with a firm grip on his wrist through the living room and the arching doorway to the trailer's tiny dining room. His Daddy looked up and grinned, slicing Kumbu's banana into the bowl of cornflakes waiting on the table. Kumbu knew why Mommy was holding his wrist so tight: sometimes he got so excited at the sight of his cornflakes and his banana and his Daddy that he lost control and jumped up on the table. He was learning not to do that. He had almost learned it. But just last week—

"Morning, sport!" Daddy's grin spread wider across the stubble of his chin. "Are we going to have fun today, like yesterday, Ralphie boy?"

More! Kumbu thought, jumping up and down just a little as he beat his free hand against his leg, and he felt Mommy's grip tighten. But he wasn't losing control today. He knew exactly how high to jump and when to stop. When they reached the table, he pulled against Mommy's grip and she lifted and he walked up her leg and swung into his high chair. It was one of the first games they'd ever learned together.

Mommy strapped him into his chair and tied on his bib. Daddy poured the milk. Then Mommy picked up his special spoon and fed him.

He loved his cornflakes. He loved his banana. He loved his Mommy and his Daddy and he loved his morning: just like yesterday morning, except brand new.

Something was going to happen today that had never happened before. That was one thing he'd learned. Even while he practiced a move that he'd practiced again and again, he always waited for it. He always watched for it. Something new was going to happen.

✳

Kyle Wilson rolled out of the sack, a little bit hung over. Something hurt. He sat up and felt under the folds of his mosquito net. Damn. He'd slept on his pistol again. Without quite opening his eyes he felt along the barrel, just making sure. Yes, the safety catch was on. But he'd better watch that. These so-called hunters he was squiring around central Africa were worth too much money to risk plugging one in his sleep. Not to mention his own worthless skin.

He tried to pry one eye open. First the right eye, then the left. But they rebelled. How much had he siphoned from his pocket flask by the campfire last night, anyway? He was supposed to keep track. No more than ten good sips per night. And none of those extra-long slurps, either. Discipline, man. Thurgood had told him straight: one more screw-up and he went on probation.

To drive home the point, the front office had paired him up with Solomon Purgis this time out, a veteran hunter nearly twice Kyle's age. No drinking buddies on this safari. Strictly business. Except hunting was more than a business to Purgis: it was an obsession.

Kyle succeeded in opening his right eye, which immediately closed again. Then he tried cracking both eyes just a little. His mosquito net turned a shaft of sunlight into a bright gauzy mist that seemed to surround him in glittering droplets of light. His headache throbbed against the glare.

Closing his eyes again, he felt under his cot for his boots. Dangerous, he knew. What if a snake had curled around them in the night? Strictly against the safety drill. After reciting it to one wide-eyed bunch of tourists after another, he knew the drill by heart.

Great White Hunters! What a joke. Not one of them had the guts to venture twentyfive feet away from the trail to track a kill. Or worse, an animal they might have only wounded. They all talked big in front of the African guides and gun-bearers, lines they'd memorized from Hollywood movies about big-game hunting in Africa. Then stayed as close to the natives as they could, twitching at every little jungle noise and wetting their safari pants if someone fired off a gun.

Deep down, they all wanted Kyle or Purgis to aim the gun, pull the trigger, then hand it to them so they could pose for the photograph. And Purgis was just the one to do it. Purgis had a house full of animal-heads somewhere, like most professional hunters, but he didn't really care about the trophy. All he wanted was the kill. Kyle had watched him opening his little pocket notebook at night by the fire, or in his tent by lanternlight. Scratch scratch. Adding one more lion, one more wildebeest, one more gazelle to his personal tally.

It made Kyle a little queasy. All he wanted was his paycheck. And his pocket flask. And his peace and quiet. Though not necessarily in that order.

"Wilson?"

Speak of the devil. Kyle found his other boot, tugged it on and thrashed his way out of the mosquito net. Purgis loomed in the door-flap, thick-necked and powerful, holding a rifle as usual.

"Look, Wilson, we got a problem. One of the black boys says we're missing one. The tall thin one, name of Trimble. Wilbur Trimble. Cot wasn't slept in. You remember him staying up by the fire last night?"

Damn. Purgis always turned in early. Campfire duty belonged to Kyle.

"Sure. He stayed up a while. Then I thought he hit the sack. I looked up and he was gone."

"Anyone else up that late besides you?"

"Sure, sure. The older couple, whatstheirname. Mott. I thought they never would get tired of regurgitating memories. And the young guy whose father . . . Parks? Pike?"

"Everyone else is accounted for, I guess. The boy says he found tracks going into the bush, but they never made it across the creek. Either he turned upstream or down, or just . . . drowned and washed away."

Kyle's headache jabbed suddenly against the inside of his skull as if a prizefighter were trapped in there, trying to punch a way out. Three quick punches. *Pro-ba-tion.*

"Any sign of—"

"Nope." Purgis sounded disappointed. "No animal sign, no blood, no smashed vegetation. Wherever he is, he's probably alive. My gut instinct is, the natives got him. Slave trade is alive and well, of course, though not exactly around here. Even our own crew ain't immune to the temptation."

"We're paying them too well for that," said Kyle. Suddenly he wished he knew exactly how much the guides and gun-bearers and kitchen staff were paid.

Purgis thought for a minute, his eyes like hard black beads in a face like tooled leather, the military haircut increasingly irrelevant to his balding skull. "Listen. You round up the dudes and dudettes and see what you can find out. I'll interrogate the black boys. We got to take care of this quick."

Kyle felt his stomach lurch and start to roll. "Right. Be right with you. Just let me . . ." He bent over to tie his boots and nearly lost last night's dinner. "I'll be right . . ." He jammed his pistol into its holster and snapped it. Then gently lowered his pith helmet over the pounding reverberation in his skull and delicately fastened the strap.

He sat still for another long minute on the edge of his cot, trying to picture Wilbur Trimble in his mind. But he'd been out in the bush too long. He'd led too many herds of timid and eager and nervous and vicious tourists into the wilds of Africa. Their faces all blended together in the gauzy haze of his brain. And it all just hurt too much.

Chapter 2

Antelopes Running

*

Wilbur awoke lying on his back in sweet-scented, swaying ferns. Trees rose majestically above him into drifts of mist, forking at odd angles and spreading their canopies much farther than the trees he was accustomed to. For a moment he just stared, thunderstruck by their beauty and strangeness.

His boots were wet, and his pants, nearly up to the knees.

Where was he?

Africa.

He hadn't just suddenly remembered. It was as if a voice had spoken inside, a deep resonant voice as strange to him as the twisting shapes of the trees. As soon as it spoke, the memories came crowding back: the long airplane ride across the Atlantic. The sweltering humidity of the Wanzani City International Airport. The nerve-wracking taxi ride to his hotel. The first awkward gathering of the safari party that night in the hotel lobby, and the terse briefing from their tour directors, Mr. Purgis and Mr. Wilson.

Then the caravan next morning, six Land Rovers and a heavily laden supply truck. They had roared through the cardboard and tarpaper slums that surrounded the city, across a rolling grassland on the paved country road the locals called a highway, and into the bush on a winding dirt road. At the base of the foothills, where the thickets of waist-high vegetation gave way to forest, the natives had set up the safari's base camp.

The first night in camp had been uneventful: getting acquainted with the others around the campfire, trying to connect names with faces, while Mr. Wilson took surreptitious sips from a hip flask and Mr. Purgis boasted about the game he had killed. Wilbur had peered politely in the flickering firelight, but hadn't really seen any dead animals in the snapshots Mr. Purgis passed around, any more than he'd really seen grandchildren in Andy and Lucretia Mott's. He'd made appropriate noises— if not exactly words— and passed them on.

Then, yesterday morning, came the first actual kill. The guides had come running into camp, calling out in their native language with a businesslike sort of excitement. One of the Land Rovers came chugging in soon afterward with a dead antelope slung across the hood. Mr. Purgis was driving and Stan Cartwright, a babyfaced shoe salesman from Pittsburgh, rode the running board, brandishing his rifle and whooping with laughter.

All the way across the plain to the foothills, from the back seat of his Land Rover, Wilbur had watched the antelopes running. They ran together like waves across the ocean, always aware of one another, never quite touching. They reminded him of the clouds he had flown over, crossing the Atlantic, then the sand dunes of the Sahara Desert: rippling, rhythmic, hypnotic, flowing shapes that formed a slowly shifting pattern in the shimmer of sun. He couldn't take his eyes off them until the endless herd had finally disappeared behind the hills.

This was what he had come to Africa to see, he'd realized, as soon as they were gone and he could think again.

As he joined the buzzing crowd that had gathered to admire the kill, Wilbur had recognized the short graceful horns and the stripes on the antelope's side and he remembered the flowing herd disappearing behind the hill. Blood oozed from a wound in the long dangling neck and trickled down the Land Rover's fender.

Wilbur had stared down at the dead antelope and swallowed. And swallowed again. As if something were stuck in his throat. Something that refused to go down.

Stan Cartwright had gripped one of the horns and levered the limp head into the air, propped one boot on the bloody fender, raised his rifle and grinned as the cameras clicked. Wilbur could only stare.

Lying on his back among the ferns, Wilbur blinked up into the mist. When his father had taken him hunting in the Indiana woods as a boy, he had never seen the deer that way. Somehow it was different here in Africa. Or he was different. But how could he have changed, mopping floors and emptying trash cans at the hospital year after year, taking piano lessons on Tuesday evenings, searching the shelves of the Cedartown Public Library for a book he hadn't read . . . What had changed inside?

Above him the mist was lifting. Parallel beams of bright sun came slanting down through the trees, lighting up the delicate patterns of the ferns around his head. Flowing, rhythmic shapes.

Yes, he realized. The living flow of the antelopes running was what he'd come to Africa to see. Not the blood-caked carcass on the Land Rover's hood.

He struggled up onto his elbows and looked around. Watching him, crouched in a semicircle among the ferns, he saw half a dozen monkeys. No, not monkeys: chimpanzees. Like Tarzan's little friend, Cheetah.

Excuse me, the biggest one said quite clearly, without moving its lips. *Did you say something?*

*

Kumbu crouched low, dug his fingers into the dark soil of his Mommy's flowerbed, uncoiled and jumped as high into the air as he could. He was aiming at the white plastic siding of the trailer, where a trail of dirty finger-marks showed how high he had jumped on other days when he and his Daddy left for morning practice. And today's mark was a knuckle's length higher than any of them!

"Way to go, sport!" said Daddy, holding out one hand. With a squeal of laughter, Kumbu slapped it and held out his own smaller hand for Daddy to slap.

Together, holding hands, they followed the boardwalk of wooden planks that threaded between the sideshow tents and trailers and carnival rides toward the giant black and orange striped tent that towered over the circus grounds: the Big Top.

"Hello, Dale. Hi, Ralph!" said Wally Scheiner, the elephant trainer, striding past in the opposite direction, wearing sweats instead of his glittering circus costume.

"Hey there, Wally," Daddy said.

Matthew Karp, the circus strong man, went jogging by in a pair of shorts, his tanned muscular chest gleaming with sweat. He gave them a smile and a nod and Daddy nodded back.

Ahead of them they saw Jimmy Doolan, old Slaphappy the Clown, limping along without his clown suit or his makeup on. They were catching up with him fast.

"Hey, Jimmy," said Daddy as they drew close. Jimmy turned to look.

"What? Oh, hi there, Dale."

"How's it going today?" Daddy asked. He and Kumbu slowed down to walk along with the old clown.

"It's the rheumatism, Dale. If it weren't for that I'd be cruisin'. But please, don't let on to Mr. Pauling that I'm hurtin'." Jimmy looked anxiously around. "He'll drop me like a lead weight. Hire some young-ster fresh out of clown school to take over my name, my face. He owns 'em both, did you know that? That last contract I signed . . . but what else could I do? I need to build up a little more social security before I can afford to retire. I just have to grit my teeth and go through with it."

"I guess so, Jimmy," said Daddy. "Sorry you're feeling poorly. But we're all going to get there someday, if we're lucky." Daddy didn't look at Jimmy now. "Well, we're headed to the Big Top. Morning practice, you know. Hang in there, Jimmy."

Kumbu and his Daddy quickened their steps again and left the limping old clown behind.

"Take it easy, you two!" Jimmy called out behind them.

Daddy lifted one arm and waved without looking back.

"Morning," said Lily Pelham, one of the ticket-sellers, walking past with Hal and Michelle Markowitz, who worked in the conces-sion stands.

"Howdy," said Hal.

"Good morning, Mr. Hardy," said Michelle. "And how are you today, Ralph? Would you like some peanuts?" She held out a hand-ful of nuts.

Daddy nodded to the three of them and pulled Kumbu past the tempting snack with a jerk on his arm.

"Not before practice, Ralph."

Now they saw Johnny Johanssen, the ringmaster, coming toward them at a trot. He was wearing a light grey suit and a tie, and sweat was running down his face.

"Morning, Mr. Johanssen," Daddy said cheerfully. "Ralph, say good morning."

Mr. Johanssen smiled, but didn't stop. "Morning, Dale." He didn't look down at Ralph at all. "Got a meeting with Pauling, and I'm late!"

"You have a good day, sir," Daddy called after him as he ran.

The very next person they passed was Mr. Pauling. He too wore a suit and tie, but wasn't hurrying at all. Two younger, shorter men Kumbu didn't recognize were walking behind him, also wearing suits. They both carried black briefcases and wore gleaming black shoes and looked around with bored, serious expressions. Mr. Pauling was busy talking on the telephone, scowling as usual, and didn't even glance at Kumbu and Daddy as he went by.

Just a second later, though, they heard his voice, as sharp and commanding as the lion tamer's whip. "Say, Hardy!"

Turning, they saw Mr. Pauling striding back toward them, followed by the other two. Kumbu had never quite understood what Mr. Pauling's job at the circus was. He didn't have an act, didn't help feed the animals or sweep out the grandstand. He was a big, red-faced man who stood almost as high above Daddy's head as Daddy stood above Kumbu, his golden hair and bushy blond eyebrows speckled with grey.

"Say," he said, much more quietly now, with a wary glance around. "Have you received any communications from a Dr. Jane Keller?"

"No, sir."

"Good. She's threatening— oh, this is Mr. Bragg, by the way, and Mr. Wascoll, our new lawyers. Dale Hardy, boys."

Daddy started to lift his hand, but Mr. Bragg gave a grim nod, Mr. Wascoll gave a stiff smile, and the hand dropped back to Daddy's side.

"Anyway, this Keller woman is threatening some kind of protest against us using Ralph here in your trapeze act. Bragg and Wascoll tell me we don't have a thing to worry about, legally speaking. But it could become one hell of a P.R. problem. Keller is a prima— primatol— you know, a scientist who studies monkeys. Teaches at a local university. My sources tell me she's stuck, career-wise, and looking for some kind of boost. Recognition in the field, that kind of thing. So if you get any communications from her, do us both a favor and don't respond. Meanwhile I want to meet with you up in my office, maybe later today. Give me a call after your morning practice."

Daddy's mouth had gone slack, but he blinked and licked his lips. "Right, sir. Right after practice. I'll call you."

Mr. Pauling looked down at Kumbu for a long moment and frowned. "This newfangled idea of Peg's better work," he growled, glancing up at Daddy again from under his bushy brows. Then he strode away, snapping his little telephone open again. Mr. Bragg gave another nod, Mr. Wascoll another smile, and they marched after him down the boardwalk.

Daddy stared over his shoulder, his jaw still hanging open. Then he swallowed and grinned down at Kumbu. "Come on, Ralph. We're not letting anything or anyone get in our way, are we? Remember: just focus on where we're at, and where we're going. What's in between will take care of itself."

Daddy's voice shook, just a tiny bit, repeating the familiar words. But Kumbu wasn't really listening to them.

For a long time now he had been hearing whispers of sound that no one else seemed to notice. Like snatches of other people's thinking that he overheard just like he sometimes overheard them talking. At first he was sure he was only imagining it. But as he grew older he seemed to hear the ghostly whispers more and more. He decided the humans around him must hear them too, and tried his best to ignore them as the humans did. It was simply part of his life in the circus.

But now Kumbu could swear he heard something else Daddy was saying underneath the bragging words and the shaky voice. Something very quiet, so quiet that it made no sound at all. Something partly angry, and partly afraid, and completely silent. Like a secret even Daddy didn't know yet.

"Dr. Keller, can you elaborate on that last statement?"

Jane's cell phone was getting so hot that she had to switch ears. "Certainly. What I meant was that chimpanzees can be extremely playful, but they are much stronger than one might assume from their size, and much more intelligent than most humans realize. In training little Ralph to play on a trapeze swing, high in the air, Ms. Tyler may be in for a surprise. Ralph may decide to change the routine just a little bit one day. Then Mr. Hardy might be extremely grateful that the Department of Animal Services suggested he use a safety net for his act."

She jotted down a note for her speech tomorrow night and went on.

"But the larger issue involves the ethics of interspecies relations. A chimpanzee in the wild behaves with a certain dignity, even nobility, no matter how clownishly you've seen them trained to act in Hollywood. The average American has never seen one outside of those awful old Tarzan movies, so has never witnessed the natural behavior pattern of a wild chimp. I have, and I assure you that training one to perform tricks in a circus is an affront to nature— and has been known to require some shockingly barbaric methods."

"But a spokesman for the circus has stated—"

"Furthermore, the United States has taken the position that the capture and sale of endangered species like the chimpanzee is an ethical violation, to the point of encouraging our trading partners in Africa to make it illegal. In allowing circuses and other animal-exploiting operations to continue exposing the public to ugly spectacles like this, we are compromising our position with even sympathetic governments abroad."

"But Professor, what about this experimental training program Ralph has been on— having his own bedroom, breakfast in a high chair at the table, his own car-seat—"

"I assure you, as one who has spent a lifetime studying these noble creatures, Ralph would much rather be sleeping in a nest he made himself up in a tree, eating fruit and leaves and seeds for breakfast, and traveling through the canopy of his native rainforest back in Africa."

"But you've seen the clips on the news of Dale and Ralph rehearsing. Ralph certainly seems to enjoy it, wouldn't you agree?"

"Ralph is still young. He will probably enjoy swinging on a trapeze right up until the moment something tragic happens. Then Animal Services will presumably take action, as they should have done long before now. But then it will be too late."

"Thank you, Dr. Keller," said the reporter, sounding relieved to have survived the interview without being attacked by wild animals.

"You're welcome. You will be covering our rally Saturday, I hope? Three p.m., on the sidewalk in front of the circus grounds."

"I'll be there."

"With a photographer?"

"You bet."

"I did mention that the rally kicks off an entire week of protests, didn't I? We'll be picketing every afternoon, leading up to a final rally when the circus opens the following weekend."

"Yes, Professor. I have it here in my notes."

Jane switched the cell phone off at last with a sigh of relief. Unfortunately, her land-line was ringing again. She let it ring while she rubbed her eyes and stretched the fingers on her telephone-answering hand. Let them ring. Whoever was calling her, they weren't about to give up now.

Two days ago she had addressed a rowdy crowd at Dade County Free the Animals, a group that bragged in its brochure that it had made the latest F.B.I. terrorist list and its phones were tapped. Tomorrow night she was scheduled to speak from the prestigious podium of the Wildlife Society of South Florida, whose members wore heirloom jewelry and designer gowns to their posh quarterly meetings. She'd been getting calls from reporters daily as the weekend rally she had organized drew closer.

It was enough to drive her up the nearest tree. She longed for the peace of the jungle, the lazy meandering of her troop of chimpanzees through the evening quiet as she trailed along, taking notes. But as soon as she pictured them in her imagination, she remembered who it was that she was doing it all for, and her nostrils flared again.

Duty calls.

Somewhere the descendants of Hamlet, Desdemona, Ophelia and Romeo were meandering the same verdant territory she remembered so well. And somewhere the poachers crouched, waiting, enticed by articles like the one in the *Entertainer* and by television shows that proved the market for live-trapped exotic animals was more lucrative than ever, in spite of governments and laws. The smuggling routes were well-established, and every smuggling ring that was exposed only left an opening for a new operation to move in.

She picked up the land-line. "Jane Keller speaking. How may I help you?"

"You can help me by stepping off a tall building," said a harsh, muffled voice, "to save me the trouble of pushing you."

"Who is this?"

"Let's just say I'm an attorney for people who prefer to settle out of court."

"And who—"

Click.

*

INDIANA MAN DISAPPEARS ON SAFARI

by Sandra Reid
Indianapolis Herald
Indianapolis, Indiana

Ever since he read his first Edgar Rice Burroughs novel at age nine, Wilbur Trimble dreamed of Africa. Growing up in tiny Cedartown, Indiana, he saw every Tarzan movie that came to town, watched every re-run of every Tarzan TV series, bought every Tarzan comic and clipped out every Tarzan cartoon strip. He's read all two dozen books in Burroughs' classic series at least three times.

This spring, the 54-year-old janitor at Cedartown's Woodrow Municipal Hospital finally got his chance to see the Dark Continent for himself. On March 17, he arrived in the central African nation of Wanzanayi for a big-game hunting safari in Babarzark Game Park, sponsored by Great White Hunter Adventure Tours.

Last Tuesday, however, he was swallowed by the African darkness when he mysteriously vanished from the safari's base camp near the end of a quiet evening around the campfire.

Park police have not ruled out abduction by terrorists, but consider it more likely that Trimble was the victim of a nocturnal predator. A military unit specializing in bush rescue operations has been searching the area since Wednesday afternoon. A reward has been offered by the Wanzanayian government, the approximate equivalent of $1,500 U.S.— a relatively large sum in this part of the world.

Tour co-director Solomon Purgis, who led a fruitless search until the team's arrival, emphasized during an impromptu press conference at the base camp that the range of conceivable explanations for Trimble's disappearance is still wide open.

"There are several possibilities," said Purgis. "None of them particularly pretty. But it's much too soon to draw any conclusions from the evidence we have so far uncovered."

Lt. Zachary Muchabe, who heads the special investigative team fielded by the Wanzanayian Army, would only comment, "We have ruled out nothing. Experience has taught us that anything is possible in country like this."

"Trimble could not have made it far on foot," added Purgis's co-director, Kyle Wilson. "I'm betting we'll find him holed up in the crotch of a tree somewhere, waiting for rescue. That's our standard advice to our safari clients if they get lost, and Mr. Trimble seemed level-headed enough to remember it."

Scott McKee, a spokesman for Great White Hunter Adventure Tours in New York, declined to comment until the investigation is complete.

"I've read everything about Africa I can get my hands on," Trimble told his hometown newspaper, the *Cedartown Gazette*, before his departure. "But none of it brings the place to life the way Burroughs did in those Tarzan novels. I still re-read them once in a while over the winter, when Indiana gets pretty darn cold and flat. But now I'm going. I want to see it for myself before I'm too old."

Trimble is a bachelor who has been a janitor all his life. The African safari was his first overseas vacation ever, and his first trip out of the country since a visit to Juarez, Mexico, during the year he spent attending Ball State University in Muncie.

Tarzan may no longer swing through the jungle from vine to vine, or ride his pet elephant across the veldt, but Africa still has its dangers. One can only hope that by some miracle, Wilbur Trimble too might have been adopted by the great apes that rescued the infant Tarzan after the deaths of his shipwrecked parents in the first Tarzan book, *Tarzan of the Apes*.

The alternatives, it seems, are too grim to contemplate.

Damn. Kyle looked away. Then tried shutting his eyes. But he still saw the grainy black-and-white photograph of Wilbur Trimble, dressed in safari gear and pith helmet— the same outfit the lanky

Midwesterner had worn nonstop since the safari began. Apparently this was the picture that had appeared in the *Cedartown Gazette* before Trimble had left home, dug out of the smaller paper's files for reprinting in the *Herald*.

The morgue. Wasn't that what they called the files of old newspaper photos?

Kyle flung the newspaper across the tent, nearly knocking over the lantern on his camp table. But he still saw it. That gaunt face with the wire-rimmed glasses, the genial grin, the greying mustache and sideburns. Once he had finally sorted it out of the disorderly crowd milling around in his head, Trimble's face had haunted him day and night. And now Purgis had to barge into his tent, his lair, his den, and slap a copy of this damn article on his camp table.

The lantern was battery-powered. He couldn't even set the damn paper on fire.

He took another slug from his flask and lay back on his cot, shielding his eyes with one bent elbow. That headache was back. *Pro-ba-tion*, it pounded, over and over, like the restless drumming of the natives in those old Tarzan movies. *Pro-ba-tion.*

Hell, he'd never even seen a Tarzan movie. Even on the antique-movie channel during some late-night drinking spree. At least he couldn't remember it if he had.

So far, no messages had arrived from company headquarters. The cute redheaded reporter who had arrived by jeep for her "impromptu press conference" had apparently contacted the front office in New York, but hadn't been able to worm a word out of McKee. Though probably she hadn't tried looking him up at the Topless Tartan Tavern after work.

The whole camp was growing daily more nervous and depressed as the missing man stubbornly remained missing. And this damn publicity wasn't going to help. Why the hell had he and Purgis allowed themselves to be sucked into giving that damn reporter a tour?

That was easy. Her freckled nose. Her copper-wire curls. The bright green eyes that had startled Kyle like an electrified spark when she took off her large round sunglasses. Purgis had responded to her prying questions just as eagerly as Kyle had, the lecherous old fart. They both should have known she'd be bad news. Literally.

And how had she happened to show up in camp a mere two days after Trimble's disappearance, all the way from Indiana, anyway? Her story about an assignment in Kenya sounded suspicious, at best.

He lay for a few minutes piecing together a paranoid certainty that this whole Trimble affair was the work of some kind of shadowy international conspiracy to ruin his day. Then he realized that Trimble's face had evaporated from the darkness behind his eyes— and it was Sandra Reid's that haunted him now.

He sat up and swung his feet to the floor with a groan, lurched across the canvas floor and retrieved the disheveled pages of the *Indianapolis Herald*. Impatiently he shuffled through the "International" section, not sure whether he was searching for evidence or the lack of it. But even in his own disheveled condition, it was impossible to miss. "Famed Snows of Kilimanjaro Disappearing Fast As Planet Warms." And Miss Reid's unmistakable byline.

Kyle slid his pistol out of its holster and checked the safety. If another jeep arrived carrying a telegram from Great White Hunter Adventure Tours, he wasn't sure what he would do. Maybe he should start his own search party of one. Head out of camp and stake out the dirt road a mile or two toward the highway.

Because if a messenger from the front office made it into camp alive, he could think of only one other person to shoot.

The human lying on the grass beside the stream under the morning mist was only sleeping. But when the browsing chimpanzees found him, they were almost too late. A pair of jackals had found him first. The bolder of the two was already sniffing at the man's fingers.

Guma saw the pale, naked fingers twitch and knew instantly what to do. Seizing a stick, he hurled it at the sniffing jackal and called out one of the traditional insults. The jackal looked up in time to duck the stick and snarled back the traditional response. But neither jackal backed away from their prey.

The other chimps looked unsure why Guma had chosen to intervene. Guma wasn't certain himself. But he had to trust his instinct; it was one of Life's greatest gifts. The others only hesitated a second.

They too had learned to trust Guma's instinct, even when they themselves felt no particular urge to act.

Each of them found something on the ground to throw— Zambi even grabbed a rotten fig— and when Guma let his second stick fly, the jackals were pelted with a barrage of sticks and rocks and fruit.

All of the chimps knew what to do next. They scattered in the mist, leaping for the lower branches of the nearest trees, and clambered rapidly out of reach as the jackals sprang at them. Only Guma remained on the ground, loping across the open grass toward the thicker forest. Both jackals followed. An insult was one thing, an assault was another. But no jackal could resist a chase.

Guma swung up into the first tree, winded but still yards ahead of the snarling, snapping jaws. From a safe branch, he looked back. The mist was beginning to clear. The other chimps had climbed down and now squatted in a protective circle around the paleskinned man asleep on the grass. Good.

The jackals trotted along behind him, panting and drooling, as Guma made his way along the branch and leapt to a neighboring tree. Tree by tree he led them gradually away from the stream. When he felt their indignation begin to falter, he scrambled up into the higher branches and abandoned them. Then he circled back to the stream and dropped into the patch of grass where the others waited.

The man was still asleep, but the morning sun came slanting through the trees now and lit up his pale, almost hairless face. A pair of clear, metal-rimmed disks shielded his eyes, catching the daylight like little glittering pools after a shower. The chimps listened in silence to the birds of the forest and the happy meandering of the stream.

Soon the man's eyelashes fluttered behind the clear disks: a pair of light blue eyes opened and looked up through the leafy branches into the light.

The chimps waited patiently, sensing the man's bewilderment, following a chain of confused remembering that brought him closer and closer to the present. It felt strange to be transported out of the cool forest morning as they extended their Gifts to encompass an awareness so different from their own. The younger chimps like Zambi and Mabu, who had little experience with humans, felt a little bewildered themselves.

Then suddenly a clear thought rang out from the man's cluttered mind, echoing in the jungle clearing as if he had spoken aloud. That took the chimps completely by surprise. And as they sat there dumbfounded, he raised his head at last.

Excuse me? Guma answered, the first to recover. *Did you say something?*

And then something even more amazing happened. The man heard. He looked around the little circle of chimps, from one watching face to the next, obviously as astonished as they were. But almost immediately, astonishment was overwhelmed by the leap and the pounce of fear. The man blinked and swallowed, tensing himself as if to jump and run, but too paralyzed to try.

Please don't be afraid, Uncle Noko spoke up hastily. *We didn't mean to startle you. We were startled ourselves, you see, by what you said. And even more by the way you said it.*

I . . . I didn't say anything, the man thought to himself, still in shock, still unaware that the chimps were listening.

But we heard you anyway, Guma replied. *It's been a long time since a human has come among us who bears the Gift.*

The man's head jerked from Noko toward Guma, though naturally neither had moved their lips. Yes: definitely the Gift. The other chimps glanced at Guma with respect, remembering why they had come to trust his instinct.

"G— gi— gift?" The man spoke aloud for the first time, in a voice that quavered and shook. The chimps could feel his mind quavering and shaking, too. Scolding himself for speaking aloud to a bunch of animals. Even worse: for answering them. When he hadn't even heard them speak. Even though animals *can't* speak. Because—

Our ancestors, Guma interrupted gravely, *have passed down to us stories of humans like yourself, who were able to communicate with us in our own way. But all were of the dark tribes. You're the first pale one we ever heard of.*

And they were never many, added Brapa, the clan storyteller. *Most were children who eventually lost the ability as they grew up. Although I understand a few wise elders did learn it, or re-learn it, by sitting alone in the forest and just listening.*

Okay, I'm dreaming, the man was thinking with a rush of relief. *That's all.* He had dreamed of Africa many times before he'd come, it seemed. And sometimes animals had spoken to him in those dreams.

The chimps looked at one another. They knew the power of dreams. Now this was beginning to make sense.

Occasionally, said Brapa, *some especially sensitive human shaman would earn the Gift through initiation— usually a female. But since the pale tribes came, our dark-skinned cousins have drawn away from us. And the few who have been favored with the Gift have used it only to track and kill us for our meat. That is their right, according to the ancient agreement, if they are hungry. But we too have the right to do what we must to survive, and we have learned to keep our distance as well.*

So, said Uncle Noko, *you can see that it came as quite a surprise to find you lying on the grass this morning, and to overhear you using your Gift.*

The man lifted one hand and pushed the clear disks in the metal frames away from his eyes. He closed his eyes and rubbed them hard. Then he looked around at the chimps again, one by one.

Okay. I'm not dreaming.

"What . . . what exactly did I say?" he stammered aloud.

That, said Guma, *was what caught our attention most of all. You said that the living flow of the antelopes running was what you had come to Africa to see. Not a dead antelope.*

Chapter 3

In the Granddaddy Tree

*

Kumbu climbed the long narrow ladder behind his Daddy, feeling the familiar excitement swell inside. He longed to scoot past Daddy and clamber up the ladder first. He knew he could reach the tiny platform at the top much faster than Daddy could. But the few times he had tried, Daddy had firmly grasped the rope tied to his safety harness and lowered him all the way to the safety net below. Kumbu had learned. Up here, Daddy was the boss.

Down below it was his Mommy, with her careful system of rewards and punishments. But all of Mommy's discipline, he realized, was only preparing him for the excitement he felt up in the lofty peak of the Big Top. One forgetful move and he was swinging on his safety rope, riding slowly back down to the net again. As he scrambled across the net to climb up the ladder again, he had plenty of time to remind himself why he should obey what Daddy said: because he always had more *fun* if he obeyed what Daddy said.

Still, sometimes he forgot. Sometimes the excitement was just too big to hold inside. Daddy would patiently remind him, lowering him back down to the net again. And then they would start all over.

Reaching the top of the ladder and stepping onto the platform behind his Daddy, holding all his excitement in a tight knot in his belly, Kumbu looked down. Far below them the safety net cast its woven shadow on the sawdust floor of the center ring. Day by day, week by week he and Daddy had practiced their routine: at first only a few feet above the net, climbing a little higher each week as the trapeze bar moved steadily up. It had been many days now since Kumbu had missed a grab and hit the net.

In fact, Daddy had been the last one to fall, Kumbu remembered with a tingle of pride. Daddy knew just how to hit the net already rolling. That had been the first game he'd taught Kumbu. Up until then, as they practiced their tumbling on the ground and then on the monkey bars, Mommy had been in charge of Kumbu's education.

Now Daddy unlashed the shiny metal trapeze bar and tested it. Smiling down at Kumbu, he gripped it in both hands, leaped lightly up off the platform and went sailing away. Kumbu tensed and waited, holding in the excitement as Daddy reached the limit of his swing, flipped around to face Kumbu and came gliding back.

Now! Kumbu leapt into empty space, grasping one of Daddy's ankles in each hand, and away they flew.

The excitement welled up and over in a slow exhale that emptied Kumbu's chest like a calm, flowing fountain of air. He felt no need to breathe in again. Flying like that felt so perfect and complete that for one long breathless moment it didn't seem that he was moving at all. And then came the moment to let go.

Kumbu filled his chest again with a quick inhale and landed on the second tiny platform, which a minute ago had been far across the tent. Then he waited. When Daddy landed on the first platform again and glanced back, Kumbu was ready. Folding one arm across his belly, he performed a dignified bow. Then he switched arms and bowed the other way. On the other platform, he knew, Daddy was doing exactly the same thing.

Bowing was one of the first games Mommy had taught him down on the ground, soon after he'd learned to scramble up her leg. But Kumbu hadn't grasped why until one day when Daddy was teaching him to do it high in the air instead. Down below, Mr. Gendron the knife-thrower and Miss Fargo, his assistant, had paused to watch. Their heads turned, following Kumbu's thrilling flight through the air without any reaction. But when he bowed, suddenly they both began clapping and whistling as if Kumbu had done something wonderful. His Mommy, watching from the edge of the ring, joined in too. A proud, warm feeling had washed over him that he'd never felt before.

From that moment, Kumbu was hooked on applause. He practiced his bows just as carefully as any of his moves in mid-air. If
anyone happened to be watching when he and Daddy practiced their
routine, he aimed an extra bow in that direction.

But sometimes he would forget what came next, after he bowed.
The next thing he was supposed to do was swell up his chest, beat on
it with his fists, and bellow as loud as he could. This was a game his
Daddy had taught him, and he could always get it right— if he didn't
forget it completely. But every time, the people watching would
answer his bellow with laughter, cutting off the applause. Maybe
that was why he kept forgetting.

No one was clapping now, even though a stranger had entered
the tent and stood watching: a woman with silver streaks in her
short dark hair, carrying a notebook. Maybe she had just come in and
had missed his bows. Kumbu reared back and pounded his chest,
bellowing long and loud. He heard the faint echo as it bounced around
inside the peak of the Big Top. But no laughter answered.

The woman with the silver-streaked hair bent and wrote something in her notebook.

But now, on the other platform, Daddy leaped into the air and
came swinging back across the tent. Kumbu tensed, concentrating.
This time, instead of grabbing Daddy's ankles in his hands, he had to
use his feet.

Now! Kumbu leaped out and grabbed hold. His arms and head
hung down. For a few seconds he closed his eyes and he was back in
the jungle, clinging to his mother's back as she swung through the
trees.

Kumbu flew.

*

Wilbur hadn't climbed a tree since junior high. Maybe grade
school. He was amazed at how it all came back: stretching up for the
next branch with one hand, hanging on while his foot searched for a
toehold, pushing himself up with his leg, then stretching up for
another branch . . .

The chimpanzees seemed to prefer to hold any serious discussion high up in what they called a Granddaddy Tree, though for
Wilbur's sake they had chosen one that was relatively easy to climb.

It was a magnificent, mossy, stout-branched old giant that stood head and shoulders above the surrounding foliage, offering a spectacular view. The higher elevation made it easier to spot a prowling predator, Wilbur guessed, since few jungle creatures could climb like the chimps could. With a sentry or two posted in the lower branches to sound an alarm, they could exchange their quiet, elegantly formal speeches undisturbed.

Quiet? Almost totally silent, punctuated only by the occasional grunt or hoot or gibber. Wilbur still needed practice, but by now, three days after the chimps had found him sleeping by the creek, he was beginning to follow most of what they said. One by one he was even learning their names. Only this morning, in a flash of understanding that could only have come from what they called his Gift, he had realized that the chimps with names of one syllable, like Min, were the females; a double-syllable name, like Guma's, indicated a male.

The sun blinded him for a moment as he hooked his leg over another limb and heaved himself up once more. Above him, among the chimps relaxing in the Granddaddy's sturdy branches, he saw Guma, Noko, Brapa and the others who had found him that first morning and escorted him back to the rest of the clan. They smiled broad, encouraging smiles, closely watching his progress up the tree.

It hadn't been easy for them to persuade the other chimps that it was safe to welcome Wilbur into their territory. Some of the older ones still bared their teeth and stalked away when he tried to greet them. And some of the mothers quickly herded their young ones out of his path when they saw him coming. But it was clear that Guma commanded more respect than any of the other ranking males, and Guma was his staunch defender.

His three days in the forest with the chimps felt like three weeks, and by now he never wanted to go back. What for? he'd asked himself, jokingly at first.

But the more he thought about it, the fewer really compelling reasons he could think of. Until finally even his memories of what awaited him back in Cedartown had begun to fade. His drab apartment over Helwig's Hardware Store, brightened with a *National Geographic* map of Africa, travel posters of Mount Kilimanjaro and Victoria Falls. The ancient bicycle he rode down to the hospital every weekday morning. His aging buddies on the janitorial staff, the younger guys who were slowly taking over as his friends retired. Their union meetings. Their bowling team. His friends among the nurses and techs and clerical staff. Even his weekly piano lessons with Miss Violet Stark, the unrequited love of his life.

With a bit of strain, he could recall a few details of the safari he had waited all his life to take: the flight across the Atlantic, the caravan into the bush, the dead antelope . . .

All of it seemed so dim and longago compared to the texture of treebark under his fingers, the tropical sun warming his skin, the watching faces of his new friends as he grunted and sweated to reach them. He smiled up at them as he struggled another foothold higher. His safari pants were holding up, so far, but his shirt hung in ragged strips and yesterday he had discarded his boots and socks for better traction as he climbed.

He was gradually growing accustomed to what chimpanzees ate. Insects and roots were the hardest to stomach, but the chimps were so sincerely concerned about his skinny ribs and limbs— especially Grandmother Min— that he pretended to enjoy it all. The chimps weren't fooled, of course: he was even getting used to the way they plucked the most secretive thought from his skull. But his hunger had slowly gone away as his stomach adjusted to the new diet.

Luckily the forest was rich with fruit, and the chimps always knew which ones were due to ripen next. Once they understood that Wilbur preferred fruit to leaves or insects, they went out of their way to make sure he was well-nourished in a style he enjoyed.

Every fruit was delicious in a different way. Wilbur recognized a few from the color photographs in *National Geographic*. Several others had been served in the base camp's dining tent by Winston, the native chef. But most of them were utterly strange and new, and every day the chimps seemed to find another one for him to try.

In a crotch not far above Wilbur's head sat Guma, eating yet another fruit unknown even to *National Geographic*. Noko crouched beside Guma, picking something out of his brother's fur. Guma spat out a large round seed that bounced off the limb Wilbur was reaching for, and grinned.

What's the hurry? Guma teased. *You'll be too tired to speak! Do you expect us dumb beasts to do all the talking?*

Wilbur smiled up at him, too exhausted to retort. But he and Guma both knew he was climbing this tree not to speak, but to listen. He had spent a good part of the past three days high in the branches, quietly taking in the wisdom and eloquence of his jungle hosts.

Finally he was settled on the branch next to Guma, with Noko on his other side; Brapa balanced just above and to his left; Mabu straddling another branch to his right; Grandmother Min a little farther out, where the branches had more spring; Kuk leaning against the Granddaddy's trunk, and a dozen others at various distances around them. Unlike the close proximity required for communicating through the human voice, distance seemed to be no obstacle to this Gift of theirs. A few chimps even sprawled far below in the neighboring trees, though these were probably on sentry duty.

This time Uncle Noko seemed to be elected to make the first speech.

Friend Wilbur, he began, *you have been making excellent progress in learning the use of your Gift. You are truly a rarity among humans, and especially the pale tribes, to be honored by Life this way. We are honored in turn to be chosen to instruct you in the ways of the forest. I thank you for paying such respectful attention when we speak, without interrupting even in your thoughts.*

But Friend Wilbur, nothing happens without a reason. It's clear to all of us, even you, I think, that we do not meet here by accident, so far from your home territory. Clearly Life has intended it. Clearly Life has a purpose here. We have been pondering for the past three days what that might be. It is my brother Guma who has the truest sense of it, as he often does, so I will ask him to explain his thoughts to you.

Guma blinked solemnly. *Friend Wilbur, just as you humans received the power of speech, Life has given us chimpanzees the Gift of communication among ourselves. Our Gift enables us to understand other creatures as well, although imperfectly. We understand the language and thoughts of your species better than we do most others, no doubt because you are so closely related to us— although I understand some humans would dispute such an obvious fact. But even such a Gift as ours cannot reach into the mind of Life itself to divine the intent behind the world or any of Life's lesser acts. We only know our purpose here is to survive, in order to reproduce, in order to evolve.*

Friend, it is rare that Life reaches down to stir something new into our age-old pursuit of these sacred tasks. But only a few days before you came, my brother Noko brought us a disturbing piece of information. An infant was kidnapped from our clan by poachers years ago, and now, by what seems an impossible coincidence, we have learned where he was taken. We have lost many beloved young ones in this way, and though our Gift sometimes allows us to communicate with them afterwards on a rudimentary level, never until now have we learned the whereabouts of a single lost child. It seems to us that Life shows a clear intent by bringing us this news, and so soon afterward bringing us a human friend with the power to help us make use of it.

Wilbur blinked. *Make use of it? How?*

No one answered for a moment. Then Grandmother Min looked up with a luminous intensity in her brown eyes that burned across the space between her branch and Wilbur's.

Friend Wilbur? she asked. *Would you be willing to travel back to your homeland across the ocean and bring our little Kumbu home?*

✳

Kyle sat brooding on his cot. He was way ahead of his carefully rationed allotment of liquor, and he wasn't sure what he would do when he ran out. If the telegram he'd been dreading arrived by then, it could be anything. Anything at all.

Someone tapped at the wooden post that supported the door-flap.

"Mister Wilson?" It was Michael Ozawek, one of the more experienced guides, a Kamba tribesman from the highlands of Kenya.

"Yeah, come in."

Ozawek's dark, wry face peered into the gloom. He did not come in. "Mister Purgis is looking for you, sir. Your Land Rover is loaded and ready."

"Of course it is. I'm twenty minutes late. Can you tell him I'm sick?"

"He knows you're sick. He just don't know you're sick of him."

Ozawek was grinning slyly, holding the door-flap wide open to let in the morning, the arrowhead-shaped tribal scars on his cheeks clearly visible. The sky outside glowed a brilliant yellow-gold that made Kyle want to crawl back under his mosquito net. He lifted his pocket flask to his lips, but it was empty.

"Michael. Take my shift this morning, all right?"

"You know my skin's too dark to tell white people where to hunt. They don't take my word for anything."

"I'll lend you my outfit. Just tell 'em you had a little too much sun."

Ozawek laughed. "That's not what you had a little too much of.

46

You hunted out. I seen it before, you know."

"Hunted out? What's that mean?"

"Like a soldier who seen too much war. I was in a war once, and I seen it there. But I seen it out in the bush on safari, too. Man makes a kill one day, or only sees one, and all of a sudden it's one too many. I seen 'em throw down the gun and just walk away. I seen one turn the gun on himself, too, and that I don't never want to see any more."

Kyle jerked. He'd been barely aware of that thought himself when it came visiting. Had Ozawek seen it in his eyes?

"Mr. Ozawek, sir. Please come in."

"No sir, thank you. I don't want Mr. Purgis to come hunting me like he's hunting you, not in the mood he's in. I'll be a trophy on the wall before I know it. You better get your boots on and come out."

Kyle reached under the cot and found a boot. He tugged it on without tying it and reached under again. This time he found a bottle. Unscrewing the lid, he re-filled his flask and capped them both.

"I think you may be right. I appreciate your advice, Mr. Ozawek. Kindly tell Mr. Purgis I—"

"Boy!" came an angry voice from outside the tent. "He hasn't made it to breakfast yet, so I know he's in there. Why are you taking so long to fetch him?"

"Mr. Purgis, Mr. Wilson say he's sick."

"I don't care if he's puking his guts out. Much as he sucks that bottle, it damn well serves him right. Go on back to your post, I'll fetch him myself."

"Yes sir," Ozawek said over his shoulder. Then he gave Kyle a wink. "Been nice to know you, sir."

"You're a true friend, Mr. Ozawek," Kyle said with a warmth that surprised him. "Thank you."

"Wilson!" shouted Purgis, shoving through the door-flap with his rifle butt. He tucked the gun under one arm and it swung back and forth as he searched the gloom for his quarry. Kyle sat still, watching the barrel's nervous silhouette. After a minute Purgis's eyes adjusted and found Kyle. The rifle hung casually from the crook of his elbow, as if ready to do the same. "You know, you're really starting to get on my nerves."

"Morning, Purgis," said Kyle, and took the first slug from his freshly filled flask. "What can I do for you?"

"Damn you, Wilson, I can't do a damn thing about that moron Trimble losing himself in the bush, but these other folks are going to get their money's worth— and you're going to do your bit, even if you're so drunk you can't stand up!"

"Come on, Purgis. I'm sure we're both on probation by now for losing one of our precious charges. Something's holding up the telegram from the front office, that's all."

The rifle barrel trembled visibly against the morning light. "*You* were on duty the night Trimble disappeared. I have six witnesses. Now get out and sit in that Land Rover and fake it, or this will be your last hunt. I'll make sure of it!"

"Ah!" Kyle grinned and took another swig. "I've been meaning to speak to you about that. I've had just about all I can stomach of you and your obscene lust for blood, guts and gore. That goes for this so-called Great White Hunter Adventure outfit, too. And for that matter, the same goes for this sadistic so-called sport of murdering animals just to put their heads on a wall back home. I think if I see one more kill, I'm going to throw up every meal I've eaten since I took this unholy job."

He couldn't see Purgis's face, but the rifle barrel was quivering wildly now. He stood up and turned his back. And took a deep breath, just in case it was his last. "Now, if you'll excuse me, I have some packing to do."

Purgis let out a slow hiss. Kyle lifted his one bootless foot as high as it would go, swept the hanging mosquito net aside and stepped unsteadily over his cot. For a miraculous moment gravity was suspended, or he would have toppled over sideways onto the cot. He knelt in the corner of the tent and opened his trunk.

"Son of a bitch!" Purgis finally growled.

Another long, silent minute went by before Kyle heard the door flap shut and Purgis's boots fading into the sunrise.

*

"Professor Keller, will the exam include any questions about chimpanzees in the circus?"

The question was meant to be humorous, and it did indeed provoke a nervous laugh from Jane's afternoon class in Primate Evolution. Jane waited until the laughter died down, waited for her annoyance with the joker to fade, and answered with a little joke of her own. "I think that's an excellent idea, Mr. Polk. But just so my exam question won't catch any of you unprepared, who can explain the relevance of chimpanzees in the circus to the overall trends of primate evolution?"

After a minute or two the class began to grow uncomfortable with the silence. Jane caught more than one hostile glance toward Greg Polk, the class smart alec.

"Mr. Polk?" she asked.

Silence. Very well; they had a few minutes left before the bell. Silence could be very educational. Besides, Jane hadn't taken a moment to relax in the nine days since she'd seen poor Ralph's picture in the *Entertainer*.

After a spell, Adam Trenton held up his hand. "Professor? A chimpanzee who learns to perform in a circus might have offspring who are more advanced, biologically— because a circus environment contains new stimuli not available in the African jungle. At least if he mates with a female from the same environment. I mean, couldn't that create a whole new subspecies?"

Adam was sweating, a hopeful grin on his face.

Jane sighed. "Nice try. Probably worth an experiment sometime. But it might take quite a few generations to produce results. Anyone else?"

More silence.

Now that the Free Ralph! campaign had escalated to daily protests outside the circus, the voice that terrorized her on the telephone had become rather routine. The calls came every afternoon right around protest time, the voice growing more and more visceral, the threats less and less imaginative. She no longer dared to go out in public except for her appearances on the picket line and occasional invitations to speak into a microphone here, at a podium there, which she gladly embraced to help publicize the campaign.

And, of course, her altogether predictable and unavoidable appearances at the lectern of her classes at Miami State.

Finally Angela Perez raised her hand. "Professor. Chimpanzees haven't evolved much in the last few thousand years, correct? It seems to me the overall trends of primate evolution are mainly relevant to the chimpanzee's cousin, *homo sapiens*. Which is rapidly destroying the habitat of chimpanzees, gorillas, baboons and all the other non-human primates to make room for itself. So the relevance of a chimp joining the circus is not a biological advance, but a step backward. A chimp taking up a lifestyle of meaningless diversion. A devolution, if you will."

English was Angela's second language, but Jane had seen her command of it put even the chair of the English department on the defensive.

"Fair enough. Perhaps we ought to take a vote. If a chimpanzee were to follow the trends of human evolution, is it a step forward for chimpdom, or back? However, I'm not sure either point of view adequately—"

Now Greg Polk had his hand in the air: the joker who had started all this.

"Yes, Greg?"

"A chimp joining the circus might be here to teach us something! Like, it's mainly children who go to the circus, right? What better way to influence humanity, you know, to stop destroying chimpanzee habitat— wild habitat in general, for that matter. Why not?"

"Greg—"

The class broke up laughing again, the lingering strain of silence shattered at last. Jane almost let out a laugh herself. Only a paranoid feeling that she would be laughing at herself held her back. And then the bell rang, the class broke up in a more literal way, and she was snapping the latches of her black leatherette briefcase and heading for the parking lot.

Thank goodness spring break was coming up. The Monday after the circus's opening show, in fact. If the campaign somehow succeeded in setting Ralph free, she would need that week off to arrange for his transfer to a suitable preserve. She had already made contact with one or two. And if the campaign failed, as appeared more likely, at least she would finally get her long-overdue opportunity to rest.

Greg Polk fell into stride beside her.

"Professor, I apologize for the jokes." Startled, Jane searched his brown eyes for yet another joke, and found none. "But seriously, I want you to know I'm behind you a hundred percent on this 'Free Ralph' deal. A lot of the kids are. You keep it up, now. Bravo!"

He peeled off at the bottom of the brick stairway as they exited from Wheeler Hall, striding away down the sidewalk without a backward glance. Jane stopped dead on the curb, staring after him. Underneath all his clowning, the joker had a serious side after all.

She only wished Dean Carlisle would share his attitude. In the academic world, publicity was always welcome. Controversy was another matter entirely.

Slipping behind the wheel of her brown Subaru, she slid her key into the ignition and paused, as she always did these days. Would the car explode when she turned the key?

Unfortunately, there was only one way to find out.

Kumbu watched Daddy's face as he hung up the phone and came back to the car. He looked pleased with himself, at first, but Kumbu looked closer. Daddy's face was smiling. But his mouth was angry and his blue eyes were afraid, as if looking out through holes in a mask. He slid into the driver's seat and gave Kumbu a twisted grin.

"Come on, Ralph, let's go home. Time for your TV show."

The car jerked into motion as if it were angry too.

Kumbu wondered why Daddy had stopped here to talk on the coin telephone instead of using the one he carried in his pocket, or the one in the kitchen at home. It had something to do with the angry and the afraid, but Kumbu didn't understand. Daddy had been angry at Kumbu before, and sometimes he said angry things to Kumbu's Mommy. More and more often now, in fact. But Kumbu had never known Daddy to be afraid, even high above the Big Top's sawdust floor.

Just this morning at breakfast Daddy had stomped out of the dining room after shouting something Kumbu didn't understand. Mommy had untied Kumbu's bib with tears glittering in her eyes. Kumbu had stretched out his arms and hugged her until she laughed.

"Don't you worry about your Daddy," she said in a quivering voice. "He'll be all right. He just needs to take a little walk before practice. That will calm him down."

Kumbu heard, but he also heard the other thing she said. Not through her trembling lips, but the other way.

Mommy was afraid of Daddy. Daddy's angry and Mommy's afraid somehow fit together into a whole thing, the way Mommy and Daddy fit together, with Kumbu in the middle. They loved each other, and they both loved him. But inside of that, like a puzzle, this other thing was hiding. The angry and the afraid.

Not everything was plain to see, Kumbu was beginning to realize. And not everything could be spoken plainly out loud, even by humans, as much as they loved to talk.

Daddy was driving fast now, swerving around another car that was in their way. Kumbu glimpsed a woman with white hair and a startled face as they flew past. Then the light at the next corner turned yellow. Daddy shoved the pedal down to the floor. The light turned red, but they roared across the intersection and kept going.

Mommy wouldn't like it if she were in the car with them. She would beg Daddy to slow down, and maybe he would. But she wasn't with them now, and Kumbu loved it.

Besides, he didn't want to miss "Jungle in the City." Marvin, the star, was the only other chimpanzee he ever saw— except the one in the bathroom mirror. Kumbu and Daddy both knew Mommy wouldn't let him watch TV until after supper. And she would be upset if he ate in a hurry. Besides, going fast meant they would get home to see her sooner. Mommy would like that, wouldn't she?

But those were only reasons. They had nothing to do with why Kumbu's Daddy shoved the pedal down to the floor, or why Kumbu loved going so fast.

Sometimes Daddy watched "Jungle in the City" with Kumbu. They would laugh together as Marvin innocently got into trouble and then, by trying to get out of it, made it worse and worse. But as soon as the show was over Daddy would click back to his favorite channel to watch the cars racing.

Each car had a number so Daddy could tell them apart as they raced. Around and around the same loop of pavement they went, so fast that they sometimes crashed. Kumbu just got dizzy trying to watch. Then bored. But Daddy got more and more excited. He would forget Kumbu, forget Mommy, forget everything except which car was which. Finally he would start shouting to encourage them.

Kumbu had figured out long ago that the people on TV couldn't hear anything except the noises on TV. But sometimes when he got nervous about a big mistake Marvin was about to make, he forgot that too.

Mommy wouldn't sit through "Jungle in the City" with Kumbu or watch the cars with Daddy, either. She liked long, slow movies that were always the same: a man and a woman talking, laughing, arguing, whispering, shouting, and talking some more. Until finally they would kiss. Mommy would sit through the whole movie hugging a sofa pillow, waiting for them to kiss— as if maybe, just this one time, they might not.

At last Daddy swung the car onto a wide street with a median down the middle studded with tall palm trees. Up ahead Kumbu spotted the giant black and orange tent. They were almost home! They were going to see Mommy and find out what she had fixed for supper! Squealing his excitement, Kumbu strained to stand up. But he kept forgetting. Daddy had strapped him into his special seat, and he was stuck.

"Stay down, Ralph," Daddy growled, even though Kumbu was helplessly buckled in. "Let's not give them the pleasure."

Kumbu heard the angry in Daddy's voice again and saw the afraid in Daddy's eyes. Then he followed Daddy's cold blue gaze, and his eyes opened wide. On the sidewalk in front of the circus, people were walking back and forth carrying white square signs on wooden sticks. Kumbu didn't know what the black marks on the signs meant, but he knew they meant something.

Sometimes Kumbu watched his Daddy reading the newspaper, or his Mommy reading a paperback book. No one had ever explained what the neat, regular rows of inkmarks meant, but if he held his hand close to them, without quite touching, he could feel them softly talking.

The pictures that interrupted the newspaper columns were clues. He had figured that out one day not long ago when Mommy and Daddy had showed him a bright color picture on the front page of a newspaper. Both of them were giggling and excited. Kumbu didn't understand why until suddenly, squinting down, he'd recognized himself in the picture.

"It's you, sport!" Daddy had laughed, pointing.

"And there's your Daddy!" said Mommy.

Yes, there they were, Kumbu and his Daddy, each holding one end of a trapeze bar, wearing the colorful matching outfits Mommy had made and smiling the smile Mommy had taught them both to smile. Mommy had cut the article out and taped it to the refrigerator. The picture was fading now, but every so often Kumbu pulled a tall stool over and sat there admiring it for a while.

Daddy shoved the pedal down and the car shot past the people on the sidewalk with a roar. The people smiled and waved.

"Goddamn busybodies," Daddy muttered under his breath. "Don't you forget, Ralph. Just focus on where we're at, and where we're going. What's in between will take care of itself." But underneath the words Kumbu felt something deeper and colder than angry, with a harder edge. That was afraid.

Then they were turning into the circus parking lot. A man in a blue uniform swung open a gate. Kumbu recognized the man, but not the uniform. The gate was a new thing, too.

Every day something new entered Kumbu's world, a new thing to wonder at. And someday understand.

✳

"Me?"

Friend Wilbur was so surprised at Grandmother Min's request that he forgot his Gift and spoke aloud. Guma and Uncle Noko both reached out to grasp an elbow, but they had chosen this branch well; there was little danger that their frail, awkward human friend might fall. Instead, the round clear disks perched across his nose gave a little lurch and dropped away through the branches.

Uncle Noko watched them fall, silently alerting the young sentries posted below. Mabu caught them in mid-air and tossed them to the sentry closest to the Granddaddy Tree's massive trunk, Yago, who tucked them tenderly between his lips and began to climb.

Friend Wilbur never even noticed they were gone. "You mean—"

Then he stopped, touching his mouth with four fingertips and a thumbtip pressed together. It was the gesture the chimpanzees used to remind him when he forgot and spoke aloud: the same one they used when they were teaching the young chimps. Friend Wilbur seemed unaware that he had used it on himself. But he frowned and swallowed and then stammered on without making another sound.

You mean, leave here— go back— leave you all, and—

Min laughed softly. *Not forever,* she said. *We hope you will return as soon as you can with our Kumbu. After that, naturally you would be welcome*

54

to stay with us for as long as you wish.

Kuk handed something shiny to Brapa, who examined it and passed it on to Guma: the set of round clear disks in their metal frames. Friend Wilbur had explained how looking through the disks helped him to see, though many of the clan remained skeptical. When Min had finished speaking, Guma gave them back to Wilbur.

My glasses! Friend Wilbur was surprised once more, but this time did not forget his Gift.

And not just welcome, Uncle Noko added, touching their human friend's knee. *Min spoke too shyly. We would rejoice to have you here with us as part of our family.*

Friend Wilbur hooked the metal frames over his ears again and looked from face to face. Water welled up in the light blue eyes behind the glasses.

Then I will go! he said. *Tell me what I need to do.*

Good, Uncle Noko said.

Excellent! said Guma.

Min gave a joyful little cry.

The entire Granddaddy Tree shook as the chimpanzees hooted and yodeled and danced in its branches. Some things, Guma thought to himself with a grin, can only be appropriately expressed with loud, crude noises, no matter how many generations of evolution have gone by.

When the cheering had died down, Uncle Noko continued.

In case you did not know it, Friend Wilbur, the humans have offered a reward for returning you to your camp. Do not go there! The tourists with guns have continued their killings in your absence. That would be difficult for you to see now that you have begun to cultivate your Gift. You must be careful from now on, wherever you go, because you have been opened to the hidden thoughts of every creature you'll encounter, large and small.

It would also be unwise, Brapa added, *for us to guide you to any of the villages nearby. The villagers would only return you to the hunting camp in order to claim the reward. We have talked about this, and we see only one possible way. We will guide you on a long journey through the bush, avoiding every village and taking you to the highway. A machine with wheels will stop for you. What do they call it again, Noko?*

A bus, Uncle Noko said. *I have seen them. Up and down the highway they go, making an obnoxious noise and an even more disgusting smell. But many* humans can ride inside.

Brapa, you forget one thing, said Guma. *Friend Wilbur, do you have money? Do you have the papers that prove to other humans who you are, or did you leave these back at the camp?*

Friend Wilbur looked blank for a second. Then he reached down and felt through the torn and dirty cloth that still hung around his waist. He smiled.

I have money, he said. *I have my passport. I even have my return ticket, right here in my moneybelt. My supervisor at the hospital, Mr. Johnson, advised me not to keep them in my pocket, but in this special pouch inside my clothes. I bought one at the airport in New York.*

Excellent! Guma said again.

Now, listen, said Noko. *Can you change the place where your airplane will take you when you return?*

I think so, Wilbur replied. He smiled. *Some people will do anything for money!* Then he cut the smile off with the same gesture he had used to stop himself from speaking. None of the chimps was smiling.

This is a sad thing, said Grandmother Min gently. *This strange hunger for money, which no one can eat. This is why so many of our brothers and sisters are no longer here with us. We understand it, thanks to our Gift, and understanding it helps us to protect our young ones from the poachers and the kidnappers. But this is one thing we wish we didn't have to understand.*

Friend Wilbur nodded thoughtfully. *Life has given you some difficult tasks,* he said. *Where is it that I should transfer my return ticket? Where will my mission take me?*

A place called Dade County, said Uncle Noko. *In a place called Florida. It is in the far south of your territory.*

I will go there, Friend Wilbur said firmly once more. *But how will I find your little Kumbu?*

Kumbu is a star in this place Dade County, Guma said. *He performs tricks in a circus. Many people will know how to find him. But if you have any difficulty locating him, remember this. The name of the circus is "Rufus Barnabas." And the name they know our Kumbu by is "Ralph."*

"Ralph?" Their human friend blinked through his glasses.

That's right, Min broke in, water spilling from her eyes. *They call my baby Ralph!*

Chapter 4

"Tall Chimp"

*

Kyle rested, leaning on his stick. It was hopeless. His trunk had wheels, but tiny ones like a toy. Fine for airports and hotels. Hopeless out here in the real world.

All that had kept him going down the miles of dirt road between base camp and the highway was his hope, his faith, finally his desperate certainty that the highway would have an asphalt shoulder where those tiny wheels could roll. And of course it didn't. By his seventh or eighth expedition into Babarzark Game Park, surely he would have noticed a detail like that. But if he had, he'd long since forgotten.

In the intervals between passing cars, trucks, and overloaded buses, he dragged his tiny wheels over cracked and patched asphalt. When he heard an engine coming, he lurched off the pavement into the mud and weeds.

Luckily, halfway down the long dirt road Kyle had heard one coming and moved aside, only to recognize a Land Rover with the Great White Hunter logo on its door. At the wheel was Michael Ozawek, grinning as he halted in a swirl of dust and motioned Kyle to get in.

"No, Purgis didn't send me," he'd said. "I struck a bargain with Winston. I thought you might need a lift just about now."

He set the handbrake and was already jumping out to help lift Kyle's trunk into the rear seat.

"Mr. Ozawek, you are not only a scholar and a gentleman. You are a true prince."

The grin vanished. "How did you know?"

Kyle's mouth opened. "I . . ."

"Only teasing." Ozawek was grinning again, a glitter of amazingly white teeth against his broad dark face. "It's only partially true. A rough translation."

"Thank God. I'm in enough trouble as it is without stirring up the natives. How far to the highway?"

"I am taking you there. From where I drop you, twentyfour kilometers to the city. Not so far. The local buses pick up everyone walking, no questions asked, if they're not already filled far above capacity. You have cash? Local currency, I mean?"

"I have enough. And Travelers Cheques for the airfare. I'll get there."

"And where is 'there'?"

"My grandmother's condo in Homestead, Florida. With any luck she'll be out of town and her houseboy will let me in."

"And if not, will you then be homeless in the streets of Florida?"

"Not too likely. But yes, it's a possibility. Even if Gram is at home, I might not be able to stand it there for long. Religion is sometimes benign, I've heard. But when it's malignant it's a terrible disease. If she knew I was coming, she would already be working on her sermon. Anyway, this time of year it's about fifty-fifty whether she's still in Homestead or already out in Idaho for the summer."

Ozawek had laughed that easy laugh and jumped back in behind the wheel. Conversation, too, was easy with Michael. It was a gift, one worthy of a prince. Walking again now with his trunk in tow, leaning on his stick, Kyle wondered why he hadn't noticed the Wakamba guide's qualities before. It would have been pleasant to have someone to talk to on this godforsaken expedition into the bush. Though somehow he doubted Ozawek was a drinking man.

The thought had no sooner leaped into his mind and bounded on again than he thought of something else. Raising his wraparound sunglasses, he stopped to look around. The lush, familiar landscape. The pale humid sky. Cattle grazing the fertile grassland along the highway to his right. Three women in bright dresses walking the stream at the far edge of the pasture, wet laundry balanced on their heads. On his left, the first low thickets of the bush country. And the long stripe of faded asphalt in between, curving just enough to accentuate the easy roll of the foothills. God, it was beautiful.

Africa had always been lovely to him, ever since he was a boy dragged here by his crazy mother. Why had he come back so many times, even after he'd become— officially, at least— a responsible adult? Not to kill it, over and over, like Solomon Purgis. It was this vast untamed beauty he had loved since the beginning: the moist abundance of the forests, the golden vista of the veldt, the wind-blown austerity of the desert. And then the breathstopping apparition of an animal: elephant, cheetah, crocodile, gazelle . . .

At that instant he remembered to watch for snakes, and looked directly down. And recoiled, almost hopping on top of his trunk as the gorgeous pattern of green and black and yellow scales winked up at him from the asphalt. But this one was dead, its coils mashed flat by the treads of a double truck-tire.

He sighed. They loved the baking heat of the pavement— often too much for their own good, when it lulled them into a trance and they no longer felt the vibration of a vehicle approaching.

Speaking of which, one was approaching now: one of those crowded local buses. He'd seen them all over Africa in his travels, but had never boarded one before. Even with Ma at her craziest. But with any luck, this one might have a little room. Kyle steered his trunk off the pavement and turned to face the windshield's twin panes, the bus driver framed in one and what appeared to be a crowd of bodiless heads tightly packed into the other. All were examining him closely as the bus braked at the last possible second and kicked and shuddered to a stop. A door in the side folded inward, precisely aligned with Kyle's dusty safari boots.

Before his eyes, a gap melted in the crowd. He dropped the walking stick he had cut for himself and stepped up onto the lowest step, dragging his trunk aboard. Before he'd finished paying the driver, the bus lurched and began to move. Step by step, amid a babble of questions, begging, and advice, a way opened. Regretting his height and bulk for the first time in all his journeys to Africa, even his shoe size, Kyle made his way into the shadowy, sweat-perfumed interior of the Dark Continent.

Somewhere in the rear of the bus, a rooster crowed.

*

Squatting beside the stream, Wilbur watched as Uncle Noko waded in, nibbled at the edge of a lilypad, then slurped up a few floating flowers. The other chimps followed one by one, pausing to drink and play a little as Uncle Noko splashed across and climbed the opposite bank. Noko kept watch while they snacked on purple lilies and satisfied their thirst.

Wilbur looked around at the verdant little valley they had just crossed. Upstream, he saw a rocky natural crossing. Downstream, a crowd of hoof and claw-marks pocked the wet mud at the water's edge where a myriad of forest creatures had stopped to drink. Uncle Noko had avoided both in favor of the floating flowerbed.

You learn quickly, I see, Zambi called to him from the water, almost entirely submerged. *But will your skill at keeping watch in the jungle be useful to you when you return to your home territory in search of Kumbu?*

I think so, Wilbur replied, trying to think back. *I mean, in Indiana, where I grew up, we don't have many deadly predators. But where I am going now I understand it is very different.*

He waded in under Uncle Noko's watchful eye. The younger chimps gaped as his safari pants trapped pockets of air like twin balloons that slowly deflated as water soaked through the fabric and the air seeped out. Splashing his face clean, wiping his glasses on the remaining shreds of his shirt, scooping up a drink in his cupped hands, then sampling the purple flowers at a leisurely pace, he ignored the stares. He was in no hurry to leave this marvelous place.

The chimps trooped out of the water and up the bank, water streaming from their fur and Wilbur's pants to form a miniature tributary feeding the stream. Uncle Noko was already leading again, sniffing at a bush that had been broken off by some large, heavy animal departing from the waterhole. Most of the footprints that left the stream, in fact, converged at that same spot to enter the forest on a wide, trampled track.

Uncle Noko followed the stream instead.

They had been traveling since early morning, though their progress resembled a typical day's random browsing for food. Today, however, all their browsing tended in a particular direction, following Uncle Noko's lead. Without a single noticeable moment of departure, the party that was accompanying Wilbur on his way had gradually left the rest of the clan behind. Now, hours later, they were on their own— Uncle Noko, Wilbur, Kuk, Zambi, Mabu, Shan, Grandmother Min's son Tunga, and Brapa. The old storyteller was observing everything closely, no doubt collecting the choice details that would make this a memorable tale for generations of listeners to come.

So far they had run across half a dozen variations on the usual chimpanzee diet that were new to Wilbur. A long green seedpod that dangled from a vine; an orange fungus that grew at the base of a certain tree, which tasted a bit chalky, but somewhat like a stale flour biscuit; a delicious but seedy fruit resembling a pomegranate; a large species of termite, which Wilbur had declined to try; a delicate yellow and orange butterfly, which he was unable to catch, to the amusement of his companions. And now the purple lilies that floated on the stream.

Along the way Uncle Noko had instructed them on the signs he used to guide them through the forest, and even Wilbur had caught one or two. He had noticed on his own how a certain kind of moss only grew on a particular species of tree, but hadn't realized that it grew only on one side. That was a handy way of judging direction down here under the canopy of leaves, where the sun only penetrated now and then.

Of course, it wouldn't have done Wilbur much good that first pitch-black night when he'd wandered away from camp. But then again, if he'd been more of a woodsman then— if he'd managed to find his way back to the campfire and his fellow "tourists with guns," as Noko called them— he never would have known what he was missing. That night seemed months ago, though it couldn't have been more than a week since his new friends had discovered him asleep in the grass.

Those "new friends" seemed like old friends now, and Wilbur was no longer the same man. And that was an understatement if he'd ever heard one.

The chimps had even given him a new name. Last night as the full moon rose, they had held a sort of farewell ceremony and adopted him formally into the clan. Grandmother Min had tucked a flower behind each of his ears, murmuring a strange new word .

Then Guma had removed the flowers and fed them to him, muttering the same new word. As Wilbur chewed the soft subtle texture of flower petals and swallowed their fragrant juices, he'd found himself repeating the strange word and realized the entire band of chimps was repeating it with him.

Tanzar! Tanzar! Tanzar! Tanzar!

Then Uncle Noko had stood up to deliver one of his somber, formal speeches. He'd begun with the new word.

Tanzar, your new name only means "tall chimp." To us, though, it means much more. It means you are different from us in only one way, and of course I'm talking about your height. We are accustomed to looking down when we teach a new member of our clan how to speak and act in a way that reflects well on the rest of us. In teaching you, we have only had to learn to look up instead. Unlike so many of the paleskinned humans we have watched as they stumble through the forest, trampling perfectly edible flowers and carving their names on the trees, you already speak and act more like a chimpanzee than a human.

So this name we thought of for you, while nothing but ordinary in every ordinary way, actually contains within it the highest compliment a chimpanzee can offer a human. You have been with us in the forest for only a few days. But already it feels as if you have been with us forever. Friend Wilbur no more, you have now become Brother Tanzar. Come safely back to us!

Guma and Min and Brapa and a few others had each taken a turn to speak as well, but Wilbur could hardly keep up with all the compliments that embellished their speeches. His new name was enough. What Uncle Noko had said kept echoing inside, reverberating with the cries and calls of the jungle that had terrified him so on that first night. The misty look in Min's eyes as she decorated him kept lingering on, along with the fragile aftertaste of flowers.

When every possible eloquence and profundity had been exhausted, the circle of small hairy bodies had crowded in on him, each stretching out an arm to touch him somewhere. Their gentle fingertips somehow conveyed even more than all their words, and Wilbur was overwhelmed with feelings that had no translations in human language.

Finally Mabu had brought out the evening's treat, a sticky, dripping beehive with a dozen honeycombs still intact. The younger chimps had immediately begun to clamor for a taste. Wilbur, though— Tanzar now till the end of his days— had only sat there, staring up through the tangled foliage at the round brilliant moon. Tears had fogged his glasses and run down into his mustache whenever he thought about leaving his new home, returning to the noises and smells of the city, boarding an airplane back to the States. But none of that could touch the feelings that hummed inside him, vibrating like a swarm of bees on the track of their stolen hive.

He still felt it now as he trailed Uncle Noko through the undergrowth, bending almost double to duck under branches that Noko cleared without bending at all. Noko never once forgot and squeezed through a gap too small for Wilbur to follow. Wilbur and the seven chimps could have been one creature, so connected were they in his mind and heart. Without even bothering to phrase it into language in his mind, he knew that all of them shared the same humming vibration of feeling.

He wondered if it would follow him back to the slums and shanties of Wanzani City, over the endless whitecaps of the Atlantic . . .

Suddenly the trees gave way and Noko and Wilbur crouched together at the forest's edge, gazing across miles of open grassland. Thirty, maybe forty yards away, a herd of antelopes browsed quietly on the green and yellow slope. One by one the other chimps reached the edge of the trees and fell silent, squinting out at the unaccustomed expanse of daylight.

Across from them, where another arm of forest jutted into the open, a leopard was slinking through the grass toward the grazing herd.

*

Kumbu sat on a tall stool in the kitchen, studying the neatly clipped square of newspaper on the refrigerator. Without looking, he stretched out one arm and pulled a banana loose from the bunch on the counter.

It was the last bunch, but his Mommy was at the grocery store right now bringing home more bananas. His Daddy was asleep on the sofa in the trailer's tiny living room. Kumbu could hear an excited voice trying to keep up as the cars roared around the track. He peeled his banana and bit most of it off, still intent on the clipping.

But this time he wasn't looking at the colorful picture he knew so well. He was looking at the little black inkmarks that covered the rest of the paper, wondering which ones meant "Ralph."

He wished Mommy would teach him how to understand the little inkmarks: she had taught him so many things. And Mommy wished she could, too. Every now and then he heard her sigh, and caught a whisper of silent yearning behind the sigh. He wasn't sure how, but somehow he knew exactly what she was yearning for.

Yet even though Kumbu knew, he didn't understand. Why couldn't Mommy teach him to read the marks? She just couldn't, and he vaguely understood that it was his fault.

But why?

Maybe if he could teach himself, his Mommy wouldn't be so sad.

The inkmarks looked a little bit like bugs marching in straight rows, although they never moved. Each row was exactly the same length. The rows of bugs formed two long columns marching down the paper, then a shorter third and fourth column above the picture. The two long columns had exactly the same number of rows: so did the two short columns.

Kumbu frowned. At first each tiny bug looked different from the rest. But glancing down the columns, he saw that some of the bugs were actually the same ones repeated. He felt a surge of excitement. He had never looked this closely at the little inkmarks before.

The bugs marched in little squads, each squad made up of a different number of bugs. But all of a sudden he caught his breath: two of the little squads of bugs were exactly the same!

Across the top of the clipping marched a line of much bigger, darker bugs. He had wondered many times what its purpose was. But now he saw another line of bugs marching across the bottom of the clipping, just below the picture. These bugs were a little bigger than the ones that made up the four columns, though not nearly as big and dark as the line across the top.

Suddenly he spotted a squad of five bugs in the line across the top that was repeated in the smaller line under the picture. He looked up and down several times, comparing them.

R-a-l-p-h. Yes: exactly the same!

He scanned down the columns, and saw the same little squad of bugs repeated one— two— three more times.

He almost fell off his stool. That was his name! He knew beyond any question, any uncertainty, any doubt. At least it was the name his human mother and father had given him. He had long ago grown used to people calling him "Ralph," though he'd always known deep inside that he was Kumbu.

And then it hit him, so hard that for a minute he couldn't breathe at all. Those same five bugs. He had seen them somewhere else. Outside the circus, coming home with his Daddy. On the white square signs those people carried on sticks. Daddy had started to take Kumbu out for a drive every afternoon, and he saw the people there on the sidewalk every time.

Free Ralph! several of the signs had said. He had no idea what *F-r-e-e* meant, but now he knew what *R-a-l-p-h* meant, and he would never forget it as long as he lived. Mommy and Daddy were going to be so proud!

This time he did fall off the stool. He was so excited that he bounced off the floor and crashed into the refrigerator, knocking over the stool, and then shot through the swinging kitchen door. Out in the dining room he let out a squeal, trying his best to shape it into the name "Ralph," as he sprang completely over the table and slid across the floor hugging his Daddy's chair. The chair skidded straight toward the arching doorway to the living room, hit the edge of the living room carpet and toppled, flinging Kumbu into the room where Daddy lay snoring.

Kumbu rolled across the carpet and leaped to his feet again with another squeal of triumph. He jumped up on the coffee table and bowed, first toward the TV, then back toward the dining room, and finally toward his Daddy. Daddy opened one eye and frowned. But Kumbu wasn't waiting for applause. He raised both arms above his head and clapped for himself.

"Dammit, Ralph, get off the table. You're standing on my remote!" Daddy snatched something out from under Kumbu's foot, and Kumbu almost fell. "And hell, look what you've switched me to."

Kumbu glanced at the TV and saw an almost naked man straddling the neck of an elephant. "Come, Cheetah!" the man commanded. A small black shape scrambled up the elephant's side and perched on the man's bare shoulder— a small black shape that looked just like Kumbu. Then the elephant lifted his trunk and trumpeted like one of the circus elephants at Wally Scheiner's cue.

"You runt, I said get off the table." Daddy was getting unsteadily to his feet, fumbling with his belt. "Off, I said!" The belt came snaking out of its loops, one by one, and suddenly Daddy swung it back and snapped it at Kumbu's legs. It stung!

Kumbu yelped and tried to grab at it, but the belt kept snapping out, stinging him again and again.

"Ralph! What is it!" Suddenly Kumbu heard his Mommy's voice on the steps outside, and a jingle of keys. "What's going on in there?"

"Dammit!" Daddy glanced toward the door, just long enough for Kumbu to grab the stinging end of the belt. The door burst open and banged against the wall. Mommy stood there looking back and forth from Daddy to Kumbu, her eyes wide and her arms full of groceries. Daddy dropped his end of the belt and backed away.

"Thank God you're home, Peg. Ralph just grabbed my belt and— went— berserk!"

*

Jane heard the cheerful little chime of her cell phone and shuddered. Lifting her picket sign a little higher, as if it could obscure the colorful billboard in front of the Rufus Barnabas Circus Spectacular, she pretended for a few more steps that she was just another picketer instead of the organizer of the protest.

The police had been unable to trace the threatening phone calls, though Detective Lopez seemed to be genuinely concerned. The calls came from public telephones at gas stations and shopping malls and supermarkets all over Dade County, always the same hoarse, muffled voice, hissing an endless variety of threats.

"The sharks are hungry tonight, animal lover. Why don't you go swimming and feed a few?"

"I hope your insurance is paid up, Professor. I understand that little car you drive tends to blow up without warning."

"Be careful next time you cross the street, Professor! All the bus drivers are eager to claim that reward."

"I wouldn't go out to your meeting tonight, if I were you. Something might happen to those precious parrots of yours."

The latest call had come on her cell phone as she was driving out on the expressway for this afternoon's picket. "Hey, meet me down in Liberty City at midnight! My gang wants to get to know you better."

She had come to dread the horrid, humorless voice, along with the ringing of either one of her phones. But still the cheerful sound persisted. Jane sighed and stepped out of the picket line to answer the call.

"This is Jane Keller. How may I help you?"

"Dr. Keller? My name is Will Pickner, and I write for the *Boston Globe*. My paper is interested in featuring your 'Free Ralph' campaign in our Sunday magazine. Do you have just a minute to talk?"

She sighed again, this time with relief. "Not exactly. We picket every afternoon outside the circus. Why don't you come down and interview some of the others as well?"

"I would, except I haven't exactly landed yet." Pickner laughed pleasantly. "My plane is still circling the airport. I thought I might get a head start on the story."

"Then meet us for dinner. We eat at a place called the Seagrass Veggie Lounge every evening after we finish picketing."

"It's in the phone book?"

"North of downtown, not far from the airport. They've started giving us the banquet table in the back room. Just ask for us."

"Sounds like the movement is growing."

"We have a lot of animal lovers in Dade County, Mr. Pickner. Every time Ralph appears on the news, we get fresh recruits."

"Then would you say—"

"I'm sorry, Mr. Pickner, that's all I have time for right now. Duty calls." She snapped her cell phone shut and raised her sign again.

Free Ralph! it demanded in neat purple lettering. Jane had blocked it out in pencil and painted it herself at the outset of the campaign. Stepping back into the picket line, she smiled triumphantly to herself.

The *Boston Globe*. This thing was really beginning to snowball. They probably had a lot of animal lovers up in Boston, too.

Much more often than not, of course, her phones rang with calls like Pickner's: fresh publicity, new volunteers, more support. Twenty-two oddly assorted animal lovers had shown up today to march in an elongated circle along the sidewalk, and every day the picket line grew longer. Every night the campaign made the Miami nightly news, on one station or another. People had begun to recognize Jane Keller wherever she went.

She shrank from the attention. Yet for Ralph's sake, she knew she could endure it. Duty calls.

"Professor!" Jim Rochdale hissed to her as they passed, going opposite directions in the line. He nodded toward an oncoming car, a green Pontiac with a white vinyl roof. "Here they come."

Jim had been the first to spot the Pontiac that almost never failed to come rumbling past the picket line about this time. In the driver's seat, even through the tinted windshield, Jane recognized Dale Hardy, the trapeze star. Though Ralph appeared regularly in the newscasts, holding Peg Tyler's hand and grinning for the cameras, Mr. Hardy seemed to shun the limelight. Strange behavior for a star circus performer, Jane had often reflected.

Beside Hardy in the Pontiac, strapped into a child's car-seat, sat Ralph. The young chimp gazed wide-eyed out the window, as if fascinated by the protest. But oddly, he didn't seem so interested in the people who had gathered to demand his freedom. Instead Ralph seemed to be staring up at the signs they carried, squinting from slogan to slogan as the car roared past on Boulevard Santa Fe. Almost as if—

Absurd. Jane shook the notion out of her head. Chimps were intelligent, but not that intelligent.

Wilbur stood up, waving both arms and filling his lungs to call out a warning to the herd of antelopes. With unexpected strength, Uncle Noko seized his belt and jerked him back down before he could make a sound. Wilbur hit the ground and toppled over backward. Lying there, winded and stunned, he felt the earth vibrating against his shoulderblades and skull with a vast drumming, as wide as the horizon, that slowly died away.

"What did you—" he stammered aloud, gasping for breath.

Uncle Noko bunched four fingers and a thumb together and gently corked Wilbur's mouth. *Exactly what I was about to ask you,* he said. *What did you think you were doing?*

It had happened so fast that Wilbur still wasn't sure. He climbed shakily to his knees and crouched among the chimps again.

I was— trying to warn them. The antelopes. The leopard was— was—

Aren't you aware that leopards also eat chimpanzee? said Tunga. *Were you trying to distract her in our direction?*

Ssshh, Uncle Noko admonished. *Yes, Cousin Leopard does occasionally feast on our brother and sister chimps. As a fellow tree-climber, we owe her the utmost respect. But that's not the point here.*

Out in the sun, Wilbur could see now, the herd of antelopes was gone. He had felt their pounding hoofs as he'd sprawled on the ground. Perhaps his warning had reached them after all.

Then he saw something else, almost invisible in the tall grass: four hooves thrust into the air. Four smooth brown limbs, one of them stained bright red. Beside the dead antelope crouched the leopard, hungrily cleaning out its rib cavity. Wilbur felt sick. He glanced at Uncle Noko with lowered brows, angry now.

Uncle Noko gazed serenely back at him. *Shall we climb a tree and discuss this, Brother Tanzar?*

Wilbur looked away.

All of us are food for someone, Noko said gently, after a pause. *The ancient agreement allows no exceptions. Even the all-knowing, all-powerful humans get eaten by some fellow creature in the end— or more likely, creatures. Even those mighty Egyptian kings inside their pyramids. Yes, we have heard about them down here in the jungle. Our cousins the camels can't resist passing on a good joke. Brapa, would you mind? You tell it best.*

Ah, well, yes, of course, said Brapa with a nervous glance and a sympathetic smile. *As I understand it, the Pharaohs had themselves embalmed with some sort of preservative— then wrapped in perfumed cloth and sealed inside a stone coffin— and then finally, or so they thought, in huge monuments of stone. Centuries later you paleskins came and disinterred them, only to seal them again inside glass cases in your museums to keep them from deteriorating. But nevertheless—*

No such luck, Noko cut in smoothly. *Centuries may go by again, but sooner or later their dried meat will indeed be cleaned off their bones by some tiny, humble creature that works hard for the privilege of eating. Our cousins the antelopes understand this, of course. Because just as it is a privilege to eat, it is a privilege to be eaten. Sorry, but you can't have one privilege without the other. That would upset the balance of things. Do you understand why?*

Wilbur shook his head. He didn't get it. He wasn't sure he wanted to.

Noko grunted softly. *I can understand why this might be a difficult concept for humans. It's called "sacrifice."*

You mean . . . a religious sacrifice? Like a sacrifice to the gods?

69

Brapa wrinkled his nose in disgust. *Not at all! That kind of sacrifice was invented by your earliest priests and kings, long before the Pharaohs. Soon after inventing themselves, they came up with the idea of placating their gods— while still retaining all their own wealth and power— by sacrificing things that belonged to others. Like the lives of animals. The concept was eventually expanded to include humans as well, usually captives from other tribes. And after a while you no longer had to be a priest or a king to sacrifice an animal. But originally even the humans understood that the only sacrifice that really counts is to sacrifice yourself. The gods, whoever they are, must know they aren't getting the real thing.*

On the other hand, said Uncle Noko, *our cousin the antelope out there . . . he made his sacrifice knowing it was for a worthy cause. The most worthy cause of all.*

Wilbur's mouth opened to make a rapid retort, but nothing came to mind except a flood of questions. He closed it.

Make no mistake, Noko went on, sober-faced. *It is the duty of every creature of every species to do our best to escape our predators. To survive, in order to reproduce. Just as it is the duty of every predator to catch and eat us if they can, for precisely the same reason. This is the ancient agreement. In exchange for the privilege of eating, all of us enjoy the privilege of feeding someone stronger or quicker or hungrier than ourselves. And even predators have predators, of course.*

But that isn't the noble cause we die for. The antelope out there was not the quickest member of the herd, you see. Perhaps he was ill. Or elderly. Or just a little slow. His sacrifice allowed the rest of the herd to get away. But he didn't die for this one herd alone. He died for all herds of antelope, everywhere. And, since antelopes do not exist alone in the world, for all the species that share their territory as well. Can you guess how we all benefit?

Wilbur's Gift was discovering no clues in Uncle Noko's kindly, cunning expression. He glanced out across the waving grass, where he could hear the leopard crunching through a bone. Then he blinked up into the bright pale sky and let his eyes drift out of focus.

"Evolution," he breathed to himself without even thinking.

Excellent! Noko said. *Although we all do our best to survive, in order to reproduce, if we should happen to fail we have the satisfaction of knowing in that moment of sacrifice that our death will improve the stock that produced us. Evolution simply cannot occur except through that sacrifice. It may not seem worth it, to a human. To those of us who are born in the wild, it's all-important.*

Evolution is the sacred task Life gave us eons ago, before antelopes or leopards existed as separate species. Evolution is what eventually separated us— antelopes from leopards from primates— long before we chimps and you humans also reached a point of departure and went our separate ways.

But . . . what about the animals I've eaten all my life? Wilbur asked, no longer resisting, but still reluctant to expose his ignorance. *When I was younger I ate my share of the deer my Dad killed, and quite a few fish I caught myself. But most of the meat we eat in America comes from the supermarket.*

Excellent question! Noko scratched himself, grinning. *And a perfect illustration of my point. Brapa? You've told the story a hundred times.*

Well, yes, said the old storyteller, *of course. Well, not long before the invention of animal sacrifice, Brother Tanzar, your ancestors succeeded in domesticating a few animals who were as tired of the hunt as they were. In exchange for food and safety, our cousins the pigs and cows and chickens and the rest agreed to sacrifice themselves. The new arrangement was an honorable one, in its way— still a willing sacrifice, and until the fateful moment I understand they ate very well indeed. But of course, our domesticated cousins were giving up the very thing that is most sacred to the rest of us: the task of evolution. And before very long the humans, naturally, forgot that this was a mutual agreement. They began to think of pigs and cows and chickens and the others as something called "property."*

Noko snorted. *Now there's a concept I wish you would explain to me some time, Tanzar!*

From that point on, Brapa continued, *the evolutionary changes in pigs and cows and chickens from generation to generation were no longer determined by what was best for them, and hence for the rest of us, but by what made them taste better to humans. A short-term gain for humans which, predictably enough, has led to some disastrous consequences in the long run. For all of us, including humans.*

A silence fell. The afternoon sun blazed down over the rolling grassland.

"Evolution," Wilbur murmured again, squinting up into the glare. In spite of himself he was beginning to understand. *So . . . when the great philosophers asked . . . what is the meaning of life . . .*

They were humans, Noko replied before the question had fully formed in Wilbur's mind. *So they were mainly concerned with their own puny, individual lives. Or at the very most, human life. What they didn't think to ask was— what is the meaning of all life? All the lives that have unfolded, all the lives now unfolding, all the lives that ever will unfold on this living world?*

The question hung there in the sunlight, reverberating silently.

Evolution? Wilbur ventured.

Exactly!

And exactly then, with a precision that would make Wilbur shudder every time he thought of it for the rest of his life, a rifle shot echoed across the golden grassland.

The leopard bounded to its feet, turned halfway around, and collapsed in a heap of black and gold fur.

Wilbur toppled backward once more and sprawled beneath the edge of the trees as if he too had been shot. The chimps scattered without a sound.

"Yes!" a voice cracked across the open. "That one's a keeper."

*

The bus jerked to yet another halt. Kyle looked up, breathing a curse. It was going to take all day to cover those twentyfour pocked and cratered kilometers to Wanzani City, thanks to the driver's ridiculous policy of stopping to pick up every single ragged, sweating pedestrian he saw.

The other passengers had made a space for Kyle about halfway back, between a woman holding a heavy basket of yams and a man with three half-naked children and a homemade cage full of ducks. Kyle was sitting with his back to the window and his trunk balanced upright between his knees. Along with everyone else, he twisted in his seat to search the brightness outside for a glimpse of the new passenger.

"I'll be damned!" he muttered, almost losing his grip on the trunk. "No fucking way!"

He twisted around the other way for a better view. The man with the three kids was frowning angrily, attempting to cover six young ears with two hands, but Kyle barely noticed. For the first time since he'd marched out of camp stinking of his last swallow of booze, he wished he had just one more.

There on the side of the road stood Wilbur Trimble— in a leopardskin loincloth.

Trimble still wore the same wire-rimmed glasses, but his feet were bare and filthy, his thin shirtless chest burned reddish by the sun. He stood leaning on a sturdy walking stick, facing the highway, but his head was turned, looking back at the wild bushland as if totally unaware of the smoking, rattling bus that waited in front of him. He raised one arm as if to punctuate some emphatic remark. But Kyle could see that his jaw wasn't moving. And who would he be talking to out there, anyway?

The bus driver honked the horn, one long blast and two short ones, and then gunned the motor. As if shoved from behind, Trimble took one long step down the dirt bank and two short steps toward the bus. Then he turned completely around and waved a last forlorn little wave at the empty wilderness behind him.

The reverberating murmur inside the bus resumed as the other passengers turned their attention back to their animals and children, their gossipy chatter and musical eruptions of laughter. Still staring out the window, stunned, Kyle saw the roadside foliage sway slightly and several small black faces peered cautiously out. They looked like children with the faces of wizened old men. He blinked, and the apparition was gone.

A commotion at the front of the bus announced the boarding of the new passenger, but Kyle didn't even look. He tipped his pith helmet down over his forehead, rested his chin on his trunk and pretended to be asleep.

From time to time, as the bus jerked into motion again and continued dodging potholes down the highway, Kyle lifted his helmet's brim and peeked out. The passengers seemed to be respectfully ignoring the oddly clad foreigner. Trimble sat half a dozen seats to Kyle's right, staring through the faces that crowded the long seat on the opposite side, through the bright windows behind them, and somewhere far beyond that. With stealthy sidelong glances from the shadows under his helmet, Kyle studied the famous missing man from head to foot.

Trimble's ribs were showing. A little thicket of chest hair stood out almost silver against his sunburn. His bony legs were covered with scratches and welts. And his loincloth— Kyle could smell it from here. But it couldn't be a fresh kill. Impossible. Permits for hunting leopard hadn't been released yet. And Trimble was obviously unarmed. Had been, Kyle knew, that night when he'd wandered out of camp. And where would he conceal a weapon now?

But no experienced hunter could mistake the smell of a freshly skinned pelt. Nor could the flies, who were beginning to buzz enthusiastically around Trimble's loins. This could mean trouble down the road. Kyle pulled the brim of the helmet down more firmly across his face.

Another stop, and a whole new crowd of passengers swarmed aboard. They staked out the long center aisle of the bus, sitting on their bundles and suitcases. One old man had brought along a folding chair. A thin, middle-aged, sick-looking woman attempted to unroll her bedroll until a chorus of disapproval persuaded her to roll it up again, muttering curses. Kyle rode the jolts of the pavement and the ancient springs of the bus, hugging his trunk between his legs and pillowing one cheekbone on his fist.

He must have fallen asleep, because the next thing he knew someone was shaking him.

"Pass port, please?"

Someone in uniform. Kyle blinked, unsure if he were dreaming, but searching anyway through his clothing for his documents. Finally, still searching, he began to cry.

"It is not necessary to weep, sir. Please, take your time."

But Kyle's tears continued to flow. His documents were gone. His money was gone. His Travelers Cheques were gone. The money-belt where he kept them was gone. Lifted, no doubt, in the crush of passengers when he'd first boarded the bus. Or just now, while he'd been asleep.

He'd meant to write down the numbers on those blasted Travelers Checques. He really had.

He looked up, prepared to babble and bluster and bawl, whatever it took to persuade the gentleman in the gold-accented brown uniform that he really did have the right to travel on this bus, whether or not he could pay for a hotel room when he arrived in the capital.

"Lost your passport?" said a deep, faintly familiar voice. Trimble sounded a little husky, as anyone would after a week in the jungle alone. "Here, use mine."

Kyle stared up through a bright blur of tears. Trimble was holding out not a passport but an engraved portrait of Benjamin Franklin, which quite tastefully decorated a hundred-dollar bill. *United States of America*, read the legend.

"Will this do, officer?"

"Ah! I see. Well, in lieu of actual paperwork, it will suffice for this particular checkpoint. I only hope you have more. Other checkpoints to come, you see."

"Then my friend and I are in good hands," said Trimble. "Thank you, sir."

"Absolutely welcome, sir."

The officer never even glanced down at Trimble's endangered-species jungle garb. Ben Franklin disappeared into a fold of the impeccable uniform. The officer saluted; Trimble returned the salute. Kyle weakly followed suit, though no one seemed to notice. Then the officer moved down the line and Trimble stood beaming down at Kyle.

"Mr. Wilson, I presume?"

After a quick review of his options, resting his closed eyes against his upturned palm, Kyle concluded that he had none. "Mr. Trimble."

"What a surprise to discover you aboard my bus!"

"A lucky one for me, all right. I sure appreciate you stepping in to help me out. Thanks a million."

"A hundred is plenty, I think. No interest required." Trimble's eyes twinkled behind their dirt-specked lenses. "Just pay me back when you can. But why is it, if you don't mind my prying, that you're leaving the safari now instead of waiting three more days for its scheduled return?"

"I— I guess I could ask you the same question."

"Fair enough. Since I was the first to leave, I suppose I might as well answer first. The problem is, I can't. I mean, not that I can't, it's just— well, no one is going to believe me."

"That I can believe. Do you know the entire Wanzanayian armed forces have been out combing the jungle for your ant-eaten corpse?"

Trimble looked delighted to hear it, then instantly repentant. "I'm sorry to— I hate putting them to all that trouble. I'm going to make it up to them, I really am. But first I have a little mission to perform."

"Only a little one."

"Yes . . . a little mission named Kumbu. It's a long story. The press is going to have a field day with it. With me too, I'm afraid. Tell me, did I make the papers yet?"

"Locally around here, yes. And someone came all the way out to base camp and did a story for the *Indianapolis Herald*."

"An excellent publication. I'm not a bit surprised. They'll get first option for a follow-up, I promise."

"So— how exactly did you survive for seven days in the bush, unarmed, without someone finding you and claiming that reward?"

"Oh, I wasn't exactly unarmed. I had my Swiss Army knife."

Reaching beneath his loincloth again, Trimble showed Kyle— and every other interested passenger— a standard moneybelt, almost identical to the one Kyle had lost. Inside, Kyle glimpsed a paper-clipped stack of Ben Franklins, a passport, an airline ticket. Trimble held up a red-handled pocketknife with a boyish grin.

Kyle smiled sardonically. "And exactly what game did you hunt with it?"

"This? Oh, none at all! I never had a chance to get that hungry. You see, I was rescued by a band of wild chimpanzees. I only used it to skin this leopard I'm wearing."

*

Guma had been staring down and contemplating the stand of mushrooms for so long that he kept forgetting which plump specimen he had decided to sample next, and had to start his deliberations all over. Just when he had finally made up his mind once more and stretched out his hand, Uncle Noko ambled up beside him, leaned over as if they had been browsing side by side all day, and nonchalantly plucked the very mushroom he had finally settled on.

Noko grinned at his brother with his cheek stuffed and his jaws busy, waiting for Guma to begin the conversation.

What conversation? Guma asked quizzically, and then suddenly his eyes sprang open. *You're back!*

Uncle Noko gave an affirmative yawn. *We escorted him to the highway, taking exactly the route you suggested. Did not encounter a single village or cross a cultivated field, as you expected. And just when we reached the road, as you anticipated, a bus came by. It stopped and he— well, we persuaded him to get on board.*

So he's off on his journey, said Guma. *An even stranger one than his adventure among us, I expect. We'll hold our first Gathering of Gifts tonight, then, at sunset. Any incidents along the way?*

Just one. Where the route you gave us came out of the forest and crossed the grassy plain. Remember?

Yes . . . well?

We saw a leopard hunting antelope. Brother Tanzar is a lover of Cousin Antelope, you recall.

Yes.

Tanzar wanted to warn the antelope to run, which I couldn't allow, of course. But then, when Cousin Leopard was feasting on her kill, someone fired a rifle and killed her.

So the killer became the kill. Interesting timing.

More interesting still was Tanzar's reaction. You would have been proud— and I can only imagine how old Brapa is going to drool over it in the telling. I had just finished explaining, you see, all about the sacrifice of the individual in the service of evolution. No sooner had we recovered from the shock of the gunshot when the hunters— to use the term loosely— came charging out of the trees to gloat over the bloody corpse. Well, our indignant Brother Tanzar went charging out to meet them, so outraged that he seemed utterly unaware that the three of them were armed with multiple deadly weapons, while all he had was—

His little red-handled knife, Guma finished for him. With the tiny folding tools inside.

The two brothers chuckled together. Guma studied the mushroom patch, considering his next selection, while Noko went on.

We watched from the treeline, of course, ready to abandon our mission and run. But we could hear him cursing them even without the benefit of our Gift. "Do you intend to eat this animal?" he demanded. "Or is this merely a sacrifice to some bloodthirsty god you worship?"

Well, one of the darkskinned gunbearers panicked and ran right then, carrying the two spare rifles. The paleskinned tourist they served held a rifle and wore a pistol on his belt, and the remaining darkskin wore a rifle on his shoulder. They both looked a little panicky too, confronted by this wild-looking paleskin rabid with inexplicable rage. But to me they looked like the type that's more likely to solve a problem by shooting it and leaving it for the jackals— except for the fact that neither could trust the other not to report him to the authorities.

"Don't you know it's illegal to kill a leopard this time of year?" Brother Tanzar shouted, and I guess both of them did know, because they looked at each other with a trapped expression that was the same in black as in white.

They backed off, as if for a better shot . . . and then I saw their heads starting to bob and nod together, and I understood that they had suddenly remembered a certain missing safari hunter and that unclaimed reward. The dark one unslung his rifle and began to circle around behind Tanzar. The pale one began talking fast, offering Tanzar "steaks" and "beer" and a nice hot "bath"— various polite forms of bribery, I gathered— if he would come back to civilization with them. And that's when our brother began to grow very angry indeed, growing several feet taller, turning bright red from the neck up, wagging his ears like an elephant—

Guma stared, trying to envision their mild and somewhat timid Brother Tanzar so enraged. The mushroom he had finally chosen hung uneaten in his fingers.

Yes? And then?

Noko grinned, enjoying the suspense.

Now, I'm convinced that Brother Tanzar had long since forgotten what we told him about the reward. I knew they were not going to harm him if they could help it. But did he know? I think he had nothing in his head at that moment except his fierce, wild love for the antelope and the leopard and the holy laws of evolution. He waited till they closed in on him. Then he sprang, grabbing the pale one's gun by the barrel and plunging it down into the dirt. And then, quick as an antelope and leopard in one, he whirled around and seized the dark one's rifle and plunged it down next to the first. Now neither rifle could be fired, you see.

But Tanzar hadn't noticed the pistol the paleskin wore, and now I saw the man unsnapping its holster. Tanzar caught my signal just in time to seize him by the wrist and twist the gun away. Our crazed brother spun his whole body around three, maybe four times, and flung the pistol high into the air. It flew over our heads into the topmost branches and by some miracle caught itself on a twig.

Now, I could see that both hunters also wore knives on their belts. But by this time they had worn out their supply of courage, and both of them decided to do the sensible thing and run for their lives. I remembered the third man and the extra rifles he carried, so I did my best to persuade Tanzar to leave the scene of his triumph and make haste toward the highway. But he was transformed. He had his little knife open when I reached him and was already busy taking the skin off the leopard. He couldn't hear me. I don't think he could even see me. I think he was in direct communication with the spirit of the leopard and doing exactly what she wanted him to do.

Guma stared in astonishment. A slow smile spread across his jowls. Noko smirked back at him. Then the brothers toppled over together in a helpless fit of giggles, grunts and guffaws.

Panting, Guma finally rolled over and sat upright again. *Now we know,* he sighed. *Now we know something is going to happen over there in Dade County Florida. That's all we know, of course. But we know that much.*

He looked around for his mushroom, sniffing in widening circles— and found it flattened in his brother's fur, glued by its own delicious juices. He squatted next to the mushroom patch again and started over.

Chapter 5

A Gathering of Gifts

*

Kumbu's Mommy cried. Sitting on the same living room sofa where Daddy had stung him with the snaking belt the night before, she held him on her lap and rocked him back and forth, back and forth. And she cried.

"Oh, Ra-alph," she sobbed, the name broken in two by her endless sobs. "Ralph, Ralph, what are we going to do? The show hasn't even opened yet, and your Daddy doesn't love me any more!"

Kumbu and his Daddy had practiced this morning in the Big Top just like always, doing the same leaps and twirls and somersaults, bowing to an imaginary audience each time they landed on the little platforms again. But the whole time Kumbu could hear Daddy roaring and raging inside, the silent angry curses echoing even across the empty distance between the two platforms. Now he wondered if Mommy had heard them too.

Daddy was so angry these days and Mommy was so afraid that Kumbu tried to stay out of the way when they were together. Angry and afraid seemed to cancel each other out in the little circus trailer, leaving only sad behind. Mommy's face, greeting him in his crib every morning. Daddy's face, swinging past in mid-air during practice. Even Kumbu's own face when he gripped the toilet seat with his toes and peered into the bathroom mirror: nothing but sad.

On the big day of his first real performance, when it was time to take his first bow, he was afraid he would hear a cracking noise inside and howl with sorrow instead.

This afternoon, Daddy had gotten up from his nap on the sofa and stamped out the door without saying goodbye. Kumbu knew he was going out driving, stopping only to make his usual call at a random coin telephone along the way. Since Mommy and Daddy had begun to quarrel, Daddy had quit taking Kumbu along on his long, aimless drives.

Kumbu shivered, remembering how it had felt to sit waiting in the car, strapped into his special seat, while Daddy talked into the telephone. It felt as if he itched all over—but inside, where he couldn't scratch. And then Daddy would come back to the car wearing that strange cold mask of a smile, with the angry mouth and scared eyes.

Kumbu used to love to go out riding with his Daddy. Now he was relieved to be left at home with Mommy. Except today, as soon as Daddy was gone, Mommy had switched off the racing cars and sunk into Daddy's place on the sofa, as if she'd only been waiting for her turn.

"Oh, Ralph," she moaned. "I don't know what I did or what I said, but your Daddy doesn't love me any more. Oh, Ra-alph, if only you could understand!"

Kumbu hugged her desperately and tried his best to tell her he still loved her, more than ever, more than he loved anyone. And Mommy understood, just like she was reading his mind.

"Oh, I know you love me, Ralph," she sniffed. "But you're just a chimpanzee. You can't understand. And sooner or later I have to admit that to myself. I tried to tell him I wanted a baby, I tried, oh I tried. But all he wants is his fame and fortune, fame and fortune. In that exact order. He'll even tell me so, when I've exasperated him enough. In that exact order, he says." And she cried again.

Kumbu clung to her, his knuckles knotted in the fabric of her tanktop blouse, his face pressed against her ribs, her heart pounding in his ears and that harsh, painful echo twisting inside his chest:

Oh, I know you love me, Ralph. But you're just a chimpanzee. You can't understand.

She let out a long, sorrowful wail. "Oh, I do love you so, Ralph, I do. My ideas for training you have worked like a dream— no, better than I ever dared to dream! But I need a real baby. I need a baby that looks like me, at least a little. A baby I can teach to walk, and then to talk, and eventually to read and write and— drive, someday, and— oh,

I've been telling myself it would be enough, training yet another animal, one that could make Dale proud, make a name for us both in this crazy circus world, but—"

She hugged Kumbu tighter and broke into deep, quaking sobs all over again.

"And meanwhile— meanwhile Mama and all my aunts keep asking— asking when is Dale going to get around to giving me kids? When is Mama going to get some grandkids? When am I going to give up this damn circus to raise some kids without *fur*, for God's sake? When am I going to settle down and live in a real house instead of this gypsy wagon? And—"

Kumbu couldn't stand it any more. With a squeal he tore himself loose from Mommy's arms and darted into the dining room and through the swinging kitchen door. The tall stool screeched as he dragged it across the floor. In one acrobatic bound, as if performing hundreds of feet in the air, he stood perched on top of the stool, ready to rip the faded clipping off the fridge.

Then he caught himself. Slowly, carefully, holding the tip of his tongue between his lips, he tore one word out of the line of bugs across the top of the clipping. Once he'd cleared the last letter, he lost patience and ripped the little scrap crookedly away from the rest. That almost spoiled it, but finally he held between his fingers the five letters that spelled his name. Waving it triumphantly above his head, he leapt from the tall stool and crossed the kitchen floor on three legs to the door.

Just then the door swung open and knocked it out of his fingers. Mommy didn't seem to notice. With a choking sob she hurried across the kitchen, tears streaming down her face. Kumbu scrambled frantically after the scrap of paper, his fingers still stinging. Mommy pushed the stool back into place at the counter, climbed unsteadily up and swung open the cabinet.

Reaching up to the top shelf, she dragged down a large bottle half-filled with purple liquid. As soon as she twisted off the cap, Kumbu could smell it. Something powerful. Something awful. Such a strong smell that all of a sudden Kumbu could hardly breathe. Mommy tilted the bottle up and took a long, gurgling swallow. She closed her eyes and knelt there for a moment, making a face. A thin shudder ran through her body. She twisted the cap back on and put the bottle away.

Then she reached into the cabinet again and took out a little spray can. She sprayed into her mouth, on either side of her neck and around her face. The strong smell of what she had drunk mingled with the sweet smell of the spray to make another smell altogether. And Kumbu instantly recognized it.

His Mommy had always liked to spray different smells on herself. Kumbu had grown used to each new smell in turn, though he'd always liked her body's true smell the best. This mingled smell of strong and sweet was the new smell that had become Mommy's familiar scent over the past few days.

Bracing her hands on the counter and stretching down with one foot, Kumbu's Mommy felt for the wooden rungs of the stool. She missed every rung and almost fell before her wildly thrashing foot finally found the floor. He thought she would be all right then. But on her way back to the swinging door she swerved and stumbled over Kumbu without seeming to see him. At the door she paused, gripping both sides of the doorway and taking a deep breath before pushing through.

Kumbu heard the TV in the living room go on again. Mommy clicked through the channels till she found one of the old movies she liked. Kumbu recognized the voices: *Moonlight Mesa*, with Blake Jameson and Samantha Collins. But it was almost over. He could tell by the music that swelled in the background and the way the two stars talked. Any minute now they were going to kiss.

He borrowed a roll of clear tape from Mommy's desk. Then he pushed the stool back over to the fridge as quietly as he could and climbed up its rungs. With trembling fingers he taped the scrap of paper back in place. At least he did his best. But somehow the crooked scrap didn't exactly fit the crooked hole in the clipping any more.

When Daddy came home, Mommy was asleep on the sofa and another program was blaring from the TV— one of those shows with an invisible audience that laughed at everything anybody said. It wasn't until Mommy was putting the leftovers away after supper that she finally noticed what Kumbu had done to their precious clipping. He hid behind a drapery in the living room and held his breath, listening. Mommy and Daddy argued for a long time, taking turns blaming each other, but even Daddy didn't think of blaming

Kumbu. And Daddy seemed to find an excuse to blame Kumbu for everything these days.

Kumbu was still discovering a new thing every day in this exciting life of his. But he wasn't sure he liked it any more. Every night now, without knowing exactly why, he curled up in his crib and cried as softly as he could.

*

Kyle Wilson woke up in a strange bed in an unfamiliar room. His head felt like it was about to break open and soak his pillow with fresh booze. His first night back in Wanzani City had been totally different from his last night before heading into the bush, a little over a week ago— with exactly the same result on the morning after.

Keenly aware of the embarrassment the nutcase in the loincloth had saved him with the timely appearance of that hundred-dollar bill, Kyle had made damn sure the cab driver at the bus station knew exactly where Trimble needed to go. So what if Trimble had been given the address by a pack of chimps out in the jungle? It was better than having no place to go at all, which happened to be Kyle's situation.

Across the river, the hotel where the safari party had spent its first night was glittering like a forbidden palace in the afternoon sun. Kyle could hear faint horns and wafting strains of African percussion beckoning the reckless. But he knew better than to venture across the bridge without a minimum fifty U.S. dollars to spend.

Visions of Trimble's open moneybelt had danced alluringly at the corners of Kyle's eyes as he closed the deal with the taxi driver, shook hands with both men and turned to walk back into the station, towing his trunk on its tiny wheels. He had successfully held in check the impulse to ask for a wee loan, though the effort left him sweating and exhausted.

Then at the last minute Trimble had craned that scrawny sunburned neck out the taxi window and called him back. "Wait a minute, Mr. Wilson! Can I drop you somewhere on my way?"

"Well, I guess that would be all right. If you don't mind a little detour, that is."

"Please, allow me. You've been very helpful."

So Kyle had squeezed himself into the back seat of the ancient Mercedes next to Trimble, hoisting his trunk across his lap. Along the way he'd entertained his host with his knowledge of the city's history and pointed out the sights: the government buildings, the colonial sites, the museums, the zoo.

The driver had grunted when Kyle explained their little detour, then suddenly swung the car down a narrow twisting alley lined with neon drinking establishments and tarpaper shacks.

Kyle saw Trimble's eyes pop open as they passed a line of predatory women whose glimmering eyes instinctively fastened on Trimble, ignoring Kyle. The skin that gleamed through calculated gaps in their garments was of every color the human gene pool has yet produced; the clothing that set off their jeweled flesh mimicked the latest high-priced fashions from Europe.

The driver stopped in front of a place called the Hippopotamus Crossing, lit up by a neon hippo in a slit skirt whose long cigarette holder was supposed to send clouds of smoke in alternating colors across the neon lettering. Kyle glanced over at Trimble under the malfunctioning sign with an embarrassed grin.

"This is it, Mr. Trimble! I sure do appreciate your help. Have a nice trip back to the States tomorrow."

"Are you sure?" asked Trimble. "I mean, this is where you're going?"

"Oh, believe me, they love me around here. They'll take good care of ol' Kyle."

As Kyle gingerly lowered the trunk onto its tiny wheels, the Hippo's tattooed Portuguese bouncer, Macao, stepped out through the open door and stood watching. He cracked his knuckles and called to someone inside. Something about the gesture stirred Kyle's memory, just beneath the surface. What was it? What had happened the last time he was here that didn't usually happen?

A second figure came to the door and stood beside Macao, looking out. With a silent flicker the neon changed color, and in the sudden wash of blue light Kyle started to remember. It was Katye, the barmaid. He recognized her profile— though that wasn't a silhouette but the actual color of her skin. Kyle had seen most of Africa and never met anyone so darkly hued. And the more he'd had to drink that night, the deeper his fascination had become.

Until finally Macao, he recalled with a sudden jolt, had escorted him out to the curb, balanced him delicately over the alley's running gutter, and toppled him in. The same gutter he was negotiating his trunk across right now.

"Say, wait a minute, Mr. Trimble."

"Please, Mr. Wilson, call me Wilbur."

"I'll make a deal with you, then. Wilbur— Kyle. Kyle— Wilbur. Okay?"

Trimble laughed. "All right, Kyle, it's a deal."

"Okay then. I've just suddenly remembered a phone call I need to make. To my grandmother back in the States, in Homestead, Florida. Bless her heart, she'll be worrying. As you know, I'm out of cash right now, and these folks here, much as they care about me, just can't afford to stake me a long distance call like that. But maybe you can. Till I get the money together to pay you back, I mean. And let me assure you, my sweet old granny's got the loot! I'll be visiting her in her condo when I get back."

"Florida?" said Trimble, his eyebrows arching behind the wire-rimmed lenses. "As it happens, I'm headed to Florida myself, the Miami area. Perhaps we can make our plans together."

Kyle hoisted his trunk again and slammed the taxi door. "Then don't let me hold you up. Driver, the Society for the Preservation of Wanzanayian Primate Habitat, please!"

And that was how Kyle had happened to have a front-row seat at Wilbur Trimble's sensational press conference in the lobby of the Wanzani General Hospital.

✱

Jane sat up straight on her living room sofa, fighting the urge to jump up and scream like a high school cheerleader.

Beside her, Jim Rochdale and Sally Martinez were already on their feet, struggling for control of the remote. To her left, Sally's husband Roger sat very pale and erect on the cliff-edge of his easy chair, clutching his fresh drink at a rather dangerous angle. At the other end of the coffee table Dr. Eugene Masebeo sat sideways across the other easy chair, one hand stretched out with his coffee cup toward a saucer on the table, unable to detach his eyes from the television for long enough to set it down.

Here they were, Jane couldn't help thinking, the core strategy committee of the Free Ralph! campaign, all gathered in one room, with two African parrots as a bonus. This would be the perfect time for the bomb to go off, wouldn't it?

On her television screen, a reporter named Vicente Cardenal stood on the highest tier of the wooden grandstand in the Rufus Barnabas Circus Spectacular's big tent, interviewing the owner of the circus, Mitchell Pauling. The volume on the TV set was turned down low, where Jane customarily kept it, but both men seemed to be having trouble filling their allotted time onscreen with appropriate noises.

The cameraman seemed to have a different problem. As interviewer and interviewee took turns fumbling for words, the camera-angle kept drifting innocently upward. Above their heads, just below the magnificent circus logo with its red pennants and golden lions, someone had painted in large crooked blue letters: *Free Ralph!*

On either side of the screen stood a burly uniformed policeman, one black, one white, both looking as uncomfortable as Pauling and Cardenal.

"I don't know," Pauling was saying when Sally finally seized the remote and turned up the volume. "I don't see how security around here can get any tighter. I mean, we're a circus. We're not used to having to patrol our perimeter at night like a damn— some kind of military base. Of course we're doing it, but then something like this happens."

"Not only did someone sneak past your security guards," said the reporter. "Apparently they carried a ladder with them, up here to the top of the bleachers and back down again. Unless they climbed that support pole somehow, I mean."

Pauling squirmed. "Well, we got plenty of ladders around here."

"And are you missing any?"

"Well, no . . ."

"But the can of paint found here this morning was definitely one purchased by your supply department."

"Yes, we're still getting things spiffed up for our opening performance this Saturday. The paint can was stolen from a storeroom, just a hop and a skip from the scene of the crime."

"So have you ruled out what they call an inside job?"

Pauling turned even redder than usual, his expression suddenly vicious, then managed to control himself. He gave a large, grandfatherly guffaw, like Santa Claus, and answered Cardenal as if the reporter was a little boy perched on his knee.

"Our staff and crew have been together a long time. The circus community is notoriously tight, you know. You should hear them talking about this latest incident— someone sneaking in and vandalizing their Big Top in the dead of night! Oh, they're angry about it, all right. If it did turn out to be someone with the circus, why you just might see an old-fashioned lynch mob in action!"

Cardenal winced, surreptitiously checked his watch, then plunged ahead. "Mr. Pauling, you may recall the last time we spoke. Have you been able to identify any employee of your circus who might be behind the anonymous death threats Dr. Keller has received?"

This time Pauling kept his face under control. He had parried this particular thrust before. "Oh. Is she still getting those?"

"As of two days ago, yes."

"Ah. Well, as I explained to you last time, that kind of publicity is the last thing any circus needs, so if one of my people does turn out to be involved, I can promise you that person will never work in the circus industry again. I know my colleagues across the country would tell you the same thing. Anyway, you'd think these animal rights wackos would appreciate what we're doing with young Ralph. He's the first performing chimp ever trained by treating him just like a human child— a highly innovative experiment we're all tremendously excited about. And Dale has readily agreed to use a safety net for each and every performance on the tour."

The camera tilted upward again, framing the crude, leftward-leaning letters for a long moment. Cardenal took the hint— seized it, in fact, Jane thought.

"Thank you, Mr. Pauling. Good luck with your opening performance, and the tour. I guess it will be a relief to pull up your stakes and hit the road?"

"Well, it is getting a little tense around here. But this Saturday we can promise a circus spectacle like you've never seen. Besides our talented little Ralph and his fantastic trapeze act, we've got dancing elephants, clown ballerinas, seals that play the trumpet, horseback riders who juggle fire, not to mention—"

"Thank you, Mr. Pauling. This is Vicente Cardenal. Back to you, Phil!"

Jane smoothly nabbed the remote from Sally and muted the volume again, ready to take charge of a strategy session that would take brilliant advantage of the suddenly altered terrain that lay ahead. But instead, the room exploded into laughter and cheers, foot-stomping and whistling and jubilant obscenities. The bomb had gone off, but it wasn't the kind she had been dreading from moment to moment for weeks now. This one had gone off in her anonymous opponent's face.

Just when their campaign had begun to lose momentum— volunteers dropping out like fallen flower petals as the heat of Florida's spring mounted, media coverage wilting as publicity for the "special hometown show" intensified— suddenly the Free Ralph! campaign seemed to have an ally inside the enemy camp.

It was too much. Without the slightest premonition that she was about to lose her mind, Dr. Jane Keller, BA, MS, PhD, suddenly leapt to her feet and stomped back and forth on the carpet, shrieking at the top of her voice like an alpha-male chimpanzee victorious over his latest challenger.

*

The sun was sinking slowly into an iridescent haze over the housetops of Wanzani City. Twilight gently tinted the buildings as the lights winked on one by one. Wilbur closed his eyes in the back seat of the taxi, dozing after his long day, and his chin bumped against his chest. Suddenly he jerked in his seat and looked around, forgetting where he was— only to find himself swaying high in the branches of the Granddaddy Tree.

Below him a familiar confluence of streams glimmered through the foliage. Green treetops swayed to the horizon. Beyond the hills, a flaming jungle sunset tinged the sky with rays of startling color. Around him sat his friends Guma and Uncle Noko, Grandmother Min, Zambi, Flor, Yago and Kuk, Shan, Tunga, Brapa and the others.

What did I just say? he asked, tingling with the feeling that no matter how ignorant or even idiotic it had been, it was the key to understanding something vitally important.

You asked, said Uncle Noko, relaxing on his favorite branch, *what the difference is between God and evolution. By God we presume you mean intelligence greater than but somehow separate from your own; by evolution we presume you mean the idea that a world like this one—* he lifted his arm and captured the grand panorama in one dramatic gesture— *can happen by pure happenstance, one coincidence at a time.*

It's not a stupid question, said Guma. *Just a question that could not possibly be asked except by a human. Difficult to translate, that is, from human language to any other idiom. It definitely requires a word.*

A word? Which word? Wilbur asked.

"God" and "evolution" are words, Guma replied with a chuckle, *which can take each other's place if the angle of the light is just right, as it is right now. Either one will do.*

But surely they aren't exactly the same? Wilbur asked, remembering all the strife and anguish he had witnessed over these two words.

In the human realm, where words must be defined precisely, and yet none means precisely the same thing to two different people, you are correct; they're not. But if you sit and allow yourself to sink slowly down through the levels of awareness, you'll find yourself in a stratum deeper than language. And there, you won't be able to detect a difference.

Wilbur tried it. A delicious silence spread over the upper branches of the tree. But then a parrot down below called to its mate in the next tree, and it seemed that the whole forest answered.

Whether you speak of God or evolution, Uncle Noko said, *what you're really talking about is a certain set of laws that govern the universe, whether set in place by a deliberate act of creation or pre-existing through some sort of random universal decree. But it's self-evident, at least to us, that it must take some form of conscious intelligence to set up a universe with laws that inevitably lead to matter, to life, to evolving awareness like yours and mine. We prefer to call this intelligence simply "Life."*

I've heard you use that word, Wilbur said, *in a way I've never heard it used among humans. Not just naming a condition, the state of being alive, but as if it's a living being itself.*

Not a being, corrected Guma. *That would make it just another name for God. Life is the thing we all have inside of us that makes us alive. It's the energy that keeps us moving, breathing, thinking, feeling, until we lie down and release it at last. But the energy of Life inside of me isn't somehow different or separate from the energy of Life inside of you. It's all one energy. It makes the green things grow, the rain fall and flow downstream and evaporate to rise again, the world turn from day to night to day and the moon swing across the sky, again and again and again.*

It even hides inside the dirt and the stones, Grandmother Min added.

Though they move too slowly for us to see, they too are alive. But Life is not just a restless, purposeless energy. It's intelligent. It communicates. It evolves.

Just as we do, Wilbur said, an awed exhilaration mounting inside as he began to understand.

There is no difference, Min said simply. *We are Life's evolution.*

Or, Guma interjected, *since in human language there is always an opposite way to say anything, Life's evolution is ours as well. But this whole discussion is a peculiarly human one, as I mentioned. Because only a human could believe that humans alone possess the intelligence to ask such a question. How could such intelligence as yours exist all alone, isolated in a universe of accident and coincidence? Rather an unintelligent notion, wouldn't you agree?*

Wilbur didn't exactly agree. But at least he possessed the intelligence to recognize that on this particular topic, he was hopelessly outclassed.

Kumbu peeked around the corner of the candy aisle, looking for his Mommy. She wasn't lost; she had only made the mistake of letting go of Kumbu's hand. Kumbu wasn't lost, either. But as soon as Mommy discovered he was missing, she was going to come looking. And then they were going to have a really good game of Hide and Seek, right here in the convenience store.

Hide and Seek had been one of his favorites when he was little, back when swinging on the trapeze was just a game, too. But none of the games Kumbu played with his Mommy and Daddy were much fun any more. And something inside of Kumbu ached all the time: something deep in his chest that weighed him down, even when he was pretending to lightly soar through the air.

Oh, I know you love me, Ralph. But you're just a chimpanzee. You can't understand.

After the argument over the torn newspaper clipping, when Daddy flopped back on the sofa to watch the cars, Mommy had swung her purse onto her shoulder and headed for the door. She hadn't meant to take Kumbu along, but he had hugged her knees until she laughed and held out one hand to let him walk up her leg.

Kumbu had not forgotten the sting of Daddy's belt last night. But that wasn't why. Settling into Mommy's safe, familiar arms, he'd almost choked on the mingled smell of strong and sweet that followed her now wherever she went. It had burned his eyes and smothered everything except a sudden understanding: wherever his Mommy was going now, she needed him with her.

Once he was buckled into his special seat, she had driven straight to the convenience store where she usually filled the car with gas. But instead of using her plastic card to pay, she'd pumped the gas and then started across the brightly-lit pavement with her purse. Kumbu had squealed until she sighed and came back to unbuckle him. With a tight grip on his hand she had marched into the store and directly to one of the sliding glass doors along the back wall.

Staring up through the glass at row after row of bottles and cans, Kumbu had realized all at once why he hadn't wanted his Mommy to go out alone. When she let go of him to tug the heavy door open, he'd grabbed his chance. Now Kumbu was hiding, and Mommy would have to seek.

"How often do you get a chimpanzee in here, anyway?" he heard her saying now from the front of the store. "I told you, I've searched the entire store and I can't find him— but the restroom is locked. He's got to be in there." She spoke louder now, growing frantic, and people were looking— turning— staring— standing on tiptoe to see. "Don't tell me you can't unlock it from the outside— don't tell me that! I think I need to speak to a manager. I think I need to speak to a manager *now!*"

Kumbu giggled and pretended to be looking at packages of pretzels and crackers and peanut brittle. He knew his Mommy would never buy anything like that for him. Only Daddy would. But at least he and Mommy were going to have some fun before she caught up with him.

Now someone was squinting down at him across the aisle: an elderly woman with faintly purple hair, who stooped and whispered to a balding man. The man adjusted a cord hanging behind his ear and leaned closer to the woman's dark red lips. Kumbu scooted around the end of the candy aisle into the next one, past cans of oil for cars, shiny metal tools, sunglasses, caps with brims.

"I said, his name is *Ralph!*" Mommy's voice echoed from the front of the store.

Halfway down this new aisle a teenaged girl watched him curiously, and the elderly couple from the other aisle had followed him, still whispering to one another.

"Does she mean *the* Ralph?" said a voice from the next aisle over, and the teenaged girl took a step closer, looking uncertain.

A man with a mean-looking face went past in a big hurry at the far end of Kumbu's aisle, but spotted him and turned back to start down the aisle. Kumbu spun around to go back the way he'd come, but immediately collided with the elderly couple, who both turned and fled as if Kumbu were twelve feet tall. Kumbu glanced over his shoulder to see the mean-faced man sprawling belly-first in the middle of the aisle— and the teenaged girl sprinting away.

He turned to run for it before the man could get up again, but right in front of him he saw his Mommy coming, her head turned to argue with the store clerk, who was following her down the aisle. Luckily it was the clerk who saw him first.

"Ralph!" Mommy yelled, but by then Kumbu was already up and over the pegboard barrier and into the next aisle. He knocked a few pegs loose and some bags of popcorn snacks fell behind him as he clambered over.

On the other side of the barrier he nearly landed in the lap of an old man in a wheelchair who was sipping from a very big cup through a long twisting straw. The big cup went over the side of the wheel-chair with a splat, the lid came off and pink liquid and crushed ice spread across the floor. The old man let out a shriek and Kumbu was off and running. The younger man pushing the wheelchair began to curse.

"It's *Ralph!*" cried a child's voice from somewhere behind him.

Up ahead, Kumbu saw the mean-faced man rounding the turn from the other aisle into this one. The mean face was growing red now and the man looked ready to strangle someone. Kumbu spun into a skidding turn, reversed direction and dashed toward the puddle of pink ice and the wheelchair again. The younger man made a grab at him, still cursing, but slipped on the spilled ice and went down with a crash. Kumbu dodged past and found his way blocked once again.

It wasn't one child but three of them, two girls and a boy, all of them calling him by name and holding out their arms to catch him in a triple-decker hug. But that was a different game. Kumbu was play-ing Run and Chase now, no longer Hide and Seek, and he was making up the rules as he went along. With all his strength he launched himself off the floor to the top of the next pegboard barrier, then to the next, and then to the next, where he gathered himself again and leapt for the top of a free-standing display of cigarette cartons.

But the display was not nearly as sturdy as it looked. Down it went with Kumbu on top, still trying to climb the tower of merchandise as it fell.

The next thing he heard was an all-too-familiar screech. "*Ralph!* You stop this nonsense, right now!"

The first to arrive at the scene of the disaster was his Mommy. That meant the game was officially over, but Kumbu was a little too excited to stop just yet. He wriggled under the pile of cigarette cartons and the toppled display, desperately trying to invent the next game he could play. He peeked out, and suddenly the thoughts froze in his head.

Pushing through the store's glass door, frowning at the mess around them on the floor, Kumbu saw two men in green uniforms and matching cowboy hats, with brass stars on their jackets and shiny black holsters on their belts. The police! He scrambled to his feet and turned to run for it one more time, but suddenly a hand clamped hard on his shoulder. He knew without looking who it was. The mean-faced man.

"Wait! Let me handle this!" said Kumbu's Mommy, clamping her own hand on his other shoulder with exactly the same amount of force. "Please!"

Standing there with a hand painfully gripping each shoulder, Kumbu stood paralyzed for a moment— and then a slow realization crept over him, tingling from the top of his head to the soles of his feet. He could feel his muscles trembling down the length of his arms and his legs: smooth, powerful muscles that propelled him through the air during his and Daddy's routine.

If he wanted to, he could— Kumbu shut his eyes tight, trembling harder— he could really *hurt* the mean-faced man. He could really hurt his Mommy, too. He could even hurt the two police officers, guns or no guns. He could knock all four of them to the floor, along with anyone else who tried to stop him, push through the door and run, and they would never catch him. Once he swung up into the trees, they would never find him in the dark.

If he played Run and Chase for real, he could easily win. But someone would get hurt. Someone would get hurt.

Kumbu wrapped himself around his Mommy's knees and started to cry. He cried hard, screaming and shaking from head to foot.

The mean-faced man let go of Kumbu's shoulder. "Get— him— out— of— here!" he demanded, turning redder by the second.

"*Ralph!*" screamed the three children. "Ralph, can we have your autograph?"

Kumbu's Mommy scooped him up off his feet and turned to face the policemen. His shoulders were shaking, but by peeking through Mommy's hair he could see their faces.

"Say, is that the real Ralph?" one of the officers asked.

"Shut up, Bob," said the other. "'Course it is. Ma'am, you heard the manager here. You're going to have to leave the premises."

"I'm willing to pay for the damage," Mommy said, glancing back at the mean-faced man. "Is that okay?"

"Don't you worry about it," said the man. Then he glared straight at Kumbu through her hair. "Just get that nasty little devil out of here!"

∗

As the taxi pulled into a semicircular driveway through a set of handsome wrought-iron gates, Kyle reached over and shook Wilbur Trimble's knobby knee. Trimble instantly straightened in his seat and blinked out at the brick building that housed the Society for the Preservation of Wanzanayian Primate Habitat. Kyle glanced at the meter and resisted the temptation to start an argument, though the ride was ridiculously overpriced.

Their sudden appearance caused a commotion inside, where the Society's staff was just about to knock off work for the night. Kyle gathered that the dozen or so paid staff and volunteers customarily sent out for a big meal at the end of the day, and tonight it was pizza. But Kyle and Trimble's taxi arrived just ahead of the delivery man, so they walked into a roomful of hungry Wanzanayians who were expecting someone else entirely.

The initial response was a full minute of utter silence. The Wanzanayians stared in shock at the tall sunburned white man in his leopardskin loincloth, ignoring Kyle completely.

"Hello," said Trimble. "My name is Wilbur Trimble, and this is

Mr. Kyle Wilson."

Out of total silence, the Wanzanayians launched into instant nonstop discussion, this time ignoring both Kyle and Trimble. For the first few minutes, no single voice was able to penetrate the uproar with a statement or question of any sort. So Trimble finally cleared his throat and tried to simply state at least his side of things.

"Wilbur— Trimble!" he roared, absolutely leopard-like, pointing a thumb at his naked chest. "Cedartown— Indiana— U.S.A.! I was given your address— because I have reason to believe— your government— has posted a reward for my safe return, and a certain group of— friends— wanted to be sure— it was your organization that claimed it!"

By the time the pizza arrived, Kyle had finally untangled the facts on both sides. Apparently the S.P.W.P.H.'s president, Dr. Herbert Taah, had gone home to have dinner with his family, leaving his second-in-command, Riza Maskari, to deal with any end-of-the-day emergencies. Within two minutes of comprehending the nature of this particular emergency, however, Mr. Maskari had whipped out his cell phone and contacted Dr. Taah for advice. And a minute after that, Maskari was handing the phone to Trimble.

"That's right, Dr. Taah— Wilbur Trimble, of Cedartown, Indiana, U.S.A. I don't know the amount of the reward, no, but yes— that's correct, the name of your organization was given to me by a band of wild chimpanzees, with the object of— that's correct, wild ones. You see, I was lost in the jungle, and they rescued me— saved my life— but of course they have no use for the money themselves— yes, they're aware of the good work you do on their behalf, and— that's right—"

After Trimble handed back the phone, it was a mere matter of seconds before Maskari and Taah worked out a plan of action. First, pizza— with the extra bonus for Kyle of a bottle of local beer. Then the hospital. A checkup, standard of course when someone was rescued from the bush country.

Kyle and Trimble climbed back into a taxi, accompanied by Mr. Maskari and several of the staff and followed by the rest in a second taxi. Dr. Taah met them on the steps of the hospital, embracing Trimble with an impulsive teary-eyed speech and then ushering him and Kyle inside, where a delegation of doctors was impatiently expecting them.

Kyle was not invited into the examining room, and had no idea what Trimble could have said to convince the doctors that he was still in possession of his faculties. But it was obvious that at least one of them was a specialist in the field of psychology, and that Trimble's gracious manners and loquacious way of speaking had made a favorable impression on everyone.

Fortunately, Kyle had no way to corroborate the troublesome part of Trimble's story, so his own sanity was never suspect. But once the team of government officials showed up, his presence turned out to be rather useful. Speaking as a representative of Great White Hunter Adventure Tours, he was able to confirm Wilbur Trimble's identity— and luckily, in the general excitement, no one asked him to confirm his own.

By the time Wilbur Trimble was officially pronounced free of all known tropical diseases, the S.P.W.P.H. had ordered a second round of pizza and beer delivered to the hospital lobby, and the press was beginning to gather. A rack of folding chairs was wheeled in by hospital orderlies when it grew obvious that the crowd was going to overwhelm the bolted-down seating in the lobby. A government representative took charge of arranging for lighting and sound, and soon the television cameras began to arrive, starting with CNN.

"Good evening, ladies and gentlemen," said the spokesman for the government, Sulaiman Golath, a dapper young man in a suit. "The government of Wanzanayi welcomes you on this happy occasion, when danger has been successfully averted and an esteemed foreign guest has been saved from peril and possible disaster in the pristine countryside of our picturesque and scenic land. I will let him tell you the story in his own words, however. Ladies and gentlemen, Mr. Wilbur Trimble of the great state of Indiana, United States of America. Mr. Trimble?"

There was no podium, though Golath had conjured the illusion of one with great success. Trimble stepped into the convergence of spotlights with an eager smile, humble and shy and yet obviously bursting to share something that had changed his life.

Sitting in the front row, caressing the moist glass of his third bottle of beer— or was it his fourth?— Kyle wondered for the first time exactly what had happened to Wilbur Trimble out there in the bush.

Surreptitiously he glanced around, scanning the faces of the press. With an almost electric shock, he recognized one: the red-headed reporter who had interviewed him after Trimble's disappearance. The *Indianapolis Herald*, wasn't it?

"Thank you, Mr. Golath," Trimble began. "Ladies and gentlemen, I don't know how to explain this. I only know I am deeply grateful to you all for giving me a chance to try. During the last week my entire world has been turned upside down, and I stand before you now shaken to my core . . ."

Chapter 6

Tanzar of the Chimpanzees

*

MISSING BIG GAME HUNTER FOUND
ALIVE IN WANZANI CITY
"Rescued by Chimpanzees," He Claims;
Reward Accepted by Local Conservation Group

by Leopold Spitz
Wanzani City Times
Wanzani City, Wanzanayi

Wilbur Trimble, the American tourist who has been missing from his big-game hunting safari in the bush country for the past seven days, has re-surfaced in the nation's capital, alive and well. Specially trained units of the Wanzanayian Armed Forces have been searching the jungle for Mr. Trimble since last Wednesday without success.

A resident of Cedartown, Indiana, Mr. Trimble came to Africa to fulfill a lifelong dream, only to disappear from his safari's base camp without a trace on his third day in the country.

The unusual part of Mr. Trimble's story is his claim that he was rescued in the jungle by a band of wild chimpanzees, who gave him food and water, taught him to communicate in "chimpanzee," and led him to a nearby highway. A privately owned bus brought him into Wanzani City at his own expense, he added.

"I am terribly sorry for any trouble or inconvenience I have caused to the lovely country of Wanzanayi," Trimble said in a statement to the press, "or to my hosts at Great White Hunter Adventure Tours. Getting lost in your magnificent countryside has been one of the finest experiences of my life, if not in fact the very finest."

The reward of approximately $1,500 U.S. offered by the government of Wanzanayi for Trimble's safe return has been claimed by the Society for the Preservation of Wanzanayian Primate Habitat (S.P.W.P.H.). Members of the group brought Mr. Trimble to Wanzani General Hospital for observation when he turned up on their doorstep, and he insists they have earned the reward.

Answering a skeptical reporter's query whether in fact the conservationists themselves had kidnapped him from his camp in order to claim the money, Mr. Trimble appeared to lose his patience.

"Now, didn't I just say I was rescued by chimpanzees after I wandered away from that camp and got myself lost? They knew I would only get lost again as soon as I made it to the city. So they told me how to find the only safe place they knew in Wanzani City."

Mr. Trimble made his way from the city bus depot to S.P.W.P.H. headquarters with the aid of a local taxi driver, again at his own expense. He was accompanied by Mr. Kyle Wilson, a fellow American and former co-director of Trimble's safari, who had coincidentally returned to the capital on the same bus.

"Quite honestly, we were completely unaware of the generous reward offered for Mr. Trimble's return to civilization," said Riza Maskari, a spokesman for the S.P.W.P.H. "We are just glad to see him safely back." A government press release confirms that the reward money has been turned over to the conservation group.

Asked whether he intends to return to the bush for the last few days of his safari, Trimble once again apologized.

"I'm sorry to say that something urgent has come up back home, and I must depart for America immediately. But I'll be back. Africa has become a second home to me during my short stay, and I leave your splendid scenery and delightful people with the deepest regret. You'll see me again, I promise!"

"Monkeyshit," growled Solomon Purgis, flinging the newspaper across his tent and jerking out his pistol to blast it full of holes. But he caught himself in time. He spun the big revolver's cylinder, just once, before holstering it again. All six chambers were loaded and ready. "Damned interfering chimpanzees! Can't they keep their paws where they belong?"

He sat scowling out through the open door-flap for a minute, listening to the familiar noises of the jungle. Then he stood up with a purposeful grunt. He opened the trunk behind his camp chair and strapped on an ammunition belt packed with pistol rounds. He filled four tin canteens from the water cooler in the corner of the tent, snapped them into their canvas jackets and hooked them securely at intervals around his waist.

Then he packed a rucksack with his hammock and tarp and mosquito net, freeze-dried military rations and mess kit, extra socks and miscellaneous other gear. His field glasses, compass, night goggles and rifle-scope were already stashed in their pouches on his ammo belt, ready for action. Raising one jungle boot to the arm of his camp chair, then the other, he made sure he had a freshly-sharpened combat knife sheathed on the inside of each calf.

He hesitated for a few minutes over his choice of rifles. His fingers rested a long time on the 30.06, caressing its black steel barrel, while his eyes closed and the theme from an old John Wayne movie thundered through his head. In the end, though, he chose the .22—lighter to carry, and plenty of firepower for small game.

He unfolded a bandolier of rifle shells and draped it over one shoulder, clipping it to the ammo belt at each end. Then he racked the other guns inside the lid of his trunk and snapped the padlock shut.

His belly bulged out a little between the ammo belt and his jungle camouflage pants. Too bad. About time he sweated a little of it off.

On the camp table under his battery-powered lantern a yellow telegram lay ripped open.

ATTENTION PURGIS AND WILSON STOP TIME'S UP STOP NEW TOUR DIRECTORS ON THEIR WAY STOP YOU'RE BOTH ON PROBATION UNTIL FURTHER NOTICE STOP DO NOT REPEAT NOT TAKE ANY TOUR PATRONS ON HUNT WHILE WAITING FOR REPLACEMENT STOP VIOLATION MEANS TERMINATION STOP SERIOUSLY THURGOOD STOP

Outside, the rain had finally quit. It was still a few hours before dark, but the moon was just past full; this would be a perfect night for tracking. Purgis smeared a little blackener across his cheeks and strolled out his door-flap. He nearly bumped into one of the black boys: Ozawek. The one who had brought him the telegram and the newspaper, both evidently delivered by the same messenger.

"Boy! Yes, you, Ozawek! Might as well tell you as anyone. I'm going out on a little extra-curricular hunt tonight. Some rabid chimpanzees on the rampage in the area, it seems."

Ozawek's eyes went wide, but he made no reply. Purgis chortled, feeling a little giddy.

"Chimpanzee is one critter I've never tracked in the wild, so this is tough to resist. But if I'm not back in time for tomorrow's first sortie, you'll have to be the one to inform the dudes and dudettes that me and Wilson have been relieved of command. No hunting sorties permitted until our replacements arrive. So I figure I'm entitled to a little— sort of a retirement celebration, let's say." He rattled out another burst of nervous laughter. "Don't tell them all that, of course. Maybe offer to drive them around for a little sightseeing. Got all that?"

Ozawek gave a stiff-necked nod that was dignified enough to qualify as a bow. "I can handle it, sir."

"Good."

Purgis had to resist the impulse to salute, as always when in the presence of a respectful inferior. The loss of his safari command was bad enough without those particular memories stalking him again. Before any of the dudes or dudettes could spot him and corral him with some bullshit complaint, he stepped around the corner of his tent and into the bush.

"TANZAR OF THE CHIMPANZEES"
PASSES HEALTH INSPECTION
American Tourist "Rescued by Chimps"
Tells His Story To Doctors, Government Reps

by Terence Ngabe
East African Standard
Nairobi, Kenya

Mr. Wilbur Trimble of Cedartown, Indiana, U.S.A., set a new fashion mark for big-game hunting visitors to the African Bush yesterday with his trademark leopardskin loincloth. Relaxing with reporters in the lobby of Wanzani General Hospital after his official examination by government doctors, Trimble was eager to dispel the impression given by initial press reports that he is, in his own words, "nutty as a loon."

The loon is a waterfowl in Trimble's part of the world which has become synonymous with mental instability because of its haunting, distinctive cry.

"I know I have no right to expect such a distinguished group of international media professionals to believe a totally unsubstantiated, off-the-wall story like mine," Trimble told his listeners with a disarming Yankee grin. "All I can do is tell you what happened."

Therein lies the rub. "What happened," as far as he recalls, is that he wandered away from his safari's base camp late one night, only to awaken on the bank of a stream the following morning surrounded by half a dozen chimpanzees. The chimps proved miraculously gifted with the ability to communicate in human language, but telepathically, without sound— a form of communication claimed by psychics and other fringe elements of the human population, but hitherto unknown among the animal kingdom.

In the ensuing days, the small group of chimps allowed Trimble to tag along as they rejoined their larger group, taught him to forage for bugs, flowers, roots, mushrooms and fruit, and eventually gave him a name in "chimpanzee," as well as a mission. Trimble's new name, "Tanzar," allegedly means "Tall Chimp." His mission is even more eccentric.

"They want me to travel back to the U.S.A. and rescue a young relative of theirs who was kidnapped by poachers," Trimble explained. To give him a head start, the chimps guided him through the bush to a major highway and— according to Trimble— gave him the Society for the Preservation of Wanzanayian Primate Habitat as a contact in Wanzani City.

"Tall tales" indeed, as Trimble's compatriots back home refer to their traditional folklore. Yet the Wanzanayian government has extended him the courtesy of paying out the promised reward to the chimpanzees' friends at the S.P.W.P.H.

Government officials balked, however, at permitting Trimble to leave the country with his famous loincloth, as it was made from the skin of a leopard killed out of season. But they declined to prosecute him for the leopard's death, accepting his claim that it was perpetrated by a European hunter he encountered out in the bush.

103

"All I had with me was my Swiss Army knife," Trimble said, countering speculations that he had killed the animal himself. "She was dead when I reached the body, though it was still warm. I knew leopard was out of season, so I tried to make a citizen's arrest. But there were two of them, both armed, and I just had my knife."

Trimble's traveling companion Kyle Wilson, the former co-director of his safari for Great White Hunter Adventure Tours, confirmed that no weapons were discovered missing after Trimble's disappearance. Since Trimble had also left his luggage behind, Wilson averted an awkward moment by offering him a set of clothes to replace the confiscated loincloth.

Wilson, also American, claims he quit the safari independently of Trimble and lost his documents and money when he boarded a crowded bus to return to the capital. The two Americans say they reconnected quite by accident when Trimble hailed the same bus after emerging from the jungle.

The American embassy has cooperated by granting Wilson a temporary passport to replace

The article ended abruptly at a charred edge where the rest of the page had evidently been used to start a fire. Beside the columns of print, a photograph showed Brother Tanzar with what looked like a piece of Cousin Leopard's fur hanging around his waist. Another man wearing a hunter's helmet tipped up a dark bottle behind him.

More trash! Grandmother Min wrinkled her nose in dismay. She really should take it to Guma and Noko before it dissolved completely. But for now, she carefully laid the rain-soaked newspaper back where she had found it in the wet black scar of sticks and ashes and charred tin cans beside the trail.

What do you think, Dar?

The younger female beside her looked up with a troubled expression. *It's a little frightening,* she said. *I don't know why.*

Because they seem to believe him, Min replied heavily. *That means it's time for us to hide. We need to be . . .*

She glanced down the valley where drifting shreds of raincloud hung low across the treetops. It had been raining since early morning. A strange, delicate light seemed to fill the forest with colors Min had never seen before. Which was impossible, given how many jungle rainstorms she had endured in all her years of roaming these hills.

Only her seasoned Gift could make sense of such an omen. Danger, yes. But not just any danger. Human danger.

We need to be drifting, Dar finished for her, *that way. With the clouds.*

Dar was the daughter of her sister Shan, not Min's own, but they often found themselves feeding together, building their nests for the night in the same tree, and finishing each other's thoughts. Today they were taking an extended ramble in search of a particular herb that was good for Min's aching joints.

You feel it too, then? Min gave Dar what she intended to be a reassuring pat. But Dar started at the touch.

I feel my fur standing up, she said. *I've never felt such a feeling. Not like Cousin Leopard who stalks the prey that's easiest, the slowest, most defenseless, simply to fill her belly. This is like— something that wants me dead, not to eat me, but for no reason at all, except—*

She shuddered, wordless, and wordlessly Min understood.

Something that feasts on death alone, Min murmured. *Not to sustain itself, to survive, to reproduce, to evolve— all that is irrelevant— but just for the savor of death itself. I have felt a danger like that before.*

Have you, Grandmother? But where?

It's the danger of humans. Not the dark tribes, who hunt because they're hungry, like any predator. It's the pale ones. I wandered too close to one of their camps one night. I had lost little Kumbu the year before, and I still missed him so badly . . . I think deep down I somehow hoped that if they caught me, they would take me where they had taken Kumbu and we could be together. Anyway, the camp dogs started barking and I panicked, so I climbed a tree at the edge of the camp. And I heard them talking.

What did they say? asked Dar.

It made my fur stand up, just like you— except I was right there, listening. They were bragging about whose head they had on display in their houses, and whose head they hoped to bring back from this year's hunt.

That's not hunting! Dar exclaimed. *Even Uncle Noko wouldn't think so!*

No, it's not the kind of sacrifice he talks about. Though I suppose even that kind of killing helps a species evolve.

I don't know. Sometimes I think Uncle Noko's ideas are sort of— stuck in the mud.

Min gently gathered up the wet, burnt newspaper. *Let's find Guma. He can help round up the others.*

But Dar was still staring down the valley, her troubled brown eyes fixed on something obscured by the clouds, invisible even to a powerful Gift like Min's. Something far away, across the river, among the distant mountains they could see from the Granddaddy Tree in clear weather.

Min waited patiently, casting her Gift in the direction of Dar's gaze, trying to form a picture of what Dar saw.

It will be all right, Dar said at last. *It will be hard at times. But it will be all right in the end.*

Wilbur stared out the window of Wanzani Air Flight 1503 into the clouds. The glass mirrored a ghostly reflection of his face, clearer whenever the wet clouds broke to allow a glimpse of dark blue ocean far below, then ghostly again.

He felt awkward in the big-game hunting outfit Kyle had loaned him, complete with pith helmet, though it was nearly identical to the one he'd worn when he landed at Wanzani International Airport a mere ten days ago. He would have felt much more comfortable wearing the skin of the hunter who had become the hunted. He could not forget for a second his friends back in the jungle, nor the mission they had entrusted to him, nor his duty to little Kumbu. But Kyle had gone to quite a bit of trouble to persuade him not to wear his loincloth on the plane.

Finally they had come to a compromise. The safari jacket chafed his sunburn; the pants were several inches too short for his long legs, and pinched a little in the stride. But underneath he felt the leathery consolation of leopardskin.

It was not the skin he had peeled from the limp corpse of the murdered leopard on his cross-country trek with the chimpanzees. That skin had begun to stiffen and stink even before he'd reached Wanzani City. He had surrendered it to one of the government functionaries after his press conference with a mixture of wild regret and civilized relief.

But Riza Maskari must have mentioned his attachment to the rotting skin to Mrs. Maskari. In the tiny guest room of the Maskari family's comfortable bungalow, where at Riza's insistence Wilbur and Kyle had spent their two nights in the capital, Riza's plump, shy wife had draped a faded cotton bathrobe over the foot of Wilbur's bed and proudly offered him a plastic shopping bag. Inside he'd found a reasonably well-preserved piece of leopardskin that smelled of mothballs, but was large enough to be cut into a loincloth.

"This belong my grandfather," she had said with a dazzling smile that eloquently filled the gaps in her English. "She kill our old cow. He hunt."

Leaning back in the tub for his first bath in over a week, Wilbur had closed his eyes and gradually relaxed into a dreamy, half-conscious state, as Guma and Min had taught him: then focused his Gift. By the time he emerged from the water he was certain he had felt the spirit of his leopard give her blessing to the substitute skin.

The jet broke through the cloud cover at last into open sky, where a bright midday sun lit the cottony topography below. But Wilbur's eyes closed again, his mind drifting back across the waves, the desert sand dunes, the equatorial jungles . . .

Until all at once he found himself blinking in the glare of a gaudy sunset, perched in the branches of the Granddaddy Tree. Back in Wanzanayi, six hours behind him, the twilight was coming on.

It had been raining, but the purple stormclouds had drifted southward, making the fierce glow on the western horizon all the more spectacular. He leaned forward to listen. Grandmother Min was speaking, and she spoke softly, as usual.

The real question, she said, *isn't whether the laws of nature are conscious and intelligent or not. They're what put us here, regardless of how or why. The question is why each individual human wants to believe that he or she can be an exception to those laws, any time they happen to be inconvenient. Looking at a view like this, the important thing isn't who created it; the important thing is who didn't. Did you invent all this amazing complexity?*

Wilbur sprayed out a fine mist of laughter and surprise. *Lord, no!*

Can you create soil, for example? Min persisted, smiling slyly.

Wilbur shook his head.

Can you make air? Or manufacture water? Can you build a tree, or bring one lost species back to life?

Wilbur looked down— several hundred feet down. Hastily he raised his eyes again, but found he couldn't meet Min's without dropping his gaze once more.

But can you at least explain how it was done? Min prodded. *Can any human?*

The scientists are working on that, Wilbur said, still unsure what she was driving at. *I mean they're all working on different aspects of the problem, but that pretty much sums up what scientists do.*

For how long now? asked Guma. *A rough guess?*

It's taken about five hundred years, I think, to learn what they know so far.

You don't count all the millennia of indigenous trial and error? Uncle Noko interjected. *The discovery of plant-breeding, ceramics, metalwork?*

More like fifty thousand years, then, Guma said.

I guess that sounds closer, said Wilbur. It actually sounded a little high. But his memories of high school were vague, and he hadn't lasted long enough at Ball State to take a science course.

Well, Grandmother Min went on. *If after all that time human science still cannot explain how the world came to be, I think we can safely say that the humans did not create it.*

No, of course not!

Yet you humans persistently seem to act as though you could easily recreate this whole complex, intricate balance of soil, air, water and living creatures if you should accidentally happen to destroy it.

Wilbur frowned. *Destroy it? How?*

Humans! said Uncle Noko with a strangled laugh. *I thought they knew everything!*

Noko, please, Guma said. *There was once a time when you didn't know everything, either.* The other chimps snickered, and Guma went on. *Brother Tanzar, the world is made of many interconnecting communities, each one a balance of many species, all put together with such delicate complexity that any sort of tampering, carried on long enough, can bring down the whole thing. It's not put here for us to use, but to marvel at, to learn from, and to play our own unique part in the balance.*

Wilbur blinked, trying to encompass a whole world in his mind at one time— and its destruction. He'd seen something in *National Geographic* that had alarmed him, something about glaciers melting, but couldn't remember anything specific.

It amazes me, Min continued quietly, *how boldly you humans go on tinkering with something you depend on for your lives, even though you couldn't possibly replace it. Now there's a leap of faith for you!*

"Say, Wilbur . . ."

He started out of his reverie. Across the aisle at the opposite window sat Kyle, leaning forward to catch Wilbur's eye over the laps of three other travelers. Kyle was dressed in a hunting outfit exactly like Wilbur's, and wore an innocent grin.

"Yes, Kyle?"

"Since I already owe you, how about loaning me enough to buy us both a drink?"

*

Jane Keller blinked as a bank of hot lights swiveled across her face, trying to hold still as Midge Twilly, the makeup artist, dabbed a powderpuff across her nose. Jane had never had much patience with the art of makeup, and at such close range it was difficult to keep the decades of disdain off her face.

"You'll do fine with just this little bit," Midge said soothingly. They were about the same age, Jane estimated, but Midge's face was such a masterpiece of casual perfection that a glimpse of it from this close might seriously damage one's confidence. At least one with less confidence in her cause than Dr. Jane Keller, BA, MS, PhD.

She glanced over at Jim Rochdale, also appearing tonight on Channel 20's "Counterpoint" segment, along with Ruby Golden, president of the Wildlife Society of South Florida. Jim too had received minimal makeup, no doubt due to his heroic good looks and smooth Florida tan. Ruby appeared to have her own makeup department in one wing or another of her North Miami mansion.

Only some last-minute armtwisting on Jane's part had persuaded the station to drop Ron Checkhoff of Dade County Free the Animals from the segment and invite Ruby instead. She hoped the campaign would not experience any negative repercussions from the switch; it had not been easy to hold the radical animal-liberation and the more mainstream factions of her supporters together. But in only two days the circus was opening its season with the big hometown show, and this broadcast could be crucial.

Across the newsroom, Midge had already finished prepping Mitchell Pauling, Dale Hardy and Peg Tyler. Ralph, of course, needed no makeup, but he and Mr. Hardy were wearing their red and blue circus costumes, and from this angle the family resemblance was truly remarkable. Jane smiled quietly and reminded herself not to mention it, at least on the air.

Mike McCarty, the host of "Counterpoint," raised an inquiring eyebrow in Jane's direction, then at Mitchell Pauling. Both gave him the thumbs-up, Pauling using both thumbs. McCarty grinned and nodded— already caught in the middle, his customary hot seat and vantage point every Thursday night at six— then passed both grin and nod along to Howard Baum, Channel 20's news director, who handed them off to his own boss, news producer Laura Chavez.

Jane watched the chain of signals roll smoothly along through its channels to the top and back down through the lower ranks like the metal ball bouncing through the mechanical maze of a pinball machine. On cue, a bell rang somewhere and the red light announcing "On the Air!" blinked to life.

Oh, these primates! How endlessly inventive they were, and how utterly predictable— at least to one who had spent her entire life studying their ways.

"Good evening, Greater Miami, and welcome to Channel 20's Nightly News at Six!" lead anchorman Bill Chandler began in his hearty voice. "Our top story tonight concerns a bad loser in a traffic accident on Interstate 95, who not only decided to leave the scene but ended up causing three more traffic peccadillos en route to felony charges, with at least one fatality. Susie?"

Camera switch to Susie Chang.

"Like everyone else in metro Miami, we're still waiting for the jury to turn in their verdict on the Roberto Vasillas drug smuggling case— but the case has adjourned for the night without a decision. Tune in tomorrow for the long-awaited answer to whether Bert Vasillas did or did not fill a hollow sculpture of his mother with cocaine before packing it up and shipping it to Miami's prestigious Galleria de los Habaneros for a high-profile exhibit."

"And Hank?"

"Somewhere out at sea, Bill, a swirl of overheated air is still making up its mind whether to smash ashore in a series of thunderstorms over the next week, or to head south and circle around into one of those huge, unpredictable superhurricanes in the Gulf of Mexico. Kind of reminds you of the Vasillas jury, doesn't it, Susie?"

The anchor team chuckled in unison.

"How about you, Leslie?"

Leslie Fielding aimed his manly grin across the sports desk and giggled. "It won't be long now, fans. Miami Dolphins spokesperson

Paul Demoe announced that his team's management is close to an agreement with the stadium maintenance workers' union, and something might be worked out as soon as this weekend that will put the Dolphins back on track for another championship season."

"All that news," McCarty wrapped it up, "plus tonight's 'Counterpoint,' pitting the Rufus Barnabas Circus Spectacular against a grassroots campaign to yank trapeze star Dale Hardy and his chimpanzee partner Ralph out of the circus lineup by Saturday's opening show . . . right after this!"

The show shifted to commercial in an eyeblink. Mitchell Pauling shot Jane a smug look that told her he'd had an inside track on this deal all along, and just couldn't wait another second to let her know it. That must be why the station had resisted so long and hard her efforts to drop Ron Checkhoff from the program— and why Checkhoff's extremist group had been invited to begin with.

But Pauling might not realize how much he had given away with that one glance. Knowing as much as Jane did about primate behaviors had proven a definite advantage before, and now she once more altered her strategy for the debate ahead.

Her mind had drifted far ahead by the time the last commercial break was over and the cameras finally swung to Mike McCarty for "Counterpoint." McCarty's mischievous eyes flicked toward Jane's and away, not quite connecting with Mitchell Pauling's either before settling on the camera directly in front of him.

"Good evening, circus-goers! Well, it's been hard to miss the controversy heating up right under our noses out on Boulevard Santa Fe in front of that big sign that reads, 'Rufus Barnabas Circus Spectacular.' You might have missed the sign, but no one can miss Mitch Pauling's gigantic tiger-striped circus tent!"

Pauling's face multiplied across a bank of monitors. He almost missed his cue, but managed to wave in time.

"And if you've followed this news program over the past couple of weeks, you've almost certainly been aware of the picket signs that read 'Free Ralph!' Those signs are the brainchild of Miami State professor and primatologist Dr. Jane Keller, whose passion for the dignity of animals has almost singlehandedly launched the 'Free Ralph' campaign."

Pauling shot McCarty a nasty look. McCarty grinned back. But

Jane knew it was her turn now on the bank of monitors. Ignoring the off-camera exchange, she nodded a graceful acknowledgement.

"This evening, we'd like to introduce our viewers to the other players in the drama— in particular, a young chimpanzee named Ralph."

Now it was Ralph's turn. Jane had never been quite this close, so she ignored Ralph's image on the monitors and studied the chimp himself. Peg Tyler had drilled him well; he actually stood up on his seat and bowed, folding one arm across his waist, first to the right and then the left.

Startled, Jane glanced across at Ms. Tyler and wondered where she'd learned so much about chimps. Was she the campaign's real opponent, rather than her surly husband or the arrogant circus-owner?

The production crew broke into spontaneous applause. Score one for Ralph, Jane thought— one point for style. Vaguely she wondered which side the chimp's points would actually come down on in the end. It was anybody's guess.

McCarty's format was simple and direct. Mitchell Pauling got his bragging rights, taking practically all the credit for Tyler and Hardy's admittedly impressive accomplishments. Then Jane got her chance, demolishing every shred of Pauling's credibility with her detailed knowledge of the lives of chimpanzees in the wild, and then some.

"While we're working to raise public awareness," she concluded, "our lawyers are working downtown to persuade a judge that a temporary injunction is needed. We're prepared to take the case to Tallahassee, if need be."

Dale Hardy followed, clowning with Ralph a little to demonstrate how affectionate their relationship was, and otherwise adding nothing to the debate.

Then Jim Rochdale took the screen with some stats about the animal training industry, the role played by abuse in its techniques, and how many chimps were in captivity, exploited by circuses and Hollywood and the experimental labs.

Peg Tyler gave a heartwrenching account of how she had purchased Ralph after he and five other baby chimps were discovered hungry and scared in a hidden compartment aboard a freighter flying the flag of Lebanon. She spoke ardently about her innovative training program and its remarkable results.

Then Ruby spoke up on behalf of the animal rescue movement, explaining how her nonprofit had helped to set up sanctuaries for wild animals like Ralph once they were rescued from the entertainment and animal testing industries.

Finally it was McCarty's turn to clown with Ralph. He always seemed to find a way to turn the spotlight on himself; it was one reason "Counterpoint" had remained so popular when other stations had long since dropped debate as entertainment in favor of police patrols on tape or celebrity interviews.

"Okay, Ralph, I think we've heard enough to be convinced that you're no ordinary chimp. The only question is, what is the appropriate place in society for a talented and dignified young primate such as yourself? And it's obvious that no one can speak to that as eloquently as you. So please. Speak directly into the mike, and tell the world where you see yourself going in life. A career in the circus? Or an idyllic retirement on a primate preserve somewhere in south Florida?"

On one of those courtroom reality shows, Jane thought, rolling her eyes, that would be considered leading the witness. But she held her breath, caught like all the others in the gentle brown gaze across the bank of monitors, and waited for Ralph's response. Even though Ralph couldn't—

Ralph smiled knowingly, reached up and removed McCarty's toupée with a thoughtful gesture, examined its label and then proceeded to try it on his own head. The entire studio melted down into helpless laughter.

Bill Chandler was the first to recover; he was Channel 20's lead anchor for a reason, after all. "Well Mike, it seems clear that Ralph is leaning toward a career change to investigative reporting. Wouldn't you say that's a fair summary?"

Across the laughter and applause Jane watched as McCarty did his best to join in the jubilation, his eyes darting back and forth from the "On the Air!" sign to his toupée. As soon as the sign went dark, he snatched back his hairpiece and stalked out.

Well, thought Jane. If she honestly added up the points made on both sides, it probably came pretty close to a draw. But regardless of the debate, Ralph had clearly carried the day.

*

Kumbu woke up crying. That was another new thing.

He'd been dreaming of the forest again: a wet and dripping jungle under a cloudy purple sky. He remembered a giant tree, so tall that it towered above the treetops for miles around. Against a fiery sunset that streaked the horizon, its high arching limbs had been crowded with chimpanzees— chimpanzees like Kumbu, though each one was different, just as Kumbu was different from Marvin, the chimpanzee on "Jungle in the City." There were big chimps and little chimps, gentle chimps and fierce chimps, loud-talking chimps and soft-spoken chimps, all patiently waiting their turns to speak.

Of course Ralph knew he'd been dreaming right away, because chimpanzees *couldn't* speak. And he hadn't actually seen them move their lips. Yet he could swear he'd heard their voices all around him, each one different from the one before, making long flowing speeches full of words he knew and many more he didn't understand.

Oddly enough, the only one who hadn't spoken was a human— a tall, awkward man in khakis who straddled a branch and looked as confused as Kumbu felt.

Lying in his crib now, Kumbu found he couldn't remember a single word, even the ones he knew. But he could picture every face. A warm glow came back to him when he recalled how it had felt to be surrounded by other chimpanzees. He loved his human Mommy and Daddy, and longed for the applause of whole crowds of human strangers. But he'd never realized before how lonely it was to live among creatures so different from himself.

The chimpanzees in his dream had touched each other freely, lovingly, reassuringly. Only Kumbu and the strange human seemed to be sitting out of reach, although the others had looked at both of them so fondly that he could still feel it.

Yet he was crying!

The last face he remembered was the one that hurt the most. He didn't know why, but the tender expression in her moist brown eyes lingered on when the rest of the dream began to fade.

He opened his eyes with a start. That was his mother! He was sure of it. So many times he had awakened with the unshakeable feeling that she was thinking about him, but never before had he been able to see her face. And this time it was not just his mother thinking about him, but the whole crowd of chimpanzees in the giant tree.

These visions would never leave him, he hoped— even if they did make him cry. They were his only link to home.

The spreading limbs and dense leaves of the trees in his dreams looked nothing like the straight trunks and trimmed heads of the palm trees here. It was hard to believe that trees could really live in such thick crowds, covering endless hills and valleys instead of standing single-file along a canal, or down the center of a boulevard . . .

Still, a palm tree was a tree, and he had always itched to climb one. Gazing out from the car as the rows of palms paraded by, he'd wondered if it might be even more fun than climbing the tall, narrow ladder under the Big Top. But his special seat kept him trapped between his Mommy and Daddy, and they kept the windows rolled up tight. And Mommy and Daddy would never understand, even if he could explain somehow.

Today he and Daddy would climb the ladder again to practice one last time before tomorrow's opening show. But practice was never new any more, he thought sadly, watching the bright shafts of sunlight walk slowly down the wall. For a while, when he and his Mommy and Daddy were first working out the routine, it had changed from week to week. Now it was exactly the same each and every time. Maybe a tiny bit more perfect, but nothing to look forward to when he woke up in the morning.

They would still keep practicing their routine every morning after the daily performances began, of course. But they could never vary it again. One small change, and Kumbu or his Daddy would go hurtling through space to catch a pair of hands, or feet, that suddenly wasn't there.

For a week now Kumbu had felt the big day approaching like elephant footsteps that shook the ground, closer and closer, though the elephant itself was nowhere in sight. Tomorrow afternoon the Big Top would begin to fill with faces and voices and smells, each one different, but gradually building up into a crowd with no one face, a roar with no single voice, an odor of mingled popcorn and sweat and sawdust with no particular scent.

Kumbu still remembered the first time he'd seen it happen, soon after his Mommy had first brought him home and introduced him to all her circus friends. As the grandstand slowly filled with excited strangers and the hum of voices expanded to fill the lofty space and the band played louder and louder and the spotlights roamed the crowd, Kumbu had felt all that excitement seeping in and swelling inside him till he could barely contain it. If Mommy hadn't buckled him into a leather harness and held on tight to his strap, he might have floated up into the air and then popped like a balloon.

Mommy had already begun to teach him those games then, and the games were already growing more interesting every day. But she hadn't met Kumbu's Daddy yet. He remembered that night, too. His slender, dark-haired Mommy had come back to the trailer with a sandy-haired man, and her dark eyes were shining. For the first time since she'd brought Kumbu home she had tucked him into his crib and then locked his bedroom door. She and the stranger had stayed out in the living room for hours with the TV turned down low, talking and giggling— just like one of those movies she liked.

Finally, when the living room grew quiet, Kumbu couldn't stand it any more. He'd climbed down from his crib and popped the locked door loose from its frame. Two dark shapes leapt apart on the sofa in the dim light of the TV, allowing Kumbu a glimpse of his Mommy's small round breasts before she covered them with her blouse. The sandy-haired man had jumped up to stand unsteadily on the sofa cushions, ready to fight or run. But in the dimness he didn't see Kumbu standing there beside the sofa, looking up.

"It's all right, Dale," Mommy had said. "I'll get it fixed tomorrow. Ralph, where are you? Come on and snuggle with us."

But Kumbu had noticed something new and strange in the flickering light. Daddy had jumped almost high enough to bump the ceiling when Kumbu reached up and touched him experimentally there between the legs. And the noise he made was loud enough to wake up the elephants next door. At least that's what Mommy said when she teased them both about it later.

Kumbu smiled to himself as he remembered, lying in his crib with his hand in his diaper, scratching his balls.

"Good morning, Ralph! How's Mommy's little— oh no, Ralph, not there! Don't scratch there!"

"Only one more day till D-Day, sport! Want to get up on the trapeze with Daddy again today?"

Chapter 7

Call It Instinct

*

Wilbur gazed down through the window of the jet, watching the coastline of Florida materialize out of the clouds like a ghostly game board far below the gleaming aluminum wing. From this altitude the beaches, the canals, the highways, the subdivisions and shopping malls all had an eerie artificial look.

Miami broke up the illusion with its haphazard patchwork of neighborhoods, downtown skyscrapers, parking lots and stadiums. Long lines of surf rolled up to the beach and broke, as if the mighty ocean was driven back over and over by the minute shadows of beachgoers thickly scattered across the white-gold sand.

Then the spidery runways of Miami-Dade County International Airport spread out suddenly beneath him, another order of magnitude closer, outlined in red, blue, purple, green and orange lights. The big jet picked out one runway from the rest and lifted its nose, dropped its tail, bounced once or twice, and they were down.

Wilbur breathed out the long flight's exhilaration and exhaustion in a long sigh, then glanced across at Kyle. Who grinned back that innocent grin, safe behind his six glasses of wine, all at Wilbur's expense. At least until Kyle secured that advance on his inheritance from his grandmother he kept promising.

Wilbur hadn't been keeping close track of Kyle's borrowing. But soon he would be running low on cash himself, and it would be time to settle accounts. He hoped Kyle's doting grandmother would indeed be waiting at the terminal to meet them— another of Kyle's promises. But he wasn't counting on it. As far as Wilbur was aware, through all the convivial chaos of their stay in Wanzani City, the young fellow never had gotten around to making that long distance telephone call to Homestead, Florida.

They put on their pith helmets and stood up as the queue of disembarking passengers jammed into the aisle began to move at last.

At the baggage claim gate, while Kyle scanned the waiting crowd, Wilbur spotted the battered safari trunk coming down the conveyor belt. He heaved it up across one shoulder, knocking his helmet slightly askew. He had just turned to look for Kyle when he heard someone call his name.

"Hello there, Mr. Trimble! Mr. Trimble!"

It took him a minute to recall her name, but he knew the voice instantly: that sharp young reporter from Indianapolis.

"You remember me from your press conference in Wanzani City, I think," she reminded him coolly, grasping his free hand with polished red fingernails that almost exactly matched her curls. "Sandra Reid. *Indianapolis Herald.*" Her own suitcase waited obediently at her heel.

"Ah— right— yes," gasped Wilbur, still searching the room with his eyes, if not for Kyle, then for something to rest Kyle's trunk on. "A surprise to see you, Miss— er, Ms.— my goodness, you beat us here!"

"Only by an hour or so," she answered cheerfully. "I waited here in baggage claim to be sure I wouldn't miss you. And thank you for asking, it's still Miss. But please call me Sandra. By the way, that trunk does have wheels, doesn't it?"

"Eh? Oh— this isn't mine. It belongs to a— friend. But you're probably right."

The trunk came crashing down on its little wheels, and Wilbur looked around once more for Kyle. And there he came, alone except for a clear plastic cup, smiling anxiously with what looked to Wilbur like bad news.

"No sign of the dear lady, I can't imagine—" Kyle caught sight of Sandra and nearly tripped over a passing suitcase in tow. "Oh! Ah . . . hey, Miss Reid, isn't it? Fancy meeting you here and all that!"

The reporter nodded with a thin smile, a faint glow in her freckled cheeks. Then she turned back to Wilbur.

"Do you need any help finding a hotel?"

"Apparently so. Mr. Wilson here was expecting his wealthy grand-mother to invite us both to stay in her condo in Homestead, but she seems to have stood him up."

"She— she must have forgotten," Kyle sputtered. "You know how older folks get. Just let me borrow enough for a call, would you?"

Sandra laughed, a lovely tinkling sound. "Surely a wealthy grand-mother is good for a collect call, after she's stood you up at the airport like this?"

"Well," Kyle said painfully, "I *am* her only grandchild, but not exactly her favorite. She's kind of— Christian. You know, the strict kind. Fundamentalist. Probably isn't here because she hasn't fin-ished her sermon yet."

"Her sermon?" Wilbur was beginning to be amused in spite of himself.

"The one she always greets me with when I dare to show up down here," Kyle said miserably, staring down at the polished tiles, his plastic cup drained down to its toothpick and cherry. He tossed it disconsolately at a trash can and missed.

It was Sandra Reid who bent to properly dispose of it.

"Well," she said. "Perhaps it's a taxi you want then, Mr. Wilson. Surely if you show up in her driveway she'll pay off the taxi driver?"

"I don't know!" Kyle said, looking up with genuine tears in his eyes.

"Taxis are that way— just follow the little icon of a taxi. Mr. Trimble, I think we could use one ourselves. You don't have a suit-case or anything?"

"No, ma'am. I didn't have time to collect my things from the safari camp. Tell you what, Kyle. I'll give you forty dollars cash for this beat-up old pith helmet. Deal?"

Kyle brightened. "Done! Wilbur, you're a pal. I'll get the rest to you later, all right?"

Wilbur handed over the cash, ducked into the nearest men's room and stripped down to his loincloth. When he returned Kyle's hunt-ing outfit he let out a breath of relief. Finally! Sandra smiled at his minimalist look and turned to lead the way.

When they stepped out together into the blinding Florida sun, she unfolded a pair of round oversized sunglasses from her purse.

Wilbur tugged the brim of his helmet down over his eyes and squinted around. Along a wide stretch of curb, shoals of travelers were arriving and departing or loitering with their luggage, waiting for rides. Here and there an animated reunion was already in progress.

Kyle was just disappearing into a yellow taxicab while the driver, a tiny Hispanic man, struggled to heave Kyle's trunk into the trunk of the cab. Wilbur sighed and gave him a hand. As Kyle's taxi disappeared into the flow of traffic, Sandra signaled to the next.

"I can help pay the meter, Miss Reid. I have a couple hundred left in my moneybelt."

"Don't worry about it, Mr. Trimble. I was taking a cab to the Matador anyway, and my editor's covering all my expenses. He liked the story I filed after your press conference. You're paying *my* way, in a manner of speaking."

"Mr. Trimble! Can I have a word with you?"

Suddenly a pack of reporters materialized out of the glare, each wielding a miniature cassette recorder and struggling for the point position. Cameras clicked madly as if someone were clattering away on an old-fashioned manual typewriter.

"Mr. Trimble, your little press conference in Wanzani City seems to have caught the world's attention. Can you comment on what brings you to Miami?"

"Mr. Trimble— I mean, Tanzar! Does it have anything to do with the mission your friends the chimpanzees assigned you?"

Beyond the siege of reporters several television news crews were converging on them too, not quite so nimble.

"Excuse me, Mr. Tanzar, but I see you're wearing leopard. What message do you think that sends to the fashion industry?"

"Mr. Trimble? Exactly what is this mission the chimps gave you, anyway? My editors have authorized me to offer you—"

Taken by surprise just before they ducked into their taxi, Sandra and Wilbur looked at one another across the yellow roof.

"Wilbur, I'd like to interview you, too," Sandra said. "But I'm on a different deadline. If you want to speak to my more desperate colleagues, I can't ethically monopolize you. Now is as good a time as any to get a few interviews out of the way."

Wilbur drew his long leg back out of the cab. "All right, gentlemen— and lady," he added with a smile at the one female in the posse.

"Slow down just a little— where do you want me to talk? You photographers might like the airport terminal in the background, perhaps? Or would you prefer an actual runway, with airplanes going by?"

He stood under an airport logo on the terminal wall and the cameras formed a semi-circle around him, so each audience could believe their favorite news source had discovered Wilbur Trimble slinking into the city and singlehandedly captured him for an interview. Behind the cameras a portable bank of lights blazed on. Wilbur took out his only prop, the famous Swiss Army knife, stood in his loincloth and smiled obligingly into the lights.

"Hello, Florida! My name is Wilbur Trimble, or at least it was. I'm here in Miami because I was rescued by a band of wild chimpanzees in the jungles of Wanzanayi. They gave me a new name, a fascinating new perspective on the world, and a mission. That's something I've never had before. My mission is to return the favor by rescuing a young relative of theirs who's in captivity right here in Dade County, Florida. My friends seemed to know all about his situation, but their only instructions were to show up here and ask. So I'm mighty grateful for this chance, so soon after my arrival, to ask all of Dade County for help. Can anyone out there help me locate a young chimpanzee who performs in a circus under the stage name 'Ralph'?"

He stopped talking, but kept smiling. A fusillade of questions burst around him from all directions, but he only smiled. A momentary silence fell. Then pandemonium broke out again as all the print reporters whipped out their cell phones and all the TV reporters stepped in front of their cameras at once to wrap the story. Sandra shrugged at Wilbur, clearly enjoying the show.

Then, in the midst of the mayhem, Wilbur saw two young cameramen look at one another with raised eyebrows. In unison they glanced down at their watches. His Gift gave a soft chime. One of the young men edged through the throng, touched Wilbur's elbow and stood on tiptoe to reach his ear.

"See that van over there with the ladder on the side and the elevator seat on the roof? Channel 20 Nightly News at Six? Just follow us. Don't worry, they all will, too, once they figure out where we're going."

Wilbur thanked him and picked up Sandra's suitcase. "Ready for that cab?"

Without a word she signaled the next taxi in line and they ran for it. The Channel 20 van peeled out ahead of them. A minute later they were on the freeway with the Miami skyline glinting on the horizon. The cavalcade of TV news vans passed them one by one.

The green sign over the exit said *Boulevard Santa Fe*, but that was only one more detail. Wilbur wasn't sure why he'd noticed or why he remembered. But his Gift knew, and he was learning to trust it.

Up ahead on the right now loomed an immense tiger-striped tent. Wilbur's Gift was silently clanging like a fire engine's bell. *Rufus Barnabas Circus Spectacular*, said a giant billboard. On the sidewalk he saw a crowd of people, and more signs. *Free Ralph!* seemed to be the prevailing theme. Wilbur stared, swallowed, then burst out laughing. As the taxi pulled up to the curb he gave Sandra a wink.

"Looks like if I want to rescue Kumbu, I'll have to take a number and wait my turn!"

Solomon Purgis found his first chimpanzee track at dawn in the drying mud between two gigantic roots that flared like flying buttresses at the foot of an enormous tree. The second track was about six feet up, printed clearly on the grey bark in brown mud. They stood out like signposts for tourists, which to Purgis's suspicious eye meant they could easily have been planted there to mislead predators. He wouldn't be surprised if chimps were that clever.

This wasn't going to be easy, he thought, squinting up the thick twisting trunk to see if he could spot any more prints. At any one of a dozen junctures, the chimp could have chosen a different route as the trunk split into gracefully sloping boughs that spread in three hundred and sixty directions. But then that was one thing he had found so tempting about this challenge: tracking a critter he had never hunted before, one as comfortable up in the trees as on the ground. Maybe more so. And if lugging this rifle and forty pounds of gear didn't get him back in shape, nothing would.

Unsnapping a pouch on his ammo belt, he clicked open a pair of battle-scarred field glasses and searched the higher branches.

He knew native poachers who bagged chimps all the time, though generally they used traps and snares. The market in chimp meat was brisk, especially among certain tribes who appreciated the flavor, and of course the export market in live chimps for research or exotic pets never really went away. No matter how many speeches the politicians gave at international treaty conferences. No matter how many busts went down on the high seas. It was called "free enterprise."

Purgis had done a little live-trapping himself between the more lucrative phases of his career. And losing his easy gig with the dudes and dudettes might mean he was headed that way again. In fact, he might be through with the safari business for good: Great White Hunter was just about the last of the safari outfits that actually employed tour directors of European descent. Anyway, picture-taking was replacing trophy-taking on safari at an alarming rate. He had plenty of acquaintances in the business who had eventually given up trying to find work. Legal work, that is.

Right now he knew of not a single war that offered employment to a man of his experience and skills. That was unusual in Africa. But lately the conflicts had been mostly ethnic, or ideological, with little chance of advancement for an outsider. And with the big multi-nationals moving in, paying off the corrupt dictators who had replaced the corrupt colonial regimes, and the corrupt bureaucrats still taking their cut, the entire continent was notoriously short of revenue.

But give it time. There were still plenty of drug-trafficking and diamond-smuggling operations cranking out untraceable cash. Even the trade in live human beings was making a respectable comeback. And the corporations and dictators were continually besieged by barefoot mobs carrying signs and whining for democracy. Someone was going to need Solomon Purgis sooner or later, and need him badly. Meanwhile, he still had a few holes to fill in his collection of trophy heads, and there was plenty of wild game to fill his belly.

He decided to make a wide circle looking for more open patches of mud. His main advantage for today's tracking was yesterday's rain, and he had all day to circle back to this tree, if it turned out to be his only lead.

*

Something— call it instinct— warned Jane to look over her shoulder just before she rounded the turn at the far end of the picket line. So she looked. And nearly groaned aloud. Not that it gave her enough warning to run, but enough to prepare her face for utter neutrality before she reached the turn and started back the other way.

After all, this was south Florida, home to every brand of bizarre, and you never knew what that was going to mean from one day to the next. As the campaign to free Ralph had heated up, she'd met some weird ones.

Striding eagerly toward her from a yellow taxi at the other end of the picket line was probably the strangest character she had ever seen in all her years in Florida. He wore a faded pith helmet, a loincloth made of disgustingly genuine-looking leopardskin, and wire-rimmed spectacles— nothing else, not even a pair of flipflops, despite the incandescent heat and the white-hot sidewalk. And he was grinning like the proverbial kid at the circus. Behind him, a young woman with coppery red curls was paying the taxi driver.

Jane nearly laughed out loud. She would have, if the stranger had not been grinning directly down the sidewalk at her. In the middle of his gaunt sunburned chest, a tuft of silver chest-hair completed the ensemble: rented for the occasion, no doubt, from a costume shop that specialized in vintage Hollywood. Tarzan had arrived on the set!

And he hadn't come alone. No fewer than four freshly-arrived television news vans had pulled to the curb either fore or aft of the yellow taxi, in addition to the three that were already here. Grateful as she was for the extra coverage, she had to admit feeling just a bit miffed that this lone fruitcake in costume could outdraw her solidly-built campaign at this stage of the game. Who could he be?

Jane was only one in a crowd of at least fifty people— a record turnout— who had showed up for today's protest after Ralph's sensational appearance on that televised pseudo-debate last night. Yet she had an unshakeable feeling that the stranger had emerged from his taxicab with his eyes already fastened on no one but her.

Of course, Jane had appeared on "Counterpoint" as well. Though introduced as the campaign's initial organizer, she had been careful to state that she was now only one of many committed activists who were dedicated to Ralph's freedom. But evidently this fellow had not been fooled.

The stranger passed the check-in station, where Jim Rochdale was handing out pre-printed picket signs. He passed Greg Polk, one of Jane's students, who was encouraging new recruits to sign up on a clipboard. He passed Ruby Golden, who was introducing half a dozen reporters to the issues of the campaign in the negligible shade of a palm tree, and strode on beside the line of protesters, his eyes still fixed on Jane.

She abandoned neutrality in a sudden panic and prepared the warmest welcome she could muster. Something about the fellow was familiar, she was slowly realizing. Her attention had been so completely focused on Ralph and the campaign that she could have passed this ludicrous get-up daily on the university campus without registering it once. Where had she seen him before? On television? A movie?

Then she had it. Two nights ago. She had seen him skip by on the television screen as she idly clicked through the channels in Jim's apartment, waiting for drinks to be mixed and snacks laid out for a final briefing before the "Counterpoint" segment. It was some kind of press conference overseas, obviously Africa, courtesy of CNN. He hadn't been wearing the pith helmet; that's what had thrown her off. But the leopardskin loincloth was enough. Any old Africa hand would have kept on clicking.

The reporters in attendance, however, had seemed unusually animated; almost all of them were smiling. A few even sported bottles of beer. And it wasn't the usual backdrop of a government podium flanked by flags, portraits of the corrupt and powerful on the walls, soldiers in dress uniform guarding the exits. So, operating on instinct, she supposed, she had clicked back to CNN to see more.

"—in their world I was a total innocent, after all," the fellow in the loincloth was saying. "Chimpanzees have their own way of doing things, and who was I to pretend I knew anything after they rescued me from my own ignorance out there in the jungle?"

God, no! She had snapped off the TV and sighed. If the damned reality shows could just keep their hands off the chimps! Well, there were uses for notoriety, after all. Whether the campaign for poor Ralph ultimately succeeded or not, there would always be the need for another campaign.

As the details came back to her, that brief clip of unfolding "news" from far away seemed more and more odd. Though of course, in this fellow's vicinity, what could be more normal?

The stranger's hand was rising from his side in a perfectly calculated trajectory as he strode closer, though his eyes never dropped to see whether Jane's hand was doing the same. But it was— even as she struggled to free her eyes from his mesmerizing stare, to glance casually aside at the passing traffic or up at the weather. The best she could do was blink furiously as she moved toward him in the picket line, helplessly drawn as if in some kind of trance.

Too late. Their hands met and linked in a precision handshake. Their eyes had never lost contact. Jane stepped out of the picket line in an effortless conversion of momentum to rest, lowering her sign, and the two of them stood gazing up past the circus billboard at the tiger-striped circus tent.

Someone had climbed the billboard and spray-painted *Free Ralph!* in blue letters across its ugly face. That was vandalism, but the line of Miami cops assigned to the protest didn't seem concerned. Perhaps the tide was indeed turning, as something seemed to whisper every time Jane looked around. Call it instinct.

Now that their eyes had broken contact, Jane was having the usual trouble thinking of something to say. No; the usual trouble on Ralph's campaign was slowing down long enough to introduce herself. The trouble she was having now was something she thought she had long left behind and forgotten: what the devil does one do or say on a date?

Absurd! With Tarzan of the Apes! She must be dreaming.

Then she remembered who she was.

"I'm Jane Keller, one of the organizers of the campaign. Isn't it a lovely afternoon for a protest?"

The stranger smiled affably. "Yes, it certainly is! I just stepped off a plane from Wanzani City, where it's about this warm and a good deal more humid." He spoke impeccably, with an amiable enthusiasm that made it hard to disagree with whatever he said. "What's the occasion, if I may ask?"

"Ralph appeared on Channel 20 last night and apparently made quite a hit."

"And was it Ralph's first time on television?"

"Heavens, no. That was weeks ago, before we started our campaign. Last night's debate was originally the circus's idea, though I think now, given the turnout today, they might be regretting it."

"Just coincidentally, I was on television myself the other night, too— my first time. I only wish it could be the last."

The conversation might have veered off track right there, but Jane smiled and steered it skillfully back to Ralph.

"Circuses do have a long tradition of training animals to do clever tricks. But recently a branch of the animal rights movement has been investigating the techniques they use to break animals of their inborn, instinctive behaviors and teach them new ones. Animal training techniques were already a closely guarded secret, but investigating them now is impossible. You literally have to plant a mole, like James Bond or something. We're working to get the laws changed in favor of total transparency, because in the case of the larger predator cats, elephants or anything dangerous, some of the methodologies uncovered have been truly horrendous."

"Cruelty to animals, in other words."

"You don't even want to know. In case you do, of course, you can get some of our literature from Ruby over there under the palm tree. But our work here is approaching its climax, because the circus launches its spring tour tomorrow afternoon with a grand opening show, right over there under that oversized tent. We're expecting our largest protest yet, though our lawyers had to work overtime to get the permit."

"I wouldn't miss it for anything! And after that?"

"The show hits the road. We're not really organized nationally, but we encourage other groups across the country to gather wherever this particular circus performs and let the local circus-goers know how they feel about the rights of animals. Meanwhile, our appeal will be dragging along through the courts. You can sign up for updates if you're— you do email, don't you?"

"I'm afraid not. I still have a mailbox up in Indiana, the old-fashioned kind, and I can get my mail forwarded. But I'm seriously considering a permanent move back to Africa."

"Back? How long were you actually there?"

The stranger laughed. "You know, it seems now like I stayed for months. But in fact I was only there for a little over a week. I had originally planned a slightly longer visit, of course; it was a trip I had dreamed about all my life. Very strange how things turn out sometimes." Suddenly he stopped short with an odd gesture, pressing the fingertips of one hand together and raising them to his lips, as if to plug an open bottle. "Oh my! I can't believe I've gone on and on and never thought to introduce myself! Please excuse me— I was born and raised Wilbur Trimble, in the humble little hamlet of Cedartown, Indiana. But I recently went through a life-changing experience and was given a new name. I've been telling reporters on two continents, so there's no reason I shouldn't tell you. My new name is Tanzar."

Jane was growing embarrassed, too. She should have mentioned by now that she'd caught that fragment of his press conference on CNN. And what about the young woman who had arrived with him? Glancing up and down the sidewalk, she spotted the redhead interviewing Ruby Golden, steno pad in hand. The television crews had staked out sections of the picket line and were also hard at work, staging interviews against the backdrop of the tiger-striped tent.

Excellent, she was thinking. With only one day to go, Ralph couldn't get too much of this! She turned back to Tanzar.

"I'll tell you what. Would you like to pick up a sign and walk the picket line a few times while I speak with some reporters? Perhaps we can talk more after the protest."

The tall man smiled and gave her a nod. "I would consider it a—"

But before he could finish, a handsome fellow with carefully coifed blond hair and a classic Florida tan broke in. "Excuse me, Mr. Trimble, Dr. Keller. We've got a camera set up over here. Would the two of you mind speaking to our audience for a few minutes about how you intend to coordinate your plans?"

Guma and Min ambled side by side along a forest glade, alert for delectables among the vegetation, but also aware that they had drifted toward the rear of the band of chimpanzees. It was the second day of the clan's migration, and Guma figured he might as well cover rearguard responsibilities as they traveled north. He took care to touch Min often. She didn't seem so strong today, and he didn't want her dropping out of his sight. Lately he had been concerned about her increasing dreaminess and lack of interest in things she normally paid attention to. Things like wildflowers and sunsets.

Except when it came to their Gathering of Gifts with Brother Tanzar each evening. She was always one of the first to arrive, always eager to begin, even if she no longer paused in mid-climb to admire the brilliant colors smoldering across the sky.

He hoped they would find an appropriate tree along their way for this evening's session. Their human brother was far away across the ocean, and the Gathering of Gifts would need all the help it could get.

Ahead of them, young Dar cast an anxious glance back, noticing Guma but fixing fiercely on his companion with waves of intensity that Min could surely feel, though she didn't seem to respond. That too was out of the ordinary for Min.

More than likely it had something to do with adopting the strange human into their clan and giving him the seemingly impossible mission of rescuing little Kumbu. Guma frowned, hoping it had not been a mistake. Yet when had the Gift ever lied? Who among the clan had spoken up even once with a misgiving or a doubt? Even those who objected to Tanzar's presence had agreed with the assignment of his mission— if only to be rid of the intruder.

No, if the Gift had been trustworthy before, generation after generation, then this too was the way forward for Guma's clan, for the evolution of their fellow chimpanzees. And if for the chimpanzees, then surely for the humans, too.

Of course, soon after they had commissioned Brother Tanzar and sent him off on his mission, the time had come to flee. It wasn't the first time the Gift had seen fit to save chimpanzees by disrupting their lives, sending them on a long pilgrimage far from their home territory. At every stop for rest or water, old Brapa seemed to come up with another tale of the ancestral migrations of the chimpanzees. And chimps had died by ignoring such an impulse to flee, especially when the sight of paleskins had been a new one in their territory.

Once upon a time it was Grandmother Min who received the deeper messages of this sort, the wisest of the clan, with the most respected Gift. Now it was also Dar, Min's spirit-daughter. Even the biggest, strongest males had learned to stand back when the two of them approached, deep in feminine communion, and by now offered the same respect to Dar when she was alone.

Guma, Min said suddenly, startling him. *I am concerned about Dar. She is so worried about me that I have not seen her even so much as glance around for food. I don't think she's eaten a bite since we came across that berry patch yesterday.*

Why don't we catch up, so you can ask her? Guma suggested, glad of an excuse to get Min moving. *Even better, walk right behind her and remind her she's hungry whenever you see something to eat.* He was snorting back a laugh now. *And eat some of it yourself, while you're nagging her, or she'll be complaining too!*

Min smiled, lured into Guma's trap, and realized she was in fact extraordinarily hungry. A sense of unknown danger behind, and not all that far, had made her reluctant to take time to nourish herself. Yet her increasing hunger was beginning to slow her down. And something else.

I'm not quite well, she told Guma shyly. *For several days now.* She giggled. *If I hadn't so successfully persuaded everyone to move, I'd like to lie down and rest a while.*

Guma stopped short and stared, motionless on all fours. His Gift was notoriously well-developed, and seldom did anyone ever take him by surprise. But if anyone did, of course, it was Min.

Kyle was virtually sober when his taxi dropped him off outside his grandmother's condominium in Homestead. It had been a long ride from the airport, and the forty dollars Wilbur had given him for his extra pith helmet wasn't going to cover it.

The driver, a Hispanic man about five feet tall, looked at the pair of twenties, then at the meter. Then up at the towering glass front of Gram's condo. Then he gave Kyle a lingering, articulate glance and started over. Cash, meter, condo, Kyle.

Kyle really had meant to call ahead from Wanzani City. And again from the Miami airport. But Wilbur hadn't mentioned it, and Kyle had a gift for indefinitely putting off unpleasant necessities. He was suddenly desperate not to ring that doorbell. Not quite yet.

"I know, *amigo,* my cash isn't quite covering it but have a little faith, will you? Look, look what I brought home with me from Africa!"

He unlocked his scuffed leather trunk on the grass beside the idling cab and lifted the lid. Item by item he spread out his nylon hammock, his stainless steel mess kit, his shortwave radio, his empty pocket flask, his set of folding cups, his camp lantern, his moccasins, his shaving kit, his collection of dirty t-shirts—

The driver reached into the trunk, picked up one of Kyle's rifles and squinted down the sights. He smiled happily and handed Kyle back the pair of twenties.

"Wait, no!" said Kyle. "I have the license for that. It's registered to me, see? You pick something else."

"*Si, si!*" the little driver said with a gigantic grin, like a kid on Christmas morning. "*Gracias, señor!*"

The driver's door slammed and the cab backed into Point Loma Drive and took off, rapidly picking up speed.

Another piece of the life he was leaving behind, Kyle was thinking as he re-packed his trunk. Better report it stolen right away. The trunk actually felt lighter as he rolled it up the driveway to the condo's fancy brick front patio.

It was Gram's second husband, a loudmouthed south Florida real estate developer, who had left her all the money— though he was just as fanatical a fundamentalist as Kyle's grandpa, the untalkative missionary doctor.

The doorbell played an arpeggio from Bach, just as he remembered. Rodolfo, his grandmother's Filipino houseboy, opened the door in full dress uniform, looking him over without comment or greeting. Or even much of an expression that Kyle could detect on that smooth, whiskerless face.

"Who is it?" Kyle heard his grandmother call.

"It's your prodigal one," Rodolfo responded, without much expression in his voice, either.

"Who, Kyle? One of his surprises!" The voice was coming closer. "Why does he never call?"

"You asked him not to call collect, mum."

"Oh yes, I did, didn't I? And that would explain— come in, Kyle dear, you've just got time for a bath before prayers."

Gram appeared in her nightie and a shimmering robe that looked like it was made of metallic foil. It matched her steel-blue eyes so well that Kyle shivered in the afternoon heat.

"Back from Africa again? So good to see you!" She leaned as though across a thousand-foot chasm to give him a peck.

"Hello, Gram. Yes, I thought I was overdue to pay you a visit."

"Hungering for spiritual sustenance, I'm sure, after your latest dalliance with the devil. Rodolfo, bring in his, um, luggage, please."

"Yes mum," said Rodolfo. Towing Kyle's trunk, the houseboy led the parade down the marble floor from the atrium to the residential wing.

"Gram, you are absolutely correct about that. 'Dalliance with the devil' hits it right on the head. No better description for old Solomon Purgis and his collection of heads."

"Heads?" Gram exclaimed.

"You bet. Heads of every animal he's ever killed, lining the walls of hell. He's obsessed with them. Passes snapshots around the camp-fire at night."

"Oh! Hunting, you mean. You know, the Bible does give man dominion over the beasts, and hunting helps keep the population down. The animal population, I mean."

"Especially the way Purgis does it."

Just in time, before the lecture shifted into sermon mode, they arrived at the end of the marble floor and the wall-to-wall carpeting of the portrait-lined hallway began. Rodolfo parked the trunk in the main guest bedroom, which was done all in white.

"Rodolfo, ask the girls to bring a laundry basket and run a load for Kyle. And fetch him some pajamas or something so he can shower. Kyle, dinner will be in about an hour in the den, beginning with prayers, of course. We're having company, so don't be late, even if you have to show up in pajamas. I just don't know how busy the girls are this afternoon."

"I'll be there, Gram."

"I know, dear, you've never missed a meal yet at my house." She patted his belly like it was a plump fuzzy poodle. "Didn't miss too many over there in Africa, either, did you?"

He had a minute or two to rest before Dolores or Hortensia or Juanita, who were all so quiet and shy that he never could keep them straight, crept in with an empty wicker basket and left it discreetly next to his trunk. No sorting was necessary; every article of clothing he owned was ready for the wash. When nothing was left in the trunk except an assortment of dented and tarnished hardware, Rodolfo returned with a set of silky white pajamas and took the basket away.

Half an hour after that, showered and sleepy in his pajamas, Kyle sat at the dining table and steeled himself for the sermon. Gram had been unusually indulgent so far— but then cleanliness was right next to godliness and in Gram's house was sometimes required to come first.

She sat at the head of the table, dressed now in sober grey and black, modestly jeweled, inspecting the place settings. Two other guests were evidently expected. Crystal glittered, china shone and silver sang. Rodolfo stood by the swinging kitchen door, waiting for a signal from inside.

"Rodolfo, give Luis Manuel another try, would you please?"

Rodolfo slid a cell phone out of his uniform and pressed a few keys. "Luis Manuel? Where are you now?" He listened for a minute and snapped the phone off. "They're waiting at the Dixie Highway traffic signal. Soon they will be passing the church."

"Thank you, dear."

Kyle knew why Rodolfo hadn't bothered to identify which church. Gram had pumped millions into the building fund for the Wholly Sanctified Church of the Holy Ghost. A decade ago they had built their immense evangelical cathedral here in Homestead. But they hadn't stopped here: Tampa, Cincinnati, Little Rock, Galveston, St. Louis. Finally their vast underground complex out west in the Rockies, where all investors were guaranteed a berth in the event of the Apocalypse. Gram was in on the ground floor of a runaway real estate enterprise, selling tickets to the Millennium.

A bell rang in the kitchen and Rodolfo brought out a wheeled tray laden with food. At that instant, a Bach arpeggio chimed from the atrium. Rodolfo abandoned the tray and headed for the front door at a rapid clip.

"Hortensia!" called Gram. "Dolores! Juanita! Come and serve the food before it's cold!"

All three came at once from different directions, and seeing them together for the first time Kyle could see why he got confused. They looked like a set of sisters, if not actual triplets. Their movements were so gracefully synchronized that it looked like choreography as they laid a steaming tortilla across each plate and pushed the serving cart around the table to invite Kyle's selection from a dozen different fillings: a rolling burrito bar.

The guests arrived, trailed by Rodolfo and a uniformed Hispanic man who had to be Luis Manuel, their driver. Luis Manuel went straight through the forbidden kitchen door, while Rodolfo seated the guests and resumed control of the serving cart.

"Kyle," Gram said, "I want you to meet my pastor, the Reverend Billy Miles. And the pastor's wife, Mrs. Billy Miles."

Kyle rose and reached across the table to shake their hands. The Reverend was a bald, portly man who grinned almost continuously, as if the skin of his face was stretched so tight that he had no choice. He grinned across the table at Kyle. "Your poor old grandma's been telling us all about you for years, son. Pleased to make your acquaintance."

Mrs. Miles was a shapely blonde who was doing everything she could to remain one in the face of insurmountable odds. "Kyle, dear, how are you? I'm blessed, thank you."

"Thank you," was all Kyle could say to that. His tortilla was stuffed, the cheese was melting in, the blend of aromas drifting upward was about to make him cry, the only thing missing now was a bottle of cold beer, and—

"Reverend," said Gram with a stern look across the table at Kyle. "Would you kindly honor us with a blessing?"

Kyle silently started to cry.

Chapter 8

Jane's Calamity

*

Wilbur was amazed. Just as his friends the chimpanzees had predicted, within an hour after touching down on American soil he had located their lost Kumbu, found allies who were already busy laying the groundwork for his mission, and spoken to a whole flock of sympathetic reporters.

And even more astonishing: Dr. Keller. She knew chimpanzees like Wilbur knew his daily route from trash can to trash can through Woodrow Municipal Hospital. He wondered if the time she'd spent studying them out in the wild might have cultivated in her the beginnings of the Gift— the way her hand had risen to meet his, without so much as a downward glance of her earnest grey eyes . . .

His only disappointment so far was having to get back into a taxi with Sandra instead of joining Dr. Keller and the others for one final strategy session before tomorrow's opening performance of the circus. But Sandra was right. He owed her an interview. Not only for anticipating his jet lag and catching an early morning flight so she could meet his plane, but also for surrendering him to the other reporters when they caught her sneaking him past their little welcome party at the airport.

She had even shepherded him around a discount store they had passed after leaving the protest, helping him pick out some civilized clothes. He had firmly resisted the idea, at first, until Sandra had changed her tack and suggested he think of it as a disguise. In a sack between them on the taxi's rear seat was Wilbur's disguise: a pair of lightweight grey slacks, a short-sleeved shirt with a tropical pattern, socks and sneakers, a baseball cap and a pair of clip-on sunglasses, plus a cheap daypack. Sandra had dropped a comb and toothbrush on top of his pile on the checkout counter without a word. Then she'd insisted on paying the bill.

He glanced across the seat. The redheaded reporter looked weary, though her makeup was still flawless. She stared out the window at the other cars, the endless strip malls and shopping centers, palm trees and canals, sucking on one tip of her oversized sunglasses. Wilbur could see her thoughtful, fretful, quick-pouncing, slow-chewing mind at work. Lining up the questions she wanted to ask him, no doubt.

But the next time he glanced across she was leaning against the door, fast asleep. Her day had been even longer than his, he remembered.

Wilbur hadn't consciously done a thing to line up all those coincidences; his Gift was nowhere near that powerful. Could Guma be doing it all from so far across the ocean? Or, more likely, Grandmother Min?

But in another second Wilbur's Gift brought the situation into perfect focus. It was Kumbu himself who was drawing them together: Wilbur, Kyle, Dr. Taah and the Maskaris, Sandra. Now Jane and her volunteers. One by one, the little chimp had effortlessly attracted the people he needed to accomplish his liberation. For what greater destiny, no one yet knew. But then, as Guma had patiently explained one misty jungle morning, even in the thickest fog it is only necessary to see a step or two ahead.

Wilbur looked out the window and his thoughts drifted back. Back across the ocean to a green, quiet place he already thought of as home, to that first night with the chimpanzees. As the violet twilight slowly faded to pitch-black African night, Guma had showed him how to weave a nest of freshly severed branches up in the crotch of a tree. Wilbur had been slow to catch on, new to the jungle lifestyle and only gradually emerging from a state of shock, but he still remembered one thing Guma had said:

The basic thing missing among the humans we see out here, Friend Wilbur—especially the ones of your tribe— is a subtle thing called respect. And I'm not just talking about courtesy or etiquette. It's much more subtle than that. Respect is an attitude that acknowledges every creature's absolute uniqueness in the world, an ingeniously engineered body and an even more miraculous self-awareness, inherited from a million generations of evolution and never to be repeated in the billion generations to come: an incalculable investment of Life in the miracle of life. It's an attitude very close to awe. And its ultimate test is to maintain one's respect even while stalking, killing and eating that creature, if necessary, in order to sustain one's own sacred inheritance of life. Respect!

But so far, since leaving the jungle, in spite of his weird costume and wild claims, Wilbur had encountered nothing but respect. Was that Kumbu's doing also, or could it mean there was still hope that his species might be capable of evolving?

At the palatial entrance of the Hotel Matador, Wilbur dug out his dwindling cash and paid the driver before regretfully leaning across to nudge Sandra awake.

After checking into their rooms, they met in Sandra's room to watch the news. Wilbur found it difficult to take the contents of a little glass window in a box all that seriously after the wide-open expanses of Africa. But Sandra insisted, clicking from channel to channel until all the newscasts had exhausted the topic of Ralph, Jane, and Tanzar— the "Wild Man of Indiana," one reporter called him— and it indeed proved entertaining, if not terribly instructive. Then they headed downstairs to the hotel restaurant for dinner.

Over dessert, Sandra slipped a spiral notebook out of her purse. She looked across the table and pinned Wilbur to his chair with a flick of her brilliant green eyes.

"Tell me something," she said. "And please speak slowly so the microphone here can pick it up." She clicked the tip of her ball-point pen and flipped to a fresh page.

It appeared that she finally had her questions ready. Wilbur was relieved to find that they bore no resemblance to the tired, titillated queries he had been answering again and again ever since his press conference in Wanzani City.

*

Jane clamped her head between her hands, fingers spread across her cheekbones, while the Channel 20 Nightly News at Six prattled on. As if to keep her face from sliding any farther down her skull. As if to give herself the clearest possible view of the unmercifully wide television screen in Jim Rochdale's black-leather-and-paisley den. As if simply to be a witness to her offense was the gravest punishment she could endure.

No one spoke. Jim cleared his throat and clicked the remote. But it was six o'clock, and Jane's calamity was on every Miami station.

What was she thinking when she allowed that costumed lunatic to be interviewed at a protest which she, Dr. Jane Keller, BA, MS, PhD, had organized— with only twentyfour hours to go before the circus's opening performance?

"After all," the runaway janitor in the leopardskin loincloth was remarking on Channel 15 in his deep, reassuring voice, "hadn't I received the clearest possible instructions from my friends, the chimpanzees who saved my life in the jungle? They told me how to find the Society for the Preservation of Wanzanayian Primate Habitat when I reached Wanzani City. Why wouldn't they also know what I should do when I landed here in Florida? Just as they predicted, all I had to do was ask."

Roger and Sally Martinez looked around at Jane with identical blank expressions and simultaneous little swivels of the neck. The onscreen picture panned slightly to the right, and there she was again, smiling stupidly at Chuck Matsuke, the on-the-scene reporter.

"So, Professor," Matsuke asked, making a sincere effort to keep a straight face. "Were you surprised when the renowned Wild Man of Indiana, by way of Africa, joined your picket line today?"

"Frankly, we've been so busy with the campaign that I hadn't been following Mr. Trimble's— adventures. But our movement to free Ralph can certainly use anybody's help."

Matsuke swung the microphone again, and Trimble's genial face with its gold-rimmed glasses and bemused expression floated once more into view. Behind him a picket sign read Minimum Wage for Chimps!

With a disgusted look at Jane, Jim clicked the remote— and there was Trimble again on Channel 8. "I wouldn't exactly say I learned their language, Jeannie," he was explaining, "since they don't use words to communicate. It was more like I accidentally tuned in to their wavelength, and they graciously consented to include me in their conversation."

"And would you say that will make you a useful member of Dr. Keller's campaign, now that you're here?"

"You and I would think so, of course. But my friends Guma and Min, little Ralph's rightful family back in Wanzanayi, well, they didn't have to 'think so.' They simply knew so, and acted accordingly."

Now the picture panned left— or was it just a clever edit?— and Jane's televised face was once more beaming out at them with idiotic delight, her eyes glazed with an infatuated rapture.

"Professor?" asked Jeannie, a young African-American with elaborately sculpted hair. "With less than a day to go before Ralph's daring debut on the flying trapeze, does Mr. Trimble's presence add to your confidence that you can persuade the circus to set him free?"

"Of course, every voice counts in this campaign," said the cheerful onscreen Jane. "Especially now that the court has ruled against us. Our appeal won't be heard for a few weeks yet."

Without a glance at Jane, Ruby Golden got up from Jim's recliner and headed for the bathroom, looking nauseous.

"Thank you, Pro—"

Jim clicked the remote again; this time they landed on Channel 12.

"—you, Professor. Tell us, was it your idea to link your campaign with Wilbur Trimble's unorthodox mission by inviting him to join today's protest, or Mr. Trimble's idea? Or—" the reporter paused to give the camera a conspiratorial smirk— "was it one of those 'synchronicities' that are getting so darned popular?"

In the background, someone passing in the picket line laughed. For the first time a hint of danger creased the serene face of the professor on the TV screen, and her grey eyes frowned.

"The key to our success so far has been our campaign's open invitation to the world. We have turned no one away who shows a genuine concern for the well-being of helpless animals like Ralph."

The picture swung right, revealing Wilbur Trimble's face and naked torso.

"And you, Mr. Trimble? Whose idea do you say it was?"

Trimble smiled, impersonating a rational human being with perfect aplomb. Then he opened his mouth. "I believe little Ralph has arranged it all, telepathically, from behind the scenes. Or as his relatives in Africa call him, little Kumbu."

The reporter faced his audience again with a smug little grin.

"This is Rick Wheeling reporting from the Rufus Barnabas Circus Spectacular, which opens its spring tour tomorrow afternoon with the traditional hometown show."

The lead anchorman looked around at his colleagues and whistled. "Whew, that's deep. Ralph and Dale meet Tanzar and Jane!"

The professional chuckles of the anchor team sounded more like a roomful of snickering college freshmen.

"And that's the News Alive from Channel 12! I'm Frank Millsap—"

"—and I'm Trudy Larson. Tune in tomorrow to catch more of what's new in south Florida!"

Jim clicked once more around the dial, but that was it for tonight. At eleven they could catch more of the same, if they were in a masochistic mood. Jim clicked the wide screen off and the little group sat in silence—except for the usually silent Dr. Eugene Masebeo.

"Leopard skin!" moaned Masebeo, with a tiny, tortured wheeze of a sigh, staring past Jim's sixteenth-floor balcony and out to sea. "Leopard skin . . ."

The rest of them sat and stared at the blank TV screen. After ten, maybe fifteen minutes of abject and dumbstruck silence, a frenzied buzzing startled them from the apartment's leather-jacketed foyer. Jim touched a button on his remote.

"Who is it?"

"It's me, Ron Checkhoff! Hey, I just saw you guys on the news, and it was, it was, like, *primo magnifico!* Like the touch of genius that's gonna put us over the top!"

Spring break, Jane kept thinking, over and over like a mantra or a prayer. Spring break couldn't possibly come too soon.

"All this we ask in the name of your beloved Son," concluded the Reverend Billy Miles, his clasped hands shaking, his voice a hoarse whisper, "our savior, Jesus Christ. May He return soon to judge His enemies and re-establish His kingdom's reign upon this sin-infested bog of selfishness and lust. Amen!"

"Thank you Jesus!" Gram fervently agreed.

"Hallelujah and amen!" Mrs. Miles chimed in.

"Thank God, now we can eat," Kyle muttered into his napkin, hoping it would go unheard. But of course one of the three serving sisters caught it and shot him a dark-eyed glance that made him jerk in his seat like a stray spark of hellfire. After the prayer the sisters retreated to the kitchen, and to the company of Luis Manuel— who was getting the better end of the deal by far, Kyle could see.

But in fact, over raw vegetable salad, cheese, olives, crackers, some sort of fish balls, a chilled tomato soup, and his custom burrito, Kyle did feel reborn. If he truly believed in a higher power, he would not have hesitated to say a prayer for one of his grandmother's altogether sinful desserts.

"Six o'clock!" Gram called out after checking her watch, and Kyle realized she'd been periodically checking it throughout the meal. "Rodolfo, the news!"

Rodolfo did not appear, but an oversized projection screen began to unroll itself through the ceiling of Gram's dining room. This was a new obsession since Kyle's last visit. With a grin of relief he realized that the topic of Gram's after-dinner sermon would not necessarily be the prodigal grandson. Though more than likely she would work him in.

"Good evening, I'm Carl Felden," a handsome anchorman was saying as the volume came up, "and welcome to the news at six . . . from a biblically-correct perspective. We have highlights of the summit talks between the U.S. and Russia, known in prophecy as the land of Gog; footage of the earthquake damage in our modern Gomorrah, Los Angeles; and a special report on how government-sponsored Bible translation in Communist China misrepresents the holy Word of God— all this and more on your Salvation Station, the Christian Prophecy Satellite Network."

Dessert arrived, pecan pie à la mode, mercifully just in time to save Kyle from laughing out loud as the day's global events and their biblically-correct interpretations unfolded on the oversized screen. Then came a series of commercials for salvation with dazzling special effects, and Carl Felden was back.

"God-fearing folks in the Miami area will want to take note of a dangerous development in a local animal-rights controversy— the 'Free Ralph' campaign."

Felden's smooth square face abruptly disappeared, replaced by a sunburned, unshaven, wildly grinning one that knocked the ice cream right off the bite of pie on Kyle's fork. Wilbur Trimble!

Felden's voice continued, offscreen. "Earlier this week we were one of the few news programs across the country to ignore the bizarre story of a big-game hunter who got lost in the African jungle— only to be rescued by a band of wild chimpanzees. It was not until he arrived in Miami today that the biblical relevance of his case became clear. Among other unlikely claims, Wilbur Trimble of Cedartown, Indiana, reports that the monkeys taught him a sophisticated tele-pathic language which enables them to overcome the limitations of their original DNA and thus evolve—" Felden paused, then repeated the word for dramatic effect— "*evolve* beyond the role God planned for them in the original Creation. Clearly a perversion inspired by Satan, wouldn't you say, viewers?"

A slowly circling picket line filled the screen, framed by a tiger-striped circus tent. Impressive turnout, thought Kyle. He saw sev-eral local TV crews at work among the crowd— then sat up straight. Wasn't that Sandra Reid?

"Mr. Trimble landed at the Miami airport this afternoon in a bla-tant last-minute attempt to use his anti-God, pro-Darwin brand of outside agitation to save the all-but-defeated 'Free Ralph' campaign— a local professor's effort to prevent a chimpanzee named Ralph from performing tomorrow when the Rufus Barnabas Circus Spectacular kicks off its spring tour. Reporter Isaac Fisk was in Miami today and spoke to Mr. Trimble at the scene of this afternoon's protest outside the circus."

"Thank you for speaking with us today, Mr. Trimble." Fisk had slicked-back hair, plucked eyebrows, and narrow, nervous eyes.

"The pleasure is all mine, Mr. Fisk," said a deep familiar voice.

"I understand you've been given a mission by these monkeys that saved your life in the jungle— making you, in effect, the first missionary to humans from a lower life-form. Is that what brings you to Miami?"

"You could put it that way, I suppose. It's quite an honor, really, after so many billions of animals have been pressed into service by humans, to be asked to give something back, and to be able to say 'yes.' Quite humbling. Although genetically speaking, by the way, a chimpanzee is quite distinct from a monkey."

"Right, of course. Speaking of genetics, then, what makes these chimpanzees way over in Africa so sure that Ralph, a would-be trapeze star here in Dade County, is their long-lost baby?" Fisk attempted a smile, but Kyle could see the sweat beginning to seep through his makeup.

"The longer you live with what they call their 'Gift,' Mr. Fisk, the more amazing you find it is. Once upon a time, you see, sir, a little baby monkey was born in a jungle garden without a tail. A fuzzy little baby whose destiny it was to be . . . well, different. That little baby— known in the most ancient books of history as baby Adam— grew up to become the common ancestor of both chimpanzees and human beings."

Isaac Fisk swallowed. "Well, that's one theory . . ."

"And let's face it, you and I aren't so different from little Ralph. You're only one more monkey without a tail, and so am I. One could even conjecture that the chimps are still living in that original garden, and what got us hairless apes thrown out was our rejection of Life's wonderful Gift. My personal opinion is that this Gift I have received is the next step in human evolution, linking us back to our beginnings, full circle— and the chimps are here to show us the way."

A crash and jangle of crockery and silverware echoed from the marble floor as the Reverend Billy Miles slumped over in his seat. His wife shrieked and began tugging at his clerical collar as the old man gasped for air and his eyeballs rolled up. Kyle's grandmother never reacted at all: just stared up at the giant screen in paralyzed shock.

"Yes," said Trimble's voice from the screen, excited now. "I think my friends the chimpanzees have sent me to introduce people once more to the Gift they gave up so long ago, so we can fulfill our common destiny as primates once and for all!"

Trimble clearly had more to say, but as he drew his next breath the camera cut hastily back to the line of picketers, the towering circus tent, and Isaac Fisk.

"There you go, believers! Straight from the monkey's mouth, irrefutable proof that evolution is Satan's pet theory— and even the beloved institution of the circus isn't safe from his evil agenda!"

Rodolfo and Mrs. Miles had the Reverend down on the floor now, flat on his back, his pearl-buttoned shirt open to the navel, taking turns giving him mouth-to-mouth. But Gram still sat frozen, staring up at the enormous screen. Now her mouth dropped open and she slowly raised one arm, working her jaw, voiceless, pointing. Kyle glanced up and saw why. Between Isaac Fisk and the shuffling picket line stood a tall woman with silver streaks in her dark hair, speaking into a megaphone. All of a sudden Kyle wished he had a drink.

"Kyle . . ." Gram said shakily.

"This is Isaac Fisk for the Christian Prophecy Satellite Network, your Salvation Station, reporting from the Rufus Barnabas Circus Spectacular in Dade County, Florida. Back to you, Carl!"

Tears came, hot and wet down Kyle's cheeks. He wished he had a sixpack.

"It's— it's blasphemy! It's— I— my . . ." Gram's face went hard and dark and she finally stammered it out. "My d-daughter, the scientist! Dammit, Kyle, I sh-should have known. I should have known she was somewhere in the middle of this!"

Kyle just cried. "M-m-mom!"

He wanted his bottle.

"I'm curious about this Gift of yours," said Sandra. "It allows you to overhear the telepathic conversations of your friends, the chimpanzees. But are you also able to pick up what nearby humans are thinking? You know, like mind-reading?"

Wilbur poked his fork into his banana pudding, but couldn't find any more slices of banana. "Well, I'm still a beginner, mind you, and a slow learner from way back— but from my limited experience I'd have to say the answer is yes and no." He laid the fork aside. His taste for civilized food had been slow to return. "The Gift is a way of projecting your thoughts to another person, and receiving the same type of communication in return. But the Gift can also be used like— like an antenna or a radar beam, aimed or cast in a particular direction to try and tune in to a particular situation."

"Like another person's thoughts."

"If they weren't consciously projected, you mean? Maybe if you really practiced . . . It's something you have to cultivate, you see. The more you use it, the more powerful it gets. It doesn't necessarily have limits."

"Let's experiment. Close your eyes and tell me what you think I'm thinking. I'll try to focus on one thing and not let my thoughts wander."

Wilbur obediently closed his eyes. He projected his Gift toward Sandra. If he'd ever married and had a daughter, he would have liked one like Sandra. But the more he tried to hold her in his thoughts, the more he kept seeing someone else instead. Someone else entirely. Unless—

He opened his eyes. "You aren't thinking about Kyle, are you?"

Sandra's green eyes went wide with amazement. "I— I kept trying not to . . ." Her pale transparent skin blushed a delicate pink.

"I'd give that young fellow a wide berth, if I were you," Wilbur advised gently. "He can't set a bottle down until it's empty. Then he can't rest until he picks up the next one."

"I noticed that right away myself." Sandra laughed that tinkling little laugh, looking down at the crumbs of her carrot cake. Then cleared her throat, the consummate professional once more. "My piece for the *Herald* is going to center around you, an Indiana native, going all the way to Africa to find your mission in life. So— do you have any family back in Indiana? Any pets? A girlfriend?"

Wilbur shook his head. "My older brother Eddie— Edward, he always wanted us to call him— he became a stockbroker in Chicago, and never came back, even to visit. I stayed with him up there one spring break while I was in college over in Muncie. But Chicago didn't appeal to me much, compared to a small town like Cedartown, and Eddie— well Eddie was still Eddie in a highrise in Chicago, only more so. It was his kind of place."

"What about your parents?"

"They both died in a snowmobile accident on a vacation trip to Michigan. Hit some thin ice under the snow and drowned."

"I'm so sorry, Wilbur. They were both the outdoorsy type, then?"

"They were, yes, and unfortunately for them, Eddie and I were not. Eddie's only interests were money, stocks and bonds, finances— the more abstract, the better."

"And you? You certainly seemed to take to the jungle lifestyle like a native."

"I was the family bookworm. Science fiction, fantasy, westerns, murder mysteries—"

"And Tarzan?" A mischievous smile lit up Sandra's freckles. "I saw your profile in the *Gazette*."

Wilbur nodded sheepishly. "Edgar Rice Burroughs was my favorite philosopher. Still is, I suppose. Eventually I graduated to biographies and travel books, a bit of anthropology, history, historical fiction— the less abstract, the better."

"Any romance?"

"Oh, I read one or two of those. Nothing that really caught my fancy, though."

Sandra glanced up abruptly from her notes, eyebrows raised, ballpoint suspended in mid-air.

"I meant," she gurgled deep in her throat, as though trying to suppress a roar, "did you have any girlfriends, you big silly galoot? Sweethearts? Love interests? Hot passionate affairs with the girl next door?"

Wilbur blushed. "Well, not exactly. I did have a lot of piano lessons."

Sandra sat back, interested now.

*

Solomon Purgis knelt beside a pool of water, tracing a glittering trickle up a steep face of rock to the source of the spring, several feet over his head. Above him the canopy of trees blotted out most of the sunlight, letting a few bright shafts through to light up the black, moist mud and the motionless water.

Around the watering hole he saw plenty of tracks: the hooves of bushpigs, claws of jackals, smooth bellyskin of a snake . . . and, almost obliterated by all the other creatures that had come here to drink, the finger-toes of at least one chimpanzee.

The terrain was rough, thickly overgrown and cut by frequent gullies and grottos like this one, but at least now he knew he was moving in the right direction. He grinned, scratching the two days' growth on his chin. Once again, just when he had all but decided he'd lost the trail, chimpanzee tracks had miraculously appeared to confirm that he hadn't.

But where did they lead from here?

Hurdling the tiny stream that was the pool's only outlet, Purgis charged full-tilt up a clay bank and used the last of his momentum to grab for a tangle of roots near the top. His boots slipped and his fingertips missed by inches and he slid back down the bank on his belly, smearing his shirt and the bandolier across his chest with a wide stripe of black clay. For a moment he lay there savoring the stink of the clay and the stinging of the grit under his fingernails.

It would all be worth it when he finally had them in his sights. With a pair of chimpanzee heads on his wall back home, everything he'd gone through to get them would become one more of his stories. Another adventure to tell when the grandchildren came for a visit. Wearily he gathered himself on his haunches and pushed himself upright with a clatter of miscellaneous gear. At his age, all the hardware he was carrying took its toll.

No hurry, he reminded himself, breathing deeply and then deeply again. After all, Kristen was in no hurry to get married and provide her papa with a grandchild. And as far as he knew he had no other offspring. Damn the girl and her endless girlfriends.

Moving farther down the little stream, Purgis sprinted once more at the clay bank and this time managed to catch hold of a vine dangling over its edge. Hand over hand he hauled himself up, rested a minute, then rolled to his feet with a grunt. Not bad for an old-timer, he congratulated himself gruffly.

From this vantage point he could see down the little winding valley of the stream to the glimmering bend of a river. He checked his compass: north-northeast. That was the general direction the chimp tracks had been headed so far. Beyond the river, through a gap in the foliage, he saw the bluegreen ridge of a chain of mountains. This was a region he had never hunted, though he had seen those mountains on the map. He was amazed that the band of chimps had made it this far so fast— and even more amazed that he was still on their track. But if they reached the mountains, his chances of catching up to them would drop close to nil.

Which presented the problem of crossing that river. Unfortunately, none of his pockets or pouches contained an inflatable raft. He did have a folding camp saw in his rucksack, but building a bridge would be far too slow.

If he were a chimpanzee, how would he handle a barrier like that?

The undergrowth grew thicker as he approached the river and the hilly terrain began to level out. When he came to the steep muddy riverbank, he took out his field glasses and scanned the opposite bank, upstream and down, but saw no sign of his quarry. Stepping over a log that had been left stranded by the last flood, he sat down to rest and consider his options.

Below him a wide expanse of brown water was traveling serenely westward. Above it, where the foliage was thinner, the startling glare of midafternoon sky marked its meandering course. But the branches from both sides of the river still met and interlaced in mid-air.

Turning sideways to straddle the log, he traced the tangle of branches on his side of the river, tracking them fork by fork to the larger and larger limbs from which they sprang, all the way down to their trunks, mapping out the possible routes a climber might take— a climber with or without fur. Then he picked the trunk that looked easiest to climb and heaved himself and his gear up off his log.

The footholds were farther apart than they'd appeared from below, he realized, stranded in a three-way crotch halfway up. If only he had a few of those steel pegs a mountain-climber carries to hammer into the ice! Luckily he had plenty of rope. On the fifth try he managed to swing one weighted end over the next branch up.

But halfway up the rope, clinging to the bark with his knees, he had a moment of panic. He was carrying too much weight. He was going to lose his grip, or faint from the exertion. Either way it was a long way to fall. Wrapping one arm around the tree, then the other, he freed one shoulder at a time from the straps of his rucksack and let it go. After a long, suspenseful pause, it struck the ground with a faint thud that reminded him not to look down.

Even after lightening his load, he had to hug the bark for several minutes to regain his strength. Not to mention his courage. But it was too late now to turn around and clamber down.

It was slow work, but in fifteen minutes he had gained the canopy and sat astride a stout branch, breathing so hard that his lungs hurt. It took another five minutes to catch his breath, and five more to stow the rope with his stiff, aching fingers. Looking down made him dizzy, one slip short of terrified, so he stared straight ahead. Inching forward with slow deliberation, he started out across the river.

*

Kumbu was supposed to be asleep in his crib. Instead he sat on the living-room carpet in his family's little trailer at midnight, humming softly, surrounded by the spread-out sections of every newspaper he'd been able to steal and hide. He'd stashed them under the mattress of his crib, in the back of the closet, behind the sofa, under the sofa cushions . . .

It had started with the papers his Mommy and Daddy left lying on the dining table after breakfast. One morning he had seen a picture of a baby holding a spoon, clearly identified under the picture as a "spoon," and had leaped up to dance across the spilled cornflakes on the table. Daddy had walloped him for that— something Daddy never used to do. But it was worth it. Now Kumbu knew how to recognize the word "spoon" when it was written down.

By now he had a list of many, many such words in his head, and his list was growing.

Of course, he'd learned to do his detective work at night instead of at the breakfast table. Frowning with a concentration deeper than he'd ever felt learning Mommy's complicated games, buzzing with an excitement more intense than he'd ever known practicing with Daddy on the trapeze, he checked each column for photographs, searched the line of little bugs under each picture for words he knew, and tried to match new objects with new words.

When he'd thoroughly ripped apart every section of every paper and carefully examined every picture and advertisement, he began to run a finger down every single column of little black inkmarks, watching for familiar squads of bugs. Every time he found one he would study the squads around it, looking for patterns. Sometimes he found a pattern that would repeat from one page to another: those he memorized so he could watch for them.

Besides the patterns of words, he was beginning to catch patterns beneath the words, too, which he could feel if he held his open palm just above the page and closed his eyes. Things that made no sense when he pieced together the meanings of the words had a deeper, hidden meaning that would come to him in a blaze of understanding when he stopped trying to figure them out. He had no idea how or why, but the more he practiced, the more quickly he understood even long, twisting strands of words.

His only worry was his Mommy. She didn't sleep so well at night any more. Twice she had nearly caught him, hurrying through the living room to the kitchen for a drink from her oversized bottle. Alerted by noises from the bedroom she shared with Daddy, twice he'd leapt up and snapped off the lamp before the bedroom door opened. Then sat quivering in the dark, hoping she wouldn't stumble out of her way and trip over his pile of newspapers.

That wasn't his only worry about Mommy, though. This morning she had come to his crib to wake him with a swollen black mark under her eye. Kumbu had winced as he caught the shock of her pain, and it went much deeper than her eye. She and Daddy had not looked at one another during breakfast, not even once. Kumbu knew they had been arguing more and more as tomorrow's opening show approached, and he grew more and more certain they were arguing about him. Somehow this was all his fault.

Just about every night as he searched the newspapers he came across his own picture— usually that same picture of him and his Daddy, but smaller and without the colors. Beside it he always saw pictures of the people carrying signs outside the circus, and sometimes the woman with silver streaks in her hair. Now he could read the signs, although "Free" was a ghostly, cloudlike idea that had taken him much longer to figure out than "Ralph."

He still felt bad about painting those words high up on the canvas wall inside the Big Top one night. The next day's papers had printed a picture of his writing— his first writing ever!— surrounded by column after column that fizzed and crackled with angry. But the hurt feelings that had welled up in him slipped away behind as he forged ahead with his newest game, mentally cataloguing word after word and the different ways they fit together.

Meanwhile, every morning he and his Daddy had been perfecting their routine on the high trapeze, so every crowd of people who came to see it would see exactly the same show. Kumbu understood why. But practicing something exactly the same way every morning and performing it exactly the same way every afternoon would never give him the fever of excitement that teaching himself words and sentences did— not to mention tracking the shifting, shadowy patterns of meaning that hid underneath.

And tomorrow at last was Kumbu and his Daddy's big debut. That was a new word he'd learned that meant "first show." And from their first show on, as they traveled from town to town in the little trailer, the crowd that swarmed into the Big Top would never be the same twice. That meant that although Kumbu's twists and somersaults would have to be exactly the same each time he did them, the applause that rewarded him would always be—

Kumbu froze. Something was going on. In the bedroom. He knew it before he heard it. But when he heard it, it wasn't the clumsy little noises that alerted him when Mommy came stumbling out for a drink. It was a heavy thud, like furniture hitting the floor. And then a growl.

"Dammit, Peg, that's the third time this week you just don't feel like it! I'm under a lot of pressure here, you know—"

A pause. Kumbu couldn't hear his Mommy answer, pleading very quietly. But he could feel it.

"Don't give me that shit about waking up the baby. He's a damn monkey without a tail, Peg, and you know it!"

And then he felt a blow.

The bedroom door banged open, but Kumbu was too stunned to jump up and snap off the lamp. This time it was Daddy coming down the hall, not Mommy. Kumbu could feel his footsteps shaking the floor. And Daddy was as angry as Kumbu had ever known him. No, angrier. Kumbu could feel it rippling through the air.

Suddenly Daddy stood blinking in the doorway, blinded by too much light. Kumbu sat motionless in the middle of the living room floor, staring up. This was his chance to run— but he only stared, shocked by what he'd heard and felt. And before he could move, his chance was gone. Daddy took two quick strides and yanked him up by one arm from his mound of newspapers.

"What the hell you think you're doing out here, messing up the floor like this? Don't you know we got rehearsals in the morning, eight-thirty sharp, and our first show at two in the afternoon?"

Kumbu knew the exact words he could use to answer, but his mouth wouldn't say them. *Give me a crayon*, he pleaded silently, *and I can write them down! I just can't say them!*

But even if he could, he knew his Daddy wouldn't understand. Daddy wouldn't care about all Kumbu had learned, sitting here by himself night after night. Mommy might care— but she would never believe it. They both loved him, but to both of them, Kumbu was just a trained animal they called "Ralph." A monkey without a tail.

Daddy bent to snatch a newspaper from the pile on the floor, letting go of Kumbu just long enough to roll it into a club. But that was enough. When Daddy grabbed for Kumbu's arm again, he had already scrambled out of the way. Before Daddy could even draw a breath to swear at him, he had scooted around the corner and into the bathroom, twisting the door-lock with a click.

The bathroom, of course, was where Daddy had been headed in the first place. He hammered for a long time on the locked door, then gave up, muttering vicious curses and vague threats about tomorrow. Kumbu heard the trailer's front door bang open as Daddy went outside.

Tomorrow he would be safe. Daddy wouldn't dare hurt him on the day of their grand debut. They had been working on their act for much too long. And besides, tomorrow he'd have his Mommy to protect him.

And Mommy would have Kumbu to protect her, too.

He waited until he heard Daddy tromp back to bed. Then he waited to make sure there would be no more arguments. Then he switched on the bathroom light and rummaged through his Mommy's makeup until he found her lipstick. Gripping the edge of the bathroom sink with his toes, he twisted the bottom of the lipstick the way he'd seen Mommy do it until he had a knuckle's length of soft red crayon to work with.

Clenching his tongue firmly between his teeth, he wrote across the mirror in tall, crooked letters that leaned slightly to the left:

FREE RALPH!

Grandmother Min gazed behind her, waiting for Dar. Up ahead where the thick underbrush of the riverbank gave way to forest she could feel Guma waiting patiently for her in turn, surrounded by his brother Noko and six stalwart young males— the traveling clan's rear guard. Ahead of them the others had spread out, browsing this new territory for snacks and succulents.

Somewhere behind them, where the river glinted under scattered patches of sun, Min's Gift still conveyed a sense of danger. And it was closing in. But nothing could have moved her from the spot where she stood rooted on all fours, still dripping wet and panting from the climb.

Guma had found this place, swimming ahead while the rest floated downstream with the current— a place where a fallen branch as big as a small tree made a natural ladder up the steep, muddy riverbank. He had clambered up and then called them to swim ashore one by one as they floated by. Guma had waited there until every single elder and young one was accounted for, helping them negotiate the slippery barkless limb with its broken-off branches.

Now Dar and another young female named Kri, the first to grasp the idea Dar had struggled to explain, were back there patting hand-fuls of river mud over their foot-marks on the bank and smoothing it down with a stick dipped in riverwater. This was a trick Min had never seen before. Of course, they had never fled for their lives from unknown danger before, either. But in all of Brapa's hoard of ancient legend, none of their ancestors had invented something as clever as this.

It was Dar, too, who had haltingly described to the elders of the clan the safe place she had dreamed, high in the distant mountains. By casting her Gift alongside Dar's, Min had dreamed it too, which gave it more weight in their minds. But the dream belonged to Dar.

Although Dar was still young— no older than Min's lost, beloved Kumbu, though it always startled her to remember it— Life had granted her spirit-daughter a Gift of breathtaking range and accu-racy that repeatedly gave Min a shiver of admiration, even awe. It was a comfort in her old age that as she grew daily more feeble in body and spirit, this younger, even more sensitive one was here to carry on.

It was Guma, on the other hand, who had used his Gift to plot the route of their migration, altering it from day to day to avoid confronting other clans of chimpanzees whose territories they were traveling through. In this clan, unlike some others, the storyteller's tales of territorial warfare were regarded as warnings, not provoca-tions.

Guma gave a nervous hoot from the edge of the trees, concerned that they were taking so long. But before Min could respond, she saw Dar and Kri coming— heard them really— no, felt their excitement over this new thing they had done.

Guma's expression showed only relief. Without waiting for the three females to catch up with him, he turned and followed the rest of the band into the trees.

Is it really so close, Grandmother? asked Kri. *This danger?*

Too close to waste your breath with questions, Dar interrupted. *Move!*

Kri gave Dar a look of annoyance, but dropped to all fours and darted ahead. Then Dar turned to Min, and the older female almost smiled. Dar's expression was so fierce that it was no surprise Kri had not paused to argue.

You too, Spirit-Mother, said Dar. *Go on!*

Right behind you, dear, said Min, still refusing to hurry, already beginning to fall behind again. Suddenly she felt so weak that she had to rely on Dar's Gift instead of her own for a sense of the urgency of their flight.

Another hoot from the thickening forest ahead reminded them not to dawdle. But as they turned together toward the treeline, something whizzed between them and a rifle shot rang out over the river. Instinctively the two friends bolted in opposite directions and fled.

Chapter 9

Just Say No to Evolution!

*

Dr. Jane Keller, BA, MS, PhD, hadn't slept all night. Nevertheless she waited stubbornly for the rattlesnake-buzz of the alarm before disentangling herself from the sweaty sheets and swinging her feet to the floor.

Coo and Caw regarded her calmly from their perch. It was only a day, they reminded her without words, a day like any other. In Africa, during her fieldwork, she had gained the ability to forget entirely what day it was, wipe the calendar's grid clean for weeks at a time, just by remembering to look around at where she was. At least until Professor Wort had assigned her to be timekeeper for her team during a waterhole watch.

Thanks, she grinned at the gorgeous preening pair. Sleep or no sleep, this was just a day. A Saturday, as it happened, and opening day for the Rufus Barnabas Circus Spectacular at that, but still. In the long run, just one more ordinary day.

Duty calls.

Facing a closetful of dignified, dark-hued outfits, befitting a professor in a dead-end career, she closed her eyes and chose. So what if the damned magistrate had ruled in favor of the circus? He'd also ruled that the Free Ralph! campaign had a right to occupy the public sidewalk, as long as it did not impede the public from entering circus property. Anyone who showed up to see Ralph's debut performance would receive an education they couldn't ignore on their way through the picket line.

Checking her appearance in the bathroom, she noticed that the silver strands in her hair blended naturally with the dark blue pin-stripe suit she'd picked.

She was bending over the fridge, trying to decide what to eat, if anything, when her cell phone rang and relieved her of the decision.

She dreaded the voice of Jim Rochdale, or Ruby Golden, Sally or Roger or any of the others. She would almost have preferred her anonymous caller. But when she heard instead the cheery bass of Wilbur Trimble articulating her name in that genteel manner of his, an odd feeling overcame her. A feeling of— well, liberation was the closest she could come. One way or the other, this would all be over soon. She dropped the phone to her polished kitchen floor and ground it gleefully under her heel.

She didn't even recall giving him her number. Had he slipped her some post-hypnotic drug or something? Was he some kind of provo-cateur, hired by that slimy Mitchell Pauling? He certainly dressed like an escapee from the circus.

The next thought that logically followed gave her a shudder. Could Wilbur Trimble be Jane's anonymous caller?

Tossing her black leatherette briefcase on the passenger seat of her brown Subaru, she circled to the rear and opened the trunk. Inside she spread a folded afghan that normally decorated her rattan settee, upon which she gently lowered two grocery bags full of ba-nanas— just in case. Then she climbed in and revved the motor.

A Saturday, like any other. And after Wilbur Trimble's disas-trous descent from the African skies, how could things possibly get worse?

Wilbur examined the telephone receiver from every angle, won-dering if he'd forgotten something crucial to its operation during his sojourn in the jungle. His first attempt to use one since returning to the human realm, where technology ruled, had gone drastically wrong. Finally he set it back on its cradle on the bedside table of his hotel room, and the beeping mercifully stopped.

Through the receiver's smooth plastic curves and miles of insu-lated wire he had sensed Jane Keller's palpable presence at the other end— no wrong number or technical malfunction— then the telltale shift in her breathing when he'd spoken her name. That had told him more than any number of angry words, though it gave him no clues as to why. His Gift was not yet that advanced, he supposed.

Sighing, Wilbur stuffed his pith helmet into his new daypack. He didn't exactly have a plan for the big day, but was suddenly grateful that Sandra had proposed a disguise, now that he and his loincloth had made their guest appearance on every newscast in south Florida. As usual, he felt awkward dressed as a human. But under his new slacks he felt the reassuring roughness of leopardskin.

He leaned back on the bed, waiting for Sandra to knock, still feeling sluggish from the long trans-Atlantic flight. He let his eyes close, just for a second— and suddenly sat up straight. Behind his closed eyelids the golden radiance of an African sunset blazed around him. Across the ocean the day was already coming to a close, though here in Florida it had just begun.

But the chimps were not relaxing in the branches of the Granddaddy Tree as usual. Instead they sat scattered across the rocks of a tremendous waterfall that roared and tumbled down a steep mossy cliff. Wilbur had seen nothing like this in their home territory during his visit. What could it mean?

For instance, Guma was saying, *most of the time we live peacefully beside our cousins the baboons. And most of the time we're content to eat plants and insects and the occasional honeycomb. But every so often when a tender young baboon gets too close, one of us gets the urge for a little meat. Not long ago a young one named Dar, the daughter of Min's sister Shan, began trying to convince us that we should give up our taste for baby baboon— simply because they're our relatives, and like us they deserve to live.*

Wilbur had seen Dar keeping company with Grandmother Min, and knew the two were close, but he hadn't been introduced. Dar was one of those who apparently preferred to avoid him.

Guma scratched, grunted, and gave a rueful grin. *To be honest, I'm not sure I could resist the temptation myself if it came along tomorrow. It's really quite a delicacy. But Dar has declared that she will no longer eat baboon, and several others of her age have joined her.*

Uncle Noko let out a snort, not quite laughter. *Ridiculous,* he growled. *They're still babies themselves. Next they'll be saying the termites deserve to live, too! One close call with Cousin Leopard will change their minds.*

We're here to eat each other, and eventually be eaten. That's the way evolution advances. They'll figure that out if they survive long enough.

Guma smiled. *We'll all know everything, if we survive long enough. Our first duty is indeed to survive, Brother Tanzar, as is yours: to survive, in order to reproduce. If we were starving, we would owe Life whatever it took to stay alive, and nothing made of meat would be safe from us then. But mere survival and reproduction is never enough. We learned long ago that listening to our elders keeps us alive and producing youngers— but to evolve, we must also listen to our young. They listen to us; the least we can do is listen to them. Who knows where the next step in our evolution is leading, if our children don't? We must at least accept the possibility that Dar may be right.*

A mutation, Wilbur muttered. A vague recollection from a longago biology class was struggling up from the depths of his mind.

A what? said Yago, a young chimp who spoke so shyly that Wilbur almost couldn't hear.

That was Darwin's word for it, said Wilbur. *One of the first human scientists to study evolution. He said that evolution happens when individuals mutate— random, accidental changes in their genes. If a mutation helps an individual survive, he or she has a better chance of reproducing and passing it along to the next generation.*

Guma grimaced. *Crude,* he said. *But close enough, for humans. We prefer to say that the changes come to those particularly able to hear the voice of Life whispering through the leaves of the forest. Like our young sister Dar. And the changes come more quickly and clearly if you're aware of the source. Perhaps that's why human evolution has gone so far astray. But if our species is still capable of evolving, thanks to youngers like Dar, surely yours is too.*

Wilbur looked down at his fingernails. They needed clipping. But when he felt under his loincloth for his Swiss Army knife, he found he was wearing an unfamiliar pair of slacks.

Of course it is, Tanzar, dear, said Grandmother Min gently. *And you're the proof!*

Sandra's firm, delicate knock brought him back to his hotel room with a start.

She looked stunning in a flowery blouse and plain green skirt, polished fingernails gripping her purse. Her other arm was raised to deliver another rap— which might have done some serious damage to Wilbur's chin had she followed through as he opened the door.

"They serve a continental breakfast downstairs if we get there by ten."

He shouldered his daypack. "All set."

She cocked her head and surveyed him from head to foot, then straightened his shirt collar and buttoned it. Wilbur hadn't even noticed it had buttons. "Not bad for a wild man from Indiana," she said.

Wilbur grinned. That was his favorite line from the dozen or so newscasts they had watched last night. Then he remembered Dr. Keller's grey eyes glancing at him during one interview, her rapt smile and attentive look as he explained his mission yet again. He winced. What could have changed her mind?

"Let's go, then."

*

Kyle opened his eyes and realized he hadn't been dreaming. That really was the voice of Juanita, or Hortensia, or possibly even Dolores, husky and pleading in his dim bedroom.

"Mr. Kyle, please wake up? We leave early today. Have one hour to drive. Mr. Kyle, are you awake?"

It was only her heavy accent that had fouled the translation. Or perhaps in his dream she really had been asking something else.

"*Si, si, si,* I surrender! I'm awake. Don't you remember the Alamo?"

Luckily, she didn't. And Kyle was now definitely awake, though the smell of coffee only reminded him that he'd had nothing to drink since leaving the airport except liquids. His grandmother's coffee would certainly not be spiked.

Whichever of the sisters it had been, she was gone as silently as she'd come. On his battered trunk he saw a vision or a hallucination of his entire wardrobe, washed, dried, folded and neatly stacked. His most presentable set of khakis appeared to be laid out on the foot of the bed. Closing his eyes again with a groan, he sat up and reached for them.

It was much too early to think, but he had no recollection at all of travel plans for today. In fact he remembered very little except the ambulance last night. Then Reverend Miles's close call with martyrdom on the dining room floor came swimming back to him. And Mrs. Miles's shrill fit of hysteria as Luis Manuel slammed the car door behind her— eerily echoed by the siren as the ponderous blue Lincoln followed the flashing red lights down Gram's driveway, turning right on Point Loma Drive.

He remembered Gram's own hoarse tantrum after the guests were gone, or most of it: the same old rabid rant about the liberal bias of the media, atheist propaganda infiltrating the schools, science teachers who taught theories as fact— nothing new since his last visit to Homestead, content-wise.

But the sharp, serrated edge in his grandmother's voice had come as a surprise. Was it because she'd come so close to losing her pastor, right at her own dining table? Was it an act, purely for Kyle's benefit? Or had the sight of her only child on television, coolly committing heresy before the world, triggered another slip in Gram's advancing senility?

Whichever it was, she must have decided on a plan of action sometime after Kyle had said good night. Action had always been her forté, after all. And sure enough, when he stumbled into the dining room he found her talking calmly on the phone, sipping coffee, surrounded by sheets of scribbled notes.

"That's right, eleven o'clock sharp," she was saying as she lifted the coffeepot with an inquiring glance at Kyle, immaculately dressed in purple and gold. "Then I can count on you? Excellent! And how many passengers can you carry?"

Dolores, Juanita, or maybe Hortensia shyly set a bowl of oatmeal on the table in front of him. Butter and maple syrup waited beside a tall glass of orange juice. Kyle wasn't anywhere near hungry yet, but he knew the penalties. A hellish eternity awaited all who refused Gram's breakfast, stretching all the way to dinnertime— because wherever they were headed today, Gram would certainly not be buying him lunch.

"Fine. I'll call your pastor and see if he can arrange for us to use the church van. If not, I'll call you back and perhaps you can explain the gravity of our cause to your wife. If she only understood how much more important this is than her Saturday shopping— heavens, now they're teaching evolution right on the news!— then she might even see fit to join us herself."

Kyle shuddered. In Gram's hands, the telephone could be a mighty persuasive instrument of torture.

God, he needed a drink.

*

Kumbu woke up and opened his eyes wide, ready for anything. Wasn't this the day? Wasn't it today that all the practicing would pay off, and the actual performances begin?

The stripes of sunlight on the wall of his room looked the same as they did every morning. He listened carefully through the wall beside his crib, but everything was quiet outside. Over the past few days the usual drowsy sunshine of the circus grounds had been filled with the noise of hammering and shouting, galloping hoof-beats and forklifts rumbling by. The quiet this morning gave Kumbu a funny shiver of excitement.

Yes: today was the day! He'd been studying the calendar in the kitchen, memorizing the sequence of numbers and days of the week and how they played together on the grid of thin lines, across and down. A little like a game his Mommy had taught him long ago, the one called Hopscotch.

One day he had spotted some boys and girls playing Hopscotch on the sidewalk, so he ran across the street to see. He wasn't going to join the game, he just wanted to see. But to get there he had to dodge two cars and a truck. He hadn't seen Mommy that angry again until he'd tried to play Hide and Seek in the convenience store.

Then, with a sudden shock, he remembered last night. With a different kind of shiver he remembered his Daddy's rage, his escape to the bathroom and his inspired revenge. Swallowing hard, he closed his eyes tightly and wished he hadn't been quite so inspired. Daddy's temper didn't scare him nearly as much as what his Mommy would do when she discovered that he'd written on the bathroom mirror with her favorite red lipstick.

He held his breath, huddled in the corner of his crib, and waited.

But when Mommy came to wake him at last, she tiptoed into his room and stared down into his crib, not angry in the least. Instead she was afraid. Afraid to touch him. Afraid to speak to him. Afraid to pick him up and help him get his costume on. He could still see the black mark under her eye, just beginning to fade, but she had forgotten it now. A new afraid covered up the old afraid, pressed between her tight lips, locked in the rigid tension of her jaw. And her breath already stank of that nasty purple stuff she drank. Kumbu had never smelled it this early in the morning.

Staring down at him with her eyes filled with fear and overflowing, she seemed so timid that Kumbu was afraid she would never touch him again: never pick him up and hold him and sing to him as she had done ever since he was little. Desperately, he tried the only thing he could think of. Giving her a shy, scared grin, he reached down into his diaper and scratched his balls.

Reacting without stopping to think, Mommy slapped his fingers away and then burst out laughing.

"All right, Ralph! I'm on to your tricks, even if your Daddy doesn't have a clue. Don't worry, I cleaned the mirror before he woke up. But you're a more amazing critter than I ever imagined, or ever could imagine. And I'm under no illusion that my training is in any way responsible. You're some kind of— evolutionary freak, I guess. A real circus freak. Come on, let's get you dressed."

After that Mommy had acted normal. No, not exactly normal: like it was all part of one endless trapeze act. Like swinging him over the bars of his crib in the morning was no different than his Daddy swinging him by the ankles way up high in the big tent. Kumbu and Daddy both had their parts to play, and she had hers. That was all.

The door to Kumbu's room swung open and banged the wall.

"Up and at 'em, sport!" Daddy sang out.

"Time for cornflakes, Ralph!" Mommy chimed in.

The big day had begun. Kumbu was ready to play his part.

Jane sped along the freeway, her spirits unaccountably lifting as the Subaru flew. She had deliberately turned the radio off before the news came on. Absentmindedly she watched the gulls circling against a heavy bank of clouds.

"Weather bulletin!" she called aloud to the hovering clouds, surprising herself with the sound of her voice, her buoyant tone, the words themselves. "This just in: no rain today!" And to her delight, a breeze sprang up and began driving the clouds eastward toward the coast. Or perhaps that was an optical illusion, since she was driving west as fast as she dared. She nearly laughed out loud at such an unscientific thought.

Approaching the Boulevard Santa Fe, she found herself in an exit-lane traffic jam that extended a couple of miles back toward the

Miami skyline. It was not yet even eleven, and the circus grounds wouldn't open till noon; the show started an hour after that. Some of the extra traffic was obviously due to circus patrons arriving early to get a good parking spot. But surely not all of it?

For a moment her heart beat faster and her brain raced with the unlikely possibility that in spite of Wilbur Trimble and his jinx, Ralph's picket line was going to set another attendance record today.

But as she inched down the exit ramp and onto Santa Fe, where a single lane of traffic merged into three northbound lanes without noticeably gaining speed, the bumper stickers on the cars around her failed to support that hypothesis. She did see six or seven that demanded *Free Ralph!* But she saw many more than that proclaiming *Jesus Saves!*

Both sides of the boulevard were already lined with cars. Pulling up over the curb onto the sandy median opposite the circus, she parked next to a palm tree. In front of the enormous tiger-striped tent, a hundred or so picketers already lined the sidewalk holding up their *Free Ralph!* signs. Approximately twice as many as yesterday, she calculated with triumphant tears in her eyes. Then she remembered it was Saturday. The weekday working folks had arrived!

But directly across the boulevard, in a vacant parking lot in front of a huge unfinished building, a much larger crowd had assembled, holding up totally different signs and banners. All of them began and ended the same way:

People Need a Safety Net Too— Free Health Care for All Human Beings! said one.

People Need a Safety Net Too— A Living Wage for All Human Beings! said another.

People Need a Safety Net Too— Freedom from Pollution for All Human Beings! said a third.

The people in the second crowd seemed to be of every ethnic variety, wearing every kind of clothes and hair, but most of them appeared Hispanic. At least three hundred people, Jane estimated enviously. And it was still early in the day.

She laughed out loud, a long and satisfying burst of utterly inexplicable amusement. Yesterday such a sight might have upset her, even angered her. But today was a new and different day for Dr. Jane Keller, BA, MS, PhD. Let the human rights movement piggyback on the animal rights movement for a change!

However, right beside that second crowd, cordoned off by a double rank of police, a third group of protesters was beginning to assemble in a newly-mown field of grass.

Jesus Is My Safety Net! said the nearest of the banners rippling over their heads.

Repent, Miami! The Judgment Cometh! read the largest, a king-size bed sheet carried on two-by-fours by two husky men.

And the most numerous, pre-printed on plastic signboards and held aloft on sticks: *Just Say No to Evolution!*

∗

Wilbur still didn't have a plan. Sandra, on the other hand, never seemed to be without one. As soon as they had exited on Boulevard Santa Fe, she'd parked her rented Buick in the first shopping center they saw. Even there, half a mile from the circus's own lot, the parking spots were filling up fast.

"I'm going to find Jane Keller," she announced, touching up her mascara in the rear-view mirror. "I can always interview you again later. But I have a hunch that my best angle on this story for today is to stick with the professor as best I can, no matter what happens."

Wilbur too harbored a strong desire to see Dr. Keller again. Their connection yesterday had been so strong, so effortless, so clear, that it was obviously going to take more than an afternoon's acquaintance to plumb its depths. Yet this morning she had cut him off before he could start. Perplexing, to say the least. But his curiosity about her would have to wait: today his mission came first. And the second he remembered that, he knew what he had to do.

"I, my dear, intend to purchase a ticket to the circus. It's been— oh, decades now since I've seen one."

"They'll be watching for you, you know."

"Of course. I did make a fairly public challenge to their right to own their fellow creatures, didn't I? That's one reason I let you talk me into this disguise. Do you think they'll recognize me?"

"Even if they do, it gives you an altogether different image than they're expecting. The press will eat it up."

With a gay wink, Sandra shouldered her purse and swung open the door. She waited while Wilbur unfolded his long limbs from the

164

car, then locked it and joined a knot of people drifting between the rows of cars toward the towering peak of the circus tent.

Wilbur cut between two parked cars and strode directly across to the sidewalk. In his slacks, sunglasses, baseball cap and tropical shirt, no one gave him a second glance. The steady flow of people toward the distant circus tent reminded him of a pilgrimage— a procession— a parade! He could have made much swifter progress had he stayed aloof, taking a parallel course through the parking lots that lined the boulevard. But his Gift told him to slow down, blend in, adopt the pace of the crowd.

Small children were part of this parade, elderly people leaning on canes, disabled people in wheelchairs, faces of many colors visibly descended from many places all over the world. Yet the air of excitement that animated each face gave them all a common expression, as though they were all relatives.

Guma would have put it much more simply. *All human children are related*, he had said once as he watched the babies tumble, shrieking, down a muddy hill. *Just like these youngsters of ours. It's growing older that puts all those different ideas in their heads. And it's the ideas that make them believe they themselves are somehow different. And so they end up thinking these ideas of difference are more important than the fact that they started out related.*

It had taken Wilbur several days' pondering to untangle that one. But watching this crowd converge— children, big and small— made Guma's meaning shine clear as crystal.

✳

Peering through his wraparound sunglasses from the back seat of Gram's slow-moving Rolls Royce, Kyle recognized the scene from last night's news. But it had grown even more loony since then: as if the circus had turned inside out and spilled its jugglers and clowns into the street, wild animals released from their cages, sideshow freaks escaping their tents . . .

The police seemed to have given up all hope of keeping the crowds of pedestrians out of the boulevard, and many drivers had simply given up and parked their cars where they could. It reminded Kyle of Africa, downtown Nairobi or Lagos or Wanzani City, when the cars had first begun taking over.

In the front seat of the Rolls, Gram was barking instructions into her cell phone and simultaneously into Rodolfo's ear as he plunged the shiny bronze-toned hood in slow motion through the crowd.

Behind her, Kyle wriggled to his knees on the velvety upholstery, his head and elbow out the window, searching the crowd for a glimpse of Sandra Reid. This was her story, wasn't it, all the way from the bush country of Wanzanayi to downtown Miami? She had to be here, didn't she, somewhere in this crowd, covering it for the *Indianapolis Herald*?

"Kyle! Are you listening?" snapped Gram, and Kyle suddenly recognized the whine of an electric window. Just in time he yanked himself back inside the car. With horrified squeals his seatmates, Hortensia, Juanita and Dolores, threw themselves against the opposite door, vainly trying to avoid Kyle's emergency landing across the laps of their spotless white dresses.

"Try to keep yourself inside the car, Kyle," said Gram calmly from the front seat, "or next time you'll be missing your head."

Despite the anarchy erupting around them on all sides, the admirable Rodolfo never lost command of the car nor succumbed to the temptation to run down a jaywalking pedestrian. But every possible parking spot appeared taken; sidewalk and street alike swarmed with a seething mass of people who'd been forced to park in one of the strip malls lining Boulevard Santa Fe and walk the rest of the way. As far as Kyle could see back toward the freeway, *Just Say No to Evolution!* signs mingled with *Free Ralph!* and *People Need a Safety Net, Too!*

But God did not intend people who ride in Rolls Royces to walk. Finally Gram's long firm finger triumphantly pointed out a space up on the boulevard's raised median, between a palm tree and an antique brown Subaru— not an actual parking place, just a half-slot created when the driver of the Subaru hadn't bothered to park as close to the palm tree as normal etiquette required. With his usual superhuman skill Rodolfo managed to squeeze the Rolls in, leaving room for at least two doors to open, one on either side of the palm tree.

To Kyle's surprise, the trunk of the Rolls was crammed with preprinted plastic signs on sticks. Gram had been busy this morning. Rodolfo kept trying to hand him an armload to distribute among the crowd he could hear singing hymns across the boulevard, while Kyle kept craning his neck the other way for a glimpse of Sandra.

"Kyle!" hollered Gram as she covered the mouthpiece of her cell phone. "Not those people, you dunce! The other side of the street! The *other* side—"

But she was too late. Kyle had already spotted a familiar spill of sprightly red curls and darted into the crowd with a stack of signs under his arm.

Just Say No to Evolution! they said. Which gave him an exquisitely wicked idea. Maybe he could sell one or two of these. Not to the pro-Creation crowd across the street, but as a souvenir to someone in one of the other camps.

Or maybe some tipsy circus-goer would trade one for a beer.

Kumbu crouched low, uncoiled and jumped as high into the air as he could. It was the day of his grand debut on the flying trapeze, and today's finger-mark on the siding of Mommy and Daddy's trailer was the highest one yet. Landing on all fours with a screech of pleasure, he spun in a circle on the wooden boardwalk and nearly knocked down the ringmaster, Johnny Johanssen.

"Whoa there, Mr. Celebrity Chimp! Damn good thing he's on our side, ain't that right, Dale?"

Mr. Johanssen gave Kumbu's Daddy an exaggerated wink and a grin as he strode past. Kumbu saw him checking his watch. The ringmaster had his costume and makeup on, so like any good circus performer he was already acting his part.

With a nervous giggle Kumbu held up his palm for Daddy to slap. But Daddy didn't seem to notice. Daddy hadn't slapped his palm and told him "Way to go!" for several mornings now, so Kumbu wasn't surprised. And he wasn't going to let it spoil the excitement of this special day.

This morning Daddy hadn't even let him let him try his jump on the way to practice. Daddy had overslept and they had to rush to be on time. Kumbu hadn't even tried to wiggle his hand out of Daddy's tight, angry grip as they hurried out the door of the trailer. Now they'd had their lunch and were on their way to the dressing room to get ready to perform. This time Kumbu had skipped out the door ahead of Daddy and seized the chance to make his jump.

Their turn in the spotlight wouldn't come till the second half of the show, but Kumbu was already tingling all over. He performed a perfect somersault-and-a-half and walked the next few steps of the boardwalk balanced on his hands.

"You crazy monkey, put a clamp on it!" Daddy growled. "You're gonna hurt yourself before you even show what you can do!"

"Quiet, jinx, you just keep those evil seeds to yourself!" scolded Miss Nitzle, the bareback rider, in her honey-sweet country drawl. Kumbu flipped back over onto his feet just in time to take a deep bow as she swept past on the wooden planks with Tom the Tumbling Midget on her shoulder. She clapped her hands and called back "Bravo! Bravo! Encore!" Tom grinned and blew a perfect smoke ring, saluting Kumbu with a miniature cigar.

Everyone they passed on the boardwalk was bursting with the same excitement: opening day of a new season! Even veterans like old Slaphappy the Clown and Kenny Barth, the grey-bearded bandleader, couldn't resist it— especially when they saw someone like Kumbu, who was performing in front of an audience today for the first time in his life, bubbling over with opening day fever. Even the carpenters, the mechanics, the ticket-sellers were vibrating with it, lit up with it, laughing and chatting happily.

Only the security force seemed immune, and today they were everywhere. Kumbu couldn't believe how many gold-trimmed blue uniforms he saw: big, serious men standing at every corner, watching every entrance and exit, on the lookout for trouble.

And one other person hadn't yet caught the fever. Even after Kumbu and Daddy left the dressing room with their costumes on, ready to spring up the long ladder when their turn came, Daddy still wore the dull, humorless face of an ordinary day. Kumbu couldn't figure out why until they met Mr. Pauling, and he was wearing it too. The two lawyers were with him, Mr. Bragg and Mr. Wascoll, looking just as bored and serious as ever.

Daddy and Mr. Pauling stopped to talk on the boardwalk. Kumbu didn't really mean to listen: it was just a game he played, watching people's lips as they talked, listening for words he could learn, trying to guess what the new words meant from other words he already knew. He rarely succeeded in catching an entire sentence. Even today he wasn't anywhere near sure.

"Don't sweat it, Hardy," Mr. Pauling murmured under his breath. "No one's going to know it was you." The big man glanced over his shoulder at the waiting lawyers and lowered his voice even more. "And even if worst came to worst, this circus has invested heavily in whoever happens to be running for office down here for years. The magistrate came through for us, didn't he? Our ass is covered, no matter what."

At least that's what it sounded like to Kumbu. But Daddy glanced down right then and caught Kumbu peering up at Mr. Pauling's lips. His eyes narrowed, studying Kumbu's face with a suspicious frown. When he nodded at Mr. Pauling and turned to continue down the boardwalk, his grip on Kumbu's hand was still tight. Still angry. And suddenly, afraid.

Kumbu shivered in the warm sunshine with a sudden chill. What if Mommy had changed her mind and told Daddy what he had written on the mirror after all?

He had no idea what Mr. Pauling's words meant, or Daddy's frown, or why it should matter if he heard or saw. But now he couldn't forget. As they started toward the Big Top again, he took apart the syllables, studied them one by one and put them back together, working forward and backward from the words he knew to the new ones, over and over and over. But that only made it all harder to understand.

Kumbu felt the fur begin to stand up all along his spine.

*

"Excuse me, Professor. My name is Sandra Reid, and I write for the *Indianapolis Herald*. Do you mind if I tag along?"

"Little Ralph needs all the help he can get," Jane automatically said, turning around with her camera-ready smile. Then she saw who it was. That young redhead who had showed up yesterday in the same taxi as the Wild Man of Indiana.

She sighed. Duty calls.

"I'm Jane Keller. I'm sorry, what did you say your name was?"

"Reid. Sandra Reid." The reporter flipped open a spiral notebook— not simply pointing a palm-size recorder, Jane noticed, like most of the print journalists she'd spoken to.

"Professor—"

"Please, call me Jane."

"Thank you, Jane. And I'm Sandra. Jane, I'm curious about your plans for young Ralph once you've sprung him from involuntary servitude here at the circus. A primate sanctuary, perhaps? I know in the past you've campaigned for at least one, here in Florida, and testified before Congress in favor of funding one at the federal level. Or, in this case, would you attempt to return Ralph to the wild?"

"Well—" Jane had to admit that the young woman had done some homework. "Good question, Sandra. I haven't met Ralph in person, so it's hard to say how easily rehabilitated to the wild he would be. Some tamed chimps grow so attached to people that they can never be truly happy among their own kind. They'll end up causing problems out in the bush for people who are seeking a genuine wilderness experience, or else they'll end up as misfits in some zoo. A primate sanctuary is a good compromise in such a case. Expensive, of course, so it's no substitute for tougher international treaties and interdiction work. But as I said, I would have to meet Ralph myself and probably get a few more expert opinions before that decision could be made."

"I see," said the reporter. Jotting a quick note, she launched another question. "But before that process can even begin, doesn't a whole other question have to be settled, probably in a court of law? I'm talking about the question of who— legally— owns Ralph."

"Ha!" Jane snorted. "That's a sticky one, considering he was part of an illegally imported shipment of contraband, confiscated by the Port Authority in New York after an F.B.I. sting, handed over to U.S. Customs, and finally 'rescued' by Peg Tyler in an open auction, backed by funds put up by the owner of the Rufus Barnabas circus, one Mitchell Pauling. But unfortunately the only claimant who might have a chance against them in court would be Ralph's nation of origin, which, as usual in cases like his, is unknown and altogether impossible to prove."

"Interesting tangle," murmured Sandra Reid, scribbling again. "Impossible to prove."

"Or perhaps not," Jane added. "There's always DNA testing. Ralph might make a good subject."

*

Halfway across the street, Kyle stopped short. He could see Sandra clearly now through the gaps in the moving picket line, wearing the big round sunglasses she'd worn during her visit to the safari camp. But she was not alone. In one hand she held the same palm-sized notebook she had scribbled in while interviewing Kyle and Solomon Purgis— ages ago, it seemed now. The pen in Sandra's other hand was poised for action as she cocked her head on that graceful neck and listened intently to a tall woman with short dark hair.

Seeing her last night on Gram's TV screen, the silver threads in his mother's hair had thrown Kyle off at first. The last time he'd seen her— four years? or was it more like six?— the dark hair had been longer, the silver only a sprinkling. And she'd apparently traded in her scholarly horn-rims for contact lenses. But the woman Sandra was interviewing was undeniably the former Dr. Jane Wilson, *née* Keller, now ten years divorced and once more teaching under her maiden name.

A taxicab edged around him. The driver didn't even glance at him; the boulevard was crawling with pedestrians and Kyle, a non-moving target, was easy to miss.

He looked both ways in a panic, his mouth suddenly dry, his brain echoing painfully with the pitter-patter of childhood memories he'd long ago strangled and left for dead. His mother dragging him by one hand up the steps of a train in Mombasa while he bawled for his Daddy. His mother losing it and thrashing him across his bare legs with a bamboo cane in front of a gang of wide-eyed African kids. His mother staring icily over the top of yet another unsatisfactory report card, her silence more cutting than the razor-edged remark he knew was coming. His mother—

A series of staccato horn-blasts cut into his reverie as another car crept past. Desperately, he spun around in the street. Where was the closest bar? Surely within a block or two. Three at the most. Florida was full of them. Thanks to a psychopathic cabdriver, he miraculously still had the money Wilbur had given him for his old pith helmet. The temporary passport issued by the American embassy in Wanzanayi would do for an ID, if anyone asked, though it was years now since he'd been asked.

Two twenties wouldn't go far in Florida, not in his present state of mind— but hey, this was America. Dressed as respectably as he was in freshly laundered khakis, no bartender was going to ask to see his money in advance. Paying his tab was a problem he wouldn't have to face until closing time. And by then a far more pressing problem would be solved. Temporarily, at least. The plan even offered the bonus of overnight accommodations in the nearest jail. Kyle grinned at the simple ingenuity of it. God bless America indeed.

Now it was only a matter of divining which direction along the boulevard would lead him sooner to the oasis he craved. He had never attempted divination for water, but luckily he possessed an infallible instinct when it came to liquor. Wilbur's Gift had its uses, no doubt. But Kyle's was infinitely more practical. He closed his eyes, feeling for clues in the darkness. His left elbow started to itch, his left kneecap twitched, and after a moment he noticed he was leaning decisively in that direction.

Then Sandra laughed. Above the crashing surf of rising and falling voices he heard a high cascading tinkle of mirth, unmistakably Sandra's. He opened his eyes. The two women swayed toward each other, both laughing helplessly, so close that Sandra's curls nearly touched his mother's nose. Beyond them the striped circus tent loomed orange and black.

Another slow-moving car veered to avoid him, honking long and loud.

Kyle closed his eyes again, but the darkness had vanished. His mother had receded once more into the blurry distance of memory. All he saw was Sandra. Clutching his armload of picket signs, he lurched blindly toward the luminous vision behind his eyes.

But when he opened them a few steps later to gauge the height of the curb, both Sandra and his mother were gone.

Ticket in hand, Wilbur took another step forward with the rest of the queue, moving up a carpeted ramp at the stately pace of a cathedral procession. And stopped to wait again. Slowly but steadily, one by one they were passing under a red and gold tasseled archway from the bright afternoon into the dim interior of the Big Top.

He'd been glad of his clip-on sunglasses when he had arrived to find a line of protesters in front of the circus— twice as many as yesterday, if not more— enthusiastically chanting "Free *Ralph!* Free

Ralph! Free Ralph!" Hoping none of them would recognize him in his disguise, he had swallowed the guilty lump in his throat and stepped through the picket line to join the one at the ticket window.

Now he was glad of the dark lenses again. On either side of the entrance, a burly security man in blue was peering closely into each arriving face. Wilbur smiled blandly and handed his ticket over to a teenaged ticket-taker, who tore it in two and handed back his half without a word or a glance.

"Thank you, miss!" said Wilbur, trying to contribute his share of festivity without attracting more than his share of attention. She didn't reply— couldn't, with that procession still coming and no end in sight. All the non-performing circus personnel were obviously just about exhausted after days of preparing to screen several thousand circus attendees for troublemakers, which seemed to make the actual screening itself fairly matter-of-fact.

Inside, the carpet underfoot turned to something soft and fluffy; even before his eyes adjusted he recognized the smell of sawdust. The heat and glare of the day outside fell behind as he entered a cool, shadowy expanse, murmurous with an expectant chatter that blended with the dull throb of air-conditioning.

The children in the queue were tiring now and beginning to complain. Not Wilbur. Every slow, shuffling step down the sawdust aisle took him deeper into a world he had not encountered since childhood, and he was discovering that although he himself had long ago forgotten it, it had not forgotten him.

His father had taken him to the circus once as a kid, probably in grade school. He remembered feeling a mounting thrill of anticipation for weeks beforehand, and talking about it for weeks afterward with his friends. He had even fantasized about growing up to be a clown. But the details of the performance itself were vague in his memory, and as far as he could recall, the circus had never come back to Cedartown for a return engagement.

Now, little by little, a distantly familiar enchantment was reawakening in him. From a colorfully bannered bandstand above the center ring a polished brass band was playing briskly, just a little faster than the line could move, which had the effect of sending his eyes roaming restlessly ahead of his feet across a cavernous space with no apparent limit, gathering millions of intricate details as if trying to link a universe of stars into constellations.

The grandstand's tiers of folding seats rose steeply behind him and stretched into dimness in both directions, spotlights twinkling across a myriad multi-colored faces, squadrons of balloons adrift toward a faraway glittery ceiling, hushed voices multiplied into a reverberating roar. An usher took Wilbur's ticket and he followed a dancing flashlight beam that climbed a narrow stairway, looping to left and right like a phosphorescent butterfly, finally coming to rest on the numbered brass plate that marked his seat.

Wilbur slipped out of the straps of his daypack and settled into the comfortably upholstered dark.

In spite of herself, Jane found herself enjoying her conversation with the young reporter, Sandra Reid. Speaking with someone so knowledgeable and yet so deferential on the subject that meant so much to her elevated their exchanges above the level of a mere interview with the press. Jane felt herself lifted to new peaks of eloquence in defense of young Ralph's right to liberty, and Miss Reid eagerly took notes.

When Jim Rochdale interrupted with an armful of signed petitions, her first impulse was irritation. She caught herself in time and accepted the pile with a bright smile and a thumbs-up. She turned back to Miss Reid, straightening the pile into a stack.

"I need to deliver these to my car so they won't get lost in all this bedlam. Why don't you walk with me? I'm parked right over there on the median."

The reporter looked up from her notes. "Let's do it."

Jane hugged the stack of papers to her pinstriped chest, dug her keys from the bottom of her purse and started across the boulevard. Sandra Reid scurried to keep up.

"Jane, I'm still intrigued by the possibility of proving Ralph's origin by means of DNA testing. Does any DNA database of African chimpanzees exist?"

"Nothing really comprehensive. But it's a project worth funding, if I could interest the primatology community's usual sources. The African governments can't afford it. Our own government is notably chintzy when it comes to animals. The universities are my best chance, I'd guess."

"But that sounds like it would take a while. What will happen in the meantime to little Kumbu?" The reporter caught herself, but not quite in time. "I mean, young Ralph?"

At the sound of the word "Kumbu," Jane stumbled and nearly tripped over the curb of the median. Papers spilled from between her fingers and caught the wind. Miss Reid leaped after them, snatching them out of the air, pinning them with one shoe as they scuttled along the asphalt. Jane meanwhile was doing the same, thanking her stars that she hadn't spilled the whole stack.

Someone else also knelt down to help: a deeply tanned young man wearing khakis, space-age sunglasses, and a panicky grin under a battered pith helmet. To free his hands, he had thrown down a stack of picket signs that read, *Just Say No to Evolution!*

Jane had no recollection of what "Kumbu" meant or why it had tripped her up. The young man, on the other hand, looked painfully familiar. Apparently he hadn't yet noticed that the woman he was helping was his mother. Or perhaps he was deliberately ignoring her. Behind his sunglasses and his outdoorsy tan and that befuddled grin, he had eyes only for Sandra Reid.

The mating habits of primates, Jane found herself reflecting numbly. It's a jungle out there.

∗

"Hello, Kyle."

Kyle looked up. Sandra stood looking down, her eyes a mystery behind the round sunglasses. But it wasn't her voice that had spoken. Bracing one hand on the bumper of his grandmother's Rolls, he heaved himself reluctantly to his feet. The picket signs he had dropped lay where they'd fallen.

"Hi, Ma."

His mother stood next to Sandra with her arms full of loose paper, smiling awkwardly, as if unsure what to say next. Kyle didn't know what to say either. He never did with Ma.

"Thanks for helping us gather up these petitions," she said. "I would hate for a single one of those precious signatures to go to waste."

"Hey. No problem."

Sandra glanced back and forth, her freckled forehead creasing in a frown. Then she smiled faintly. Sympathy, or amusement? It didn't matter. Kyle Wilson was a joke in Sandra Reid's eyes, no matter what he said or did. Had been all along. He had just been too stubborn to see it until now. Or maybe he just hadn't been sober enough.

"You dropped something," said Ma, pointing at the heap of picket signs. Then she had to read one out loud, just to drive in the punchline. "Just say *no* to evolution!"

Sandra let out a polite little laugh, and Kyle squirmed. "I've been helping Gram. A little. You know, just to earn my keep."

"I might have known she was behind these." Ma glanced over at the anti-evolution crowd. "Evolution is pretty controversial right now in Florida."

"Yeah. We saw you on the news. On the Salvation Station."

"And is this . . ." She pointed at the bronze-colored Rolls.

Kyle nodded. "Can't you tell by her plates?"

The two women turned to examine Gram's license plate. *REPENT!* it commanded.

"She would find the last parking space this side of hell," said Ma.

Kyle and his mother laughed together. They always could when it came to Gram. When it came to Gram, they seemed to have no other choice.

"Gram spotted it," he said. "But only Rodolfo could have squeezed one of Gram's cars into it."

"You must have all had to get out on one side!"

"Yeah."

Ma's nervous glance darted toward the circus tent, checking on her picket line, then measured the relative sizes of the two crowds across the boulevard. Finally her grey eyes settled on Gram's license plate again.

"And how is your grandmother doing?"

"The same. If you hadn't showed up on the news last night, first thing this morning I would've been starting out for hell on foot, just to get that damn sermon out of my ears."

"Still not ready to repent, Kyle?"

Kyle snorted. "And get a car like hers, so I can ride around preaching to the ignorant masses? No, thanks."

"Still in the big-game hunting racket, then?"

"Well . . . Africa is still gorgeous. I can't get it out of my head when I come back to the States. And hunting's the only way I can afford to get there, it seems. But this time out I lasted three days and quit. I think for good. Like I hit some invisible wall."

"Well, hallelujah!" said Ma, her voice full of jeering disbelief— as if unable to hear him finally say what she'd long ago given up begging and badgering him to say.

"I just couldn't get up and do it again. One more Land Rover-load of the ignorant masses, looking for a new experience, namely killing? No, thanks."

Kyle's voice quivered and he fell silent, remembering. Sandra Reid cocked her head, studying him from behind her opaque lenses.

"So why Florida?"

This time it was Sandra's voice that surprised him. He hesitated, improvising something persuasive and sincere. Then she took off her sunglasses, startling him even more, and the piercing green of her eyes stopped him cold.

"Gram's the only one who'll take me when I show up broke," he confessed. "Or drunk. She's never given up on my soul, I guess. Even Ma quit putting up with me."

But Sandra was blushing now, closing her notebook and stowing it away in her purse. "I'm sorry, I didn't mean to pry. And I'm intruding on your reunion. Always curious— I guess you can see why I ended up in the news biz. I'll finish my interview with you later, Dr. Keller. Nice to see you again, Kyle."

"No— wait!" Kyle swallowed a lump of something close to panic. All he wanted was to retire to a cool, dark barroom for a round of beers with Sandra— and she was going to abandon him to the company of his mother?

"No, please—" Ma sounded just as rattled at the prospect. But she caught herself and cleared her throat, looking calm and professional again. "I take it you two have already met?"

Sandra gave Kyle a teasing glance and answered for both of them. "I interviewed your son for a piece I wrote recently for the *Herald*. I was on assignment in Africa, and while I was there I covered the disappearance of an Indiana native from Kyle's safari. Who's here today, incidentally; I believe you met him yesterday."

Ma blinked. "Yesterday?"

Chapter 10

Kumbu, Come Home!

*

Kumbu waited in the tunnel, holding his Daddy's hand, while the booming voice of Johnny Johanssen finished announcing their act. Listening to the hypnotic phrases echo around the big tent made it suddenly hard to stay awake.

". . . making their *grand debut* in the trapeze department of the Rufus Barnabas Circus Spectacular . . . *never before seen* under canvas anywhere . . . ready to *rock the world* of aerial artistry with *unmatched daring* and courage under fire . . ."

Daddy's eyes were closed and he still gripped Kumbu's hand a little too tightly, muttering something under his breath.

"Here they are, the sensational *interspecies* trapeze team of . . . *Dale and Ralph!*"

A long drumroll ended with a cymbal-smash that jolted Kumbu's eyes wide open. He had to gently tug Daddy's hand twice before Daddy too jerked awake. They jogged together up the tunnel into the waiting spotlight, still holding hands. The audience was applauding thunderously, whistling and stomping on the wooden grandstand. Here and there a voice called out, "Go Dale!" "You show 'em, Ralph!"

Waving with their free hands at the dim faceless thundering, Kumbu and his Daddy jogged once around the center ring. When they reached the tunnel's mouth again they dropped hands and raced toward the tall ladder, pretending it was a real race. As a warm-up, cued by the band and timed to another cymbal-smash, they each

178

performed a cartwheel on the way.

Daddy reached the ladder first and started climbing, with Kumbu close behind, as they had rehearsed it so many times. For one endless moment, climbing that long narrow ladder was Kumbu's whole universe. Closing his eyes, gripping rung after rung with his hands and his feet, he let the sounds of the band and the crowd fade away until he was just practicing with his Daddy again, concentrating on getting the routine exactly right.

At last they reached the top and stepped onto the little platform. Far below Kumbu saw the safety net and its woven shadow. While Daddy unlashed the trapeze bar and tested it, Kumbu studied the crowd. From this height all he could see was colors: random ever-changing colors as the spotlights swept restlessly around the arena.

Grasping the trapeze bar in both hands, Daddy gave Kumbu a tight smile, leaped lightly up off the platform and went sailing away into space. Kumbu crouched on three hands, holding his breath as the red and blue figure shrank into the distance, flipped around to face him and came gliding back.

It seemed like no time at all had gone by since this morning's rehearsal. Kumbu was ready to fly again.

Suddenly Jane had to sit down.

"You remember Wilbur, right?" said Kyle. "Surely you couldn't forget a guy in a leopardskin loincloth showing up at your protest?"

Right behind her, thank goodness, was the bumper of her trusty Subaru. *Free Ralph!* it said in bright red letters. *Save the Manatees!* in blue. And in yellow on black: *Bring Back the Everglades!* Gratefully Jane sank down and let the car's rear springs support her weight, clutching her petitions against her chest, taking her first real rest of the day. Possibly the entire week.

"You okay, Ma?"

The reporter, Sandra Reid, gently took the petitions and began straightening the pile once more into a stack.

"I'll— I'll be all right," Jane murmured. She found her waterbottle dangling on its shoulder-strap and unscrewed the lid. The water revived her, trickling cool and alive down her throat. "Yes, I believe I do remember. Tanzar of the Chimpanzees."

The reporter cleared her throat. "Wilbur Trimble is his actual name."

"And— he was the fellow from Indiana who got lost from Kyle's safari?"

"Right," said Kyle.

"And saved by a band of wild chimpanzees?"

"Yeah," said Kyle. "Well, that's—"

"Who taught him a telepathic language, and then gave him the address of the Society for the Preservation of Wanzanayian Primate Habitat."

Kyle glanced uncomfortably at Sandra Reid, whose eyes at that moment were closed, her brow troubled.

"I believe Wilbur's story," said the reporter with a long sigh. "I attended the press briefing he gave at the Wanzani City hospital, and have interviewed him extensively since then. Frankly it's the most bizarre story I've ever covered. But once you've talked with Wilbur you understand that the man either simply does not lie, or he has been utterly changed by something that happened to him. Or both. In fact I believe he was somehow chosen for this experience— and for the mission he was given— because of his unusual personal qualities. Kyle?"

Kyle nodded. "Definitely . . . unusual. The perfect word for Wilbur. Even before he wore that leopard thing."

"I saw what they did with you two on the newscasts last night," Sandra went on. "Quite clever, really. Television as a medium lends itself so perfectly to smearing a character and stretching the truth. But this time the bastards couldn't be closer to the truth. Wilbur was sent here on a mission that happens to run absolutely parallel to yours. In fact there's only one difference. The chimpanzee you're trying to save from the circus is named Ralph. The chimpanzee Wilbur is supposed to bring back to his family is named Kumbu."

Jane lowered her face into her open palms and groaned. "So I really am that— that— that *lampoon* I saw last night on the news? God, I feel like I'm turning into my mother. The one thing I swore I would never be is a missionary."

Sandra turned to a fresh page in her notebook. "Wait a minute. I'm just a little slow. I'm starting to figure out that Kyle learned to love Africa when he was living there with you, presumably while you did your fieldwork with the chimpanzees. And if you don't mind my prying just a wee bit more— where exactly did your mother serve as a missionary?"

"In Kenya. And Nigeria. And in Libya, a little," Jane said tonelessly.

"You left out the Congo," said a familiar and altogether unexpected voice. Jane raised her head, hoping it was a hallucination. Heatstroke, even. But no: resplendent in gold and purple stripes, her mother stood serene and shaded beneath a wide straw hat. "Kyle, haven't you dropped something?"

"Yes, Gram." Kyle scrambled to pick up the spilled protest signs.

"We only lived in the Congo for a month, Mother," said Jane. "But Miss Reid's intuition is correct. I originally signed up for fieldwork in Africa because I remembered how lovely it was when I was growing up there. Just like Kyle. Nowadays, of course—"

"It was a godforsaken jungle," her mother interrupted curtly. "And I mean *literally*. Populated by superstitious savages and ignorant witchdoctors, infested with poisonous insects and snakes and bloodthirsty predators. I could hardly wait to get back to the States for a month or two on furlough every few years. If it wasn't for the dreadful need that Paul and I saw there . . ." Her eyes drifted away for a moment into the past, then snapped back into focus. "But while we were busy over there, little did we realize how busy the missionaries of Satan would be over here, transforming our Christian nation into a more godless wilderness than Kenya, Nigeria, Libya and the Congo put together!"

The steel-blue eyes narrowed to gunslots, swiveled and homed in on Jane. "Now, Jane, dear. What kind of garbage have you and this idiot Trimble been feeding the press?"

＊

High up in the darkness of the second balcony of the grandstand, Wilbur unzipped his daypack and groped for the opera glasses Sandra had lent him. The clowns had been hilarious; the acrobats had been astounding; the tightrope-walkers had been mesmerizing. But most of the precisely choreographed sequence of circus acts had involved animals. Watching the seals clap their flippers on cue, the elephants clumsily dancing, the lions and tigers sullenly obeying the whip, he had felt a heavy, helpless sensation in the pit of his stomach. He could not forget what Dr. Keller had told him about how performing animals were trained.

Surely it was possible to put together an equally thrilling sequence of acts featuring only human performers, who had joined the circus of their own free will?

It wasn't until the ringmaster raised his red-fringed golden megaphone and announced the debut performance of Dale & Ralph that Wilbur had felt a sudden need to be closer to the action— to see it all in greater detail, participate more deeply in the opulent drama unfolding below— and remembered Sandra's miniature binoculars.

That longago trip to the circus in Cedartown had become one of the few childhood memories that included his absentee father, a traveling dealer in kitchen cutlery. Unlike their occasional hunting trips, however, in this one the old man appeared only as a figure in the background: indistinct, even immaterial, a reassuring presence which nevertheless was not entirely present. Now, sitting in the darkness holding the binoculars to his eyes, Wilbur felt that same sense of an invisible presence just behind him, watching over him and reminding him of his mission.

His Gift. That same humming vibration he had felt in the jungle. Connecting him to each of the chimpanzees in Kumbu's extended family through the medium of their own Gifts. And not just when the sun set over the jungle, but any time he took a moment to stop and turn his attention inward, as he was doing now.

A cymbal crashed, and far below him in the center ring two small figures in red and blue raced toward a tall, flimsy-looking ladder and began to climb. He zeroed in with his binoculars: first on the larger one that led the mad upward scramble— Dale— and then on the smaller, darker one that followed up the ladder. Finally they reached a tiny platform up in the higher reaches of the spacious tent. Almost immediately, the larger figure leaped out and launched itself across the towering emptiness toward a second, similar platform.

A lone spotlight swung, tracking Dale, while the snare drum rolled. But Wilbur's binoculars remained fixed on the smaller figure left behind: Ralph.

No, he reminded himself. *Kumbu.* Not Ralph.

And then, remembering why he was here, he projected the

thought a little more firmly. *Kumbu, come home!*

The little red and blue figure on the high platform jerked visibly. Through the binoculars Wilbur saw a small baffled face looking to left and right, looking down across the crowd, even up at the empty canvas above. Finally the little chimp turned all the way around to look behind him, clearly mystified.

Kumbu! Your family loves you! Your homeland needs you! Kumbu, your Gift is calling you home!

The larger red and blue figure reached the platform again on its return swing, and in the field of his binoculars Wilbur watched Kumbu leap out and seize Dale's ankles. Out in the spotlight, sailing through space, the two joined figures twisted oddly to the left and then the right. Wilbur didn't dare attempt another communication while they dangled so precariously in mid-air, but he was clearly getting through.

After a breathless moment they reached the second platform and effortlessly alighted. They bowed together in the spotlight, rotated ninety degrees and bowed again. The crowd whistled and clapped and roared.

Kumbu, listen. I've come to take you home. Home to the forest. But the decision is up to you.

Dale looked down at Kumbu as if waiting for something. But Kumbu stood staring out over the crowd without moving. Wilbur saw Dale stamp his foot. Then he took one more bow, untied a lashed trapeze bar and launched himself once more across the tent. He almost reached the first platform again before whirling around and swinging back to Kumbu for the second time.

Again the little chimp leaped out to grasp Dale's ankles— this time with his feet. The crowd gasped in unison. One woman screamed. Kumbu now seemed to have stopped trying to look around to see who was calling to him. The two red and blue figures soared back toward the first little platform, and at the limit of the swinging arc, Kumbu released Dale's ankles and flew on alone.

As soon as the two figures separated, Wilbur saw the costumed chimpanzee spin himself around, one complete revolution in mid-air, before landing on the platform— a little off-balance, it seemed. He stood there with one hand on the ladder, once more staring intently down at the crowd, scanning in a slow circle as if searching for something. Or someone. And then Kumbu— or Ralph— remembered to bow.

Then came the applause: low and clamorous, echoing around the huge canvas tent, slowly rising to a screaming, whistling crescendo.

*

"Hey, Ma!" whispered Kyle, while Gram was busy lecturing Sandra Reid about the latest ploy of Satan. "You got a floor I can sleep on, by any chance? Just one or two nights?"

Rodolfo and Gram's three maids stood listening gravely as Gram's lecture shifted automatically into sermon mode, holding their signs erect and looking virtuous— though Kyle knew they had heard the sermon a hundred times before. Even the part about him.

Ma gave him a teasing smile. "You prefer my sermons to Gram's for a while, you mean?"

Gram turned and snorted over her shoulder, savagely spitting the words like bitter-tasting seeds: "The greatest sorrow of my life is to have a daughter who spurns salvation, repudiates her Creator, and then goes off to Africa trying to prove that Adam and Eve were the offspring of monkeys. The only sermon I have for you, Professor, is that hell is hottest for those who mislead the innocent!"

Then she shot a steely glance at Kyle. "Not that that's an alibi for innocents who are given ample opportunity to straighten out their steps. Hell is plenty hot enough for you, too, young man."

Gram turned to Sandra again. "The book of Genesis explains all we need to know about the origins of God's Creation, young lady— six days, and on the seventh day, He rested. This scientific obsession with fossils and dinosaurs and Stone Age artifacts is nothing but an egotistical distraction from the real meaning of life, which is personal salvation. Evolution is nothing but a modern-day superstition, which my only child seems to find irresistible. If you find Creation so amazing and wonderful, Jane dear, you might find its Creator even more so. A God who can bring into being a million species, from whales to butterflies, is perfectly capable of doing so in a day or two, or in the blink of an eye, if it suits Him. Scattering a few fossils around would be child's play, in comparison. It's all in the Good Book. One would think you'd never been exposed to it."

"I was exposed to it as much as I could stand," snapped Ma, "and

184

more. Your Sunday School classes had more to do with my taking an interest in science than you can ever imagine. Superstition! Why don't you look into the origin of your Bible, while you're talking about the origins of things? It's as much a human artifact as any Stone Age arrowhead. Fossils and dinosaur bones are the artifacts of Creation itself, and they clearly spell out that your six days actually took millions of years of mutation, adaptation, trial and error. Evolution may not have all the answers yet, because science itself is still evolving, but at least we scientists are humble enough to admit we don't know everything. *Yet.*"

Ignoring Ma's outburst, Gram fixed her eyes on Sandra again with a greedy look: a predator on the scent of fresh prey. "The only essential question," she announced, "is salvation. Just look around at the mess we sinners have made by our pitiful efforts to 'evolve.' Are we ever going to get anywhere on our own? Can this random, hit-or-miss process of trial and error possibly save us from ourselves, or is some outside force our only hope? An outside force that happens to have created us in the first place, and then sacrificed the most perfect man who ever lived to redeem us? I think the answer is obvious. What do you think, Miss Reid?"

Sandra took a deep breath, and plunged. "Now, wait, you two. Hasn't it occurred to either of you that you may be talking about the same thing, in different languages? I don't find the ideas of Creation and evolution so incompatible myself. One is a mythic account, told around the tribal campfires of the ancient Hebrews, with all the poetic symbolism and magical numerology that makes their language so unique. The other is told in the modern language of biology and geology and physics. Why couldn't evolution simply be the method God used to invent Creation, and the six days just a poetic metaphor? Why couldn't real salvation be an evolutionary leap, like choosing to follow Christ's example and give away all your possessions?"

Gram's eyes flared wide and her lips tightened. Then her eyes shrank to malevolent slits and her mouth snapped open. But nothing came out.

"Say, you've been talking to Wilbur, haven't you," said Kyle, forgetting his firm intention to keep out of it. "I mean, Tanzar."

Sandra gave him a warning look, but it was too late. Gram's eyes lit up again.

"Ah yes, Mr. Tanzar! At long last, the missing link!"

Kyle wanted to crawl under the bumper of Gram's Rolls Royce and hide.

"Your modern scientific superstitions play the same role in Satan's plans as the primitive superstitions Paul and I had to contend with in the mission field. Those multitudes of blacks living and breeding and dying without ever hearing the good news of Jesus Christ— going off to hell in the end without ever being offered a chance at heaven. And then on top of that, the droughts and famines and diseases carrying them off so much the sooner. Paul and I could hardly bear it!"

"Your late husband," Sandra ventured. "Has he been gone long?"

"Aaah!" Over the years, the melodramatic wail that Kyle knew so well had been tamed to a sigh. But it still sliced through to his core. "To me, it's like the Lord took him yesterday. Such a kind, compassionate soul, so devoted to the Lord's work, and I was privileged to be his wife and helpmeet—"

"He held on as long as he could," Ma cut in. "He was a doctor, and after a while he couldn't stand the faces of the mothers when he told them there was nothing he could do. Believing all those babies were going straight to hell was the worst part. Finally, right before we were due to go home on furlough, he committed suicide."

"Suicide?" Gram exploded in a shrill fury. "You jealous child! His plane went down in the bush. He was the only one aboard. Write this down, please, Miss Reid. We had established seven bush hospitals in Kenya— our last assignment. Paul spent three weeks every month making the rounds of them all in his single-engine Cessna, showing those heathen villagers the love and humility of Christ. No one but a jealous child could ever believe such a dedicated Christian would commit suicide, deliberately cutting short his service to the Lord, and damning himself to eternal hellfire besides!"

People on both sides of the boulevard were starting to glance across at the median. Kyle wanted to crawl underneath the Rolls and keep crawling, all the way to the front bumper— then creep out into the sunshine and run.

"I'm sorry, Mother. I'm only informing Miss Reid what the coroner decided, based on the police report."

"That coroner? An African, and not even Christian?"

"His race and religion had nothing to do with it. There was simply no mechanical reason for Daddy's plane to flip over like that."

"Jealous, jealous child! That was purely an act of God— taking Paul home to glory!"

Kyle lifted one foot to the bumper of the Rolls, pretending to adjust his shoelace. Then he lurched forward and stood up on Gram's bumper to his full height, scouting the crowds across the street for a cooler, an icechest, anything that might contain cold beer—

Turning to a fresh page of her notebook, Sandra gave him a look that told him to calm down and be patient. Looking down into her green eyes, Kyle suddenly realized that Sandra's cool glance was enough: was more than enough. That he could be very calm and extremely patient, as long as he was waiting for another glance like that one. And that he wanted nothing on Earth more than to make Sandra proud.

Kumbu looked around from the tiny platform under the peak of the big tent, blinded by the spotlight that followed his every move, listening as his first real applause dwindled away. This was it: the moment he'd been practicing for, fantasizing in his crib at night, yearning for as the feeling slowly grew that his human parents considered him— deep down, under Daddy's lust for applause and Mommy's longing for a child— just a monkey. A monkey without a tail.

But even at its peak, when the frenzy of clapping and stomping and whistling was loudest, the applause he had craved for so long had felt oddly distracting. Because just a few minutes before, while he was waiting to leap out and grab Daddy's ankles for his first swing, Kumbu had heard a voice. A voice that knew him by his real name. And though he knew it was hopeless, he could not help searching the hundreds of craning faces beneath him for its source.

I can see you love the circus, the voice spoke up again, startling him once more. *You love the spotlight and the applause. You love your human parents, too. And you have a right to. You were raised here. But is this what you were born for?*

He knew the voice was in his head, because it had made no sound. That in itself was not so unusual. But this voice was different from the ghostly whispers that had become part of the background of his life: so different that it spooked him. This was someone who had found a way into his head and spoke to him quite clearly in the private place inside, using his own true name, the name he'd been given at birth.

Kumbu, your family misses you. They sent me here to bring you home. But you don't have to leave this life behind if you don't want to. The choice is up to you.

It wasn't a frightening presence, trying to whisper its way into his head and take over, or lure him into a trap. It wasn't a dangerous or evil or sinister voice. In fact, it felt kind and soothing. But it was definitely mysterious. Who in the entire world knew him as Kumbu, not Ralph?

But it was his own response to the voice that had scared him the most. That lateral spin at the end of his second swing, right after he let go of Daddy's ankles with his feet— that wasn't part of their routine. Kumbu had done it without thinking, searching the crowd for the source of that mysterious voice. What had he expected to see, spinning around like that, so high in the air? And his landing on the platform had been a little shaky, with no momentum to spare.

The safety net was stretched across the ring below, as it had been for all their rehearsals. But Daddy would have been disappointed, and Mommy too, and all his other circus friends, if he had fallen in front of the crowd.

Of course, even without a fall, Daddy would probably be upset with him anyway. This was no time to be adding something new to their long-practiced, carefully perfected routine.

Which reminded him. He had just taken his bows. After his first swing he had been so spooked that he forgot, and now he'd almost forgotten again. Kumbu reared back and beat his fists against his chest with a triumphant bellow. The crowd broke into laughter.

This was the one part of the routine that had always made him uncomfortable. He didn't understand why it made people laugh— but then he rarely understood when people laughed. And why shouldn't people laugh at Kumbu, anyway?

All of a sudden, the strange voice in his head was back.

They aren't laughing at Kumbu, little brother. They're laughing at Ralph.

It was true. They were laughing at Ralph! Why had he never

realized it before?

When Daddy's next swing brought him back to the little platform, this time dangling upside down by his knees, Kumbu was surprised to discover how upset he actually was.

"You little pisser!" he hissed as Kumbu leaped out and grabbed him by both wrists. His face had turned red from hanging down, and the tight smile had twisted into a grimace. He glared down into Kumbu's upturned eyes, spewing a continuous spray of angry as they soared together high above the crowd. "Saving it up for the big debut, eh? Showing off your genius talents with a little improvisation, eh? Messing with the routine just when we've got it down? Add a little twist whenever it suits you—"

When they reached the end of their long arc, Kumbu took extra care to let go of Daddy's wrists and land on the tiny platform exactly as they had practiced it. But Daddy shot him one more furious glance and snarled, "Let me show you how it's done, monkey!"

Kumbu could only stare as he sailed away toward the other platform. In the middle of his swing he let go, spun around in a double somersault that Kumbu had never seen him try before, reached out for the bar again and missed. A look of desperate hatred burned across the emptiness between them. And Kumbu's Daddy fell.

The crowded Big Top went silent as Daddy curled into a ball and plummeted down into the safety net. It seemed to take him forever to fall. The net stretched and tossed him back up into the air once, twice, three times before he caught the heavy rope around its edge and swung himself down to the sawdust floor.

Kumbu saw a movement at the mouth of the tunnel far below, then a face, and recognized his Mommy. Daddy started toward the tunnel at a run, limping a little, just as Mommy started out to meet him. But when they met, Daddy brushed past her and kept going. Mommy stood hesitating for a long moment, gazing up at Kumbu. Then she turned and ran after Daddy, catching up with him just before they both disappeared into the tunnel.

Nobody else moved. Then, down in the second balcony of the grandstand, someone stood up and slowly moved along a row of knees to the aisle. Standing there with his head bent back, staring directly up at Kumbu, a tiny man took off his shirt, then his pants, and stood wearing nothing but a loincloth. At this distance Kumbu couldn't be sure, but the tiny man somehow looked familiar. Without ever lowering his gaze, he positioned a whitish helmet on his head and fastened the strap under his chin.

But Kumbu was not the only one who saw. From every entrance to the big tent, security men in blue uniforms began to move at an urgent trot toward the grandstand stairs.

Kumbu! the voice in Kumbu's head repeated, firm but kind. *It's time to decide. You can stay if you want. But your family needs you. If you're coming, I'll meet you outside. Some friends you haven't met are waiting out there to welcome you.*

The voice came from the man in the loincloth. Kumbu wasn't sure how he knew, but he knew.

At that exact moment the spotlight found him again. Somberly, blinking in the glare, Kumbu took off his red and blue costume, folded it neatly and laid it down on the little platform. Dressed only in his fur now, he looked around at the audience, which had remained breathlessly silent since his Daddy had fallen. Then he climbed onto the narrow ladder and started up. The spotlight followed him.

Above the little platform, the ladder was anchored to a thick steel cable: one of the guy wires holding up the tent's massive center pole. Kumbu grabbed the cable and kept climbing. When he reached the junction of guy wires at the center pole, he paused and looked around.

Far below, the man in the loincloth had somehow eluded his pursuers, reached the bottom of the stairs and started toward the nearest exit. A squad of security men was heading for the exit at a run.

From the mouth of the tunnel, just then, a larger group of blue-uniformed men appeared. At their head Kumbu recognized the chief animal trainer, Milt Guffey, carrying a rifle. Every single man had his eyes fixed on the peak of the Big Top where Kumbu dangled, unsure where to go next.

He chose another cable at random and started down again. Where the cable passed close to a sturdy rope that maneuvered a bank of red, green, blue and yellow lights, Kumbu leaped across the gap and followed the rope. He was trying to dodge the spotlight's glare, but every time he changed course it soon caught up with him again.

He leaped from the rope to a heavy wire connected to one of the huge loudspeakers high above the crowd, then slid down the wire to a big metal box where dozens of wires converged, right above the heads of the circus band.

Kenny Barth, the bandleader, saw him coming and threw up both hands, which confused the musicians— at least the ones who were still paying attention. They had just launched into a tune that might have been "Happy Days Are Here Again" when Kumbu crashed into the metal box and all the lights in the big tent went out. The horns and drums kept playing for a few seconds in the sudden darkness, which drowned out the startled, swearing, scuffling sounds of Kumbu escaping down the side-tunnel that served as the musicians' entrance.

Behind him, the music trailed off into an uncertain silence. Even the dull hum of the air conditioners had stopped. Here and there Kumbu heard a nervous applause beginning to break out. And then, as if suddenly awakened from a trance, the whole tent broke into an explosion of clapping, stomping, whistles and shouts of "Go, Ralph!"

"Free Ralph!" someone else shouted, and other voices picked it up.

*

Still elated by his success at crossing the river through the tree-tops— and his first sighting of actual chimpanzees, even if he had missed his shot— Purgis clambered down a long angling branch to the crotch where the tree's gigantic trunk divided into six.

It would have made a good place to rest, far better than the place where he'd slung his hammock and mosquito net the previous night. But it was still mid-afternoon and too soon for stopping, no matter how weary he was. If he unfurled his hammock for a nap, he would never prod himself into motion again before nightfall, and those damn chimps would regain the lead they had lost by his unorthodox river-crossing.

He was closing in on them, he knew— at least on the two female laggards he had nearly blasted. If the recoil of the .22 hadn't almost knocked him off the limb he was straddling, he wouldn't have missed. But bagging a female would have only spurred him on after a male to complete the set, and he would still be out here soaked with sweat, lugging his rifle and his remaining gear, tracking chimp.

Safe on the ground again, he marked the location of his descent and began ranging back and forth in widening arcs, searching for spoor. Any clue would do— chimpanzee scat, footprints with fingers, a raided termite mound, even a telltale dislocation of flora.

Then something stopped him cold, glistening beside a lichen-covered boulder: fresh scat. But not chimpanzee. No, this belonged to one of the big cats. He bent to inspect it more closely.

Damn the luck! A leopard. It was a good thing he'd come down when he did. His movements up in the branches were much too cumbersome to escape an encounter with a tree-climbing cat that size. Even on the ground, of course, he'd have to stay alert. He unslung the .22 and checked its action: loaded and ready.

For a second he regretted leaving behind his beloved 30.06— but only a second. Even that instant of distraction could have been fatal. Continuing to widen his arcs, he listened, sniffed the forest air, scanned the lower branches and the ground, his rifle-barrel alert.

The ground sloped downward for a few paces now, and he felt it begin to soften underfoot. A prime spot to look for prints! Sure enough, on one of his arcs he spotted a footprint with suspiciously long fingers— and just ahead of it, the marks of chimpanzee knuckles. He followed, and almost immediately found more. Then, a few feet off to the right, a parallel set of tracks. Both sets were small for a chimp. This had to be the two lagging females, very likely an old grandmother and her eldest daughter, doing their best to keep up with the band's migration. The tracks disappeared as the terrain began to rise again, but their direction was clear.

Purgis frowned, pondering his options. Risking a gunshot would tip off the males who were leading the band, a mistake he'd made before, back there at the river. On the other hand, how to outflank this rearguard of weakness?

He wished he knew more about the habits of chimpanzees. Why a migration, this time of year, and where to? It was the kind of information he had eagerly absorbed for years about lion, giraffe, wildebeest and rhino. With chimpanzees, he wouldn't even know who to ask. The poachers would clam up if anyone came asking; strictly proprietary information, more outlaw than assault rifles or black-market diamonds or raw opium. And for that matter—

Wait a minute: quietly, now. He could swear he'd heard something up ahead. The trees seemed to be thinning toward some kind of clearing, where a little daylight intruded on the afternoon twilight of the jungle. Trying to step only on protruding rocks or roots, he focused all his senses on the clearing ahead, his finger tensed on the trigger of the .22.

*

Wilbur strained against the ropes, surreptitiously trying to reach the moneybelt under his loincloth where he carried his trusty Swiss Army knife. But all he accomplished was to pull the knots tighter and rub his bound wrists raw. The two clowns had done a good job of tying him to the chair. Across the little storeroom they sat playing cards on a stack of boxes, wearing their painted faces and outlandish costumes. A security man in a blue uniform stood guard outside in the corridor, opening the door at random intervals to check on him.

On the shelf next to Wilbur an open box was half-full of red rubber noses of every shape and size. *GREASEPAINT*, read the stenciled lettering on another box. *MISC. PROPS*, another one said.

"Hit me," said the clown wearing the bright red wig and enormous purple shoes, holding up three fingers. The clown wearing green dreadlocks and a pink tutu dealt him three fresh cards.

Wilbur wondered how Kumbu had fared in the uproar that had followed Dale's plunge into the safety net. He himself hadn't managed to get very far. As soon as he'd stepped through the exit, momentarily blinded by the brightness outside, two security men had materialized on either side and seized his elbows. They had marched him around the girth of the big tent to a door that led into a labyrinth of passages underneath the sawdust-covered floor. This storeroom had apparently been the handiest place to hold him.

Hold him for how long? He had asked the two surly clowns as they were tying him, but they'd kept their painted mouths shut. No sooner had they finished and dealt themselves their first hand of cards than the lights in the little room had blinked and gone out. In unison, the two of them had let out a string of altogether unprofessional curses. But their voices were all but washed away by an immense wave of applause that rumbled across the ceiling overhead. Wilbur had smiled, sensing that Kumbu was somehow responsible.

One of the clowns must have taken advantage of the dark to swap his cards for a new hand, or perhaps both of them, because when the lights finally flickered on again they'd begun arguing bitterly. The argument went on and on until at last they had sullenly agreed to start the game over.

The return of the lights had told Wilbur's Gift that Kumbu was free, if not yet out of danger. But he didn't dare attempt to use his Gift to reach Kumbu now, lest he lure the little fellow into a trap. Kumbu was free— but Wilbur's hands were still bound, and now the ropes were beginning to chafe badly.

"All right, hit me again," said the clown in the red wig and purple shoes. His partner obliged.

Out in the corridor Wilbur heard voices and footsteps approaching, and the door banged open. A large red-faced man wearing a Hawaiian shirt flanked by two shorter, paler men in business suits came crowding into the tiny space.

The clown in the red wig and purple shoes said, "Yes! Hit me again!"

The red-faced man swept the cards to the floor. "Outta here, clowns. Clear us some space, will you?"

"Hey, hey, hey!" moaned the clown who'd just been hit. "I was about to win that one, you—"

"Shhh!" said the clown in the dreadlocks and the tutu, gathering up the cards. "That's no way to talk to the boss, Arnie!"

But the boss was already leaning on the cleared stack of boxes, looking Wilbur in the eye with a venomous sneer.

The two men in suits looked nervous. "Mr. Pauling, please be careful," said one. "You're already—"

"I'll handle this," said Mr. Pauling, his eyes fixed on Wilbur.

"But don't you understand—" the other underling started to say.

Mr. Pauling ignored him. "Listen, Trimble, my attorneys have advised me that the law doesn't permit me to hold you against your will unless I'm performing a citizen's arrest. But I think you'll agree that it's a little too soon to involve the authorities. I'd rather settle this man to man. Why don't you save us both the trouble by handing over the chimpanzee known as Ralph, right now? I happen to have the papers to prove the animal is now my sole property."

The attorneys exchanged an uneasy look behind Pauling's back.

They tiptoed to the door and their footsteps fled down the corridor. Wilbur smiled, though his wrists were beginning to go numb. "I'm sorry, but I have no such animal in my possession. You have my permission to search me, if you like."

"I can produce a videotape of you claiming you've come to Miami specifically to 'rescue' the chimpanzee in question on half a dozen different newscasts. Not only that, I think I could easily round up a couple hundred witnesses to swear you were seen standing up in the audience and changing into your famous loincloth at exactly the time young Ralph was incited to commit an act of insubordination against all his careful training."

"It's possible that you claim ownership of a chimpanzee named Ralph," Wilbur answered. "But the chimpanzee I saw performing in your circus today is not Ralph. His name is Kumbu, and he belongs to no one but himself."

Pauling's nose wrinkled and his bushy eyebrows arched; he turned to his attorneys, but all he found was a pair of clowns. He turned back to Wilbur with an angry growl.

Just then a cry went up in the corridor outside. "Hey! It's that damn monkey! That way! He went that way!"

The storeroom door banged open again and Pauling went charging out, followed by the two clowns and the security man on guard in the corridor. No one bothered to close the door.

Wilbur sat tied to his chair, once more tugging at the knots, vainly trying to twist free. Had he spoken Kumbu's name too emphatically just now, and accidentally communicated to the chimp where he was being held? He closed his eyes and concentrated on sending Kumbu away in some other direction instead— worrying the whole time that the sheer intensity of his concentration was drawing Kumbu closer instead.

By and by he heard footsteps approaching in the corridor, accompanied by an odd squeaking sound. He watched the open door. The footsteps proved to belong to a petite young woman with dark eyes and dark hair, who looked down at the floor as she dragged a huge suitcase along on squeaky wheels. As if she suddenly felt him watching, she looked in through the storeroom door. Her mouth fell open and she froze in her tracks.

Wilbur smiled. "I would offer to help, miss, but unfortunately

I've been tied up by a couple of clowns."

She stared, frozen in place. Her face looked vaguely familiar, but Wilbur couldn't be sure; she wore a bandage taped to her cheekbone and her lower lip was swollen. A bruise was fading under one eye. Fresh tears stained her face and her eyes were bloodshot with immeasurable grief. After a moment she stepped through the door, maneuvering her suitcase after her, and softly shut the door.

"You're— you're Ralph's— friend, aren't you? I saw you on TV. I'm sorry, I forget your name."

Then he remembered. He'd seen her on one of the newscasts in Sandra's hotel room. He nodded his head, a bit awkwardly, since that was the only part of himself he could move.

"I'm pleased to meet you. They call me Tanzar. And aren't you Peg Tyler?"

She looked nervously back at the closed door. "Nice to meet you, too." She smiled a melancholy smile. "Really it is. I know it sounds strange, coming from me, but I appreciate what you're doing for Ralph. Or— what's his real name again? You said it on the news."

"Kumbu."

"Kumbu. Yes. Kumbu does deserve to be free, doesn't he?" Her dark eyes glistened. "I do love him a lot. And then I realized something. Lying awake last night, sometime in the wee hours, after I got up to use the bathroom and saw what he'd—" She hesitated, gave Wilbur a timid glance, then took a breath and went resolutely on. "What he'd written on my mirror."

Wilbur only nodded. He had no idea Kumbu knew how to write. But if Guma and Min could read, why not?

"I— I realized I've got to love little— Kumbu— just a little bit more, and let him go. No matter how much I coddled and pampered him as if he were my own child, rather than a critter I was training, he never really belonged to me. He can never really belong to anyone but himself."

"A courageous thought. I hope you were able to sleep after that."

She shook her head. "I still had a lot more to think about after that." She looked down at her suitcase, fidgeting. "You know, animal trainers get trained, too, when they're young and getting started. But some of the methods I was taught never seemed quite right. I don't know about other trainers, but I chose this career because ever since

I was a toddler I've been crazy about anything with fur. I would do anything to work with animals, and by now I guess I have. Chimps are smarter than a lot of critters, though, you don't have to—" she swallowed and looked away— "hit them so much. Or . . . use the electric prod." Wilbur saw a tear slide down her nose. "That's why I picked them as my specialty. And then I was lucky enough to find Ralph. Kumbu, I mean."

She gave him a wry smile, and something shone through the distraught dark eyes. "From the very beginning, tiny as he was, Kumbu was different from the other chimps I'd trained. Smarter, yes, but something more. He seemed to look into your eyes and speak to you. Not just understand you, *speak* to you. I don't think I ever had to discipline him once. He took to performing like human children take to playing games. And then last night I found out— I found out he was even more— *unusual* than I thought. It gave me quite a shock."

"I can see how hard it is for you to give him up."

"Oh, I'm giving up more than Ra— Kumbu. I'm quitting the circus. I'm leaving Dale. My career. My home. I'm done with all of it." Tears were flowing freely now.

"Where will you go?"

"Home to mother, of course. But if I were you, I'd be thinking about getting out of here myself."

"Ah, yes, that was my very next question. I've got a knife, but I'm afraid I carry it in a place you—"

"I've got one too," she interrupted, and from between the buttons of her blouse she drew a kitchen paring knife. She stepped behind Wilbur and the ropes dropped to the floor around his chair. Wilbur caught a strong odor composed equally of alcohol and perfume as she leaned close.

"Tell me, do you have any idea where Kumbu is now?" he asked.

She shook her head. "That's what everybody wants to know, isn't it? But Dale signed the paper. He doesn't belong to us any more. Not that he ever really did."

She stashed the knife again and picked up the handle of her suitcase. "If Dale comes along here, do me a favor and don't tell him you saw me." She opened the door a crack and peeked out, looked both ways and stepped into the corridor.

Wilbur grinned. "Don't worry! I have no intention of staying. But

I think I'd better find a hiding place and try my luck after dark. Do you have one to recommend?"

She glanced back the way she'd come. "They all went that way," she said. "Follow me."

Wilbur looked around. "Wait a minute." He grabbed a couple of red rubber noses and stuffed them into his moneybelt. Then he ripped open the box labeled *GREASEPAINT*.

*

Dar was worried about Min. Her spirit-mother's steps were flagging. The ground grew moist, flowering in little patches of color, sending up little signals of scent, and danger was closing in behind them as they trailed farther and farther behind, bringing up the rear of the clan's migration.

She shuddered. Human danger, according to Min.

Something else was hanging in the dank afternoon air, something almost as dangerous, but recently departed, already several hours gone: Cousin Leopard. Dar's Gift told her not to be concerned about it. But dear Min, the eldest grandmother of her clan and especially close to Dar these last few years . . . All she could do was hope it was not too much farther, this place she and Min had both seen in their dreams, and stay with Min in the rear, no matter how much her fear urged her forward.

It didn't help that her beloved elder insisted on teaching her, even now. A new herb, never seen in the clan's old territory, its healing virtues and other uses. Stories brought to mind by the journey, legends of similar journeys undertaken generations back. Insights drawn up from the deeper pools of instinct by Min's extraordinary Gift, powerful truths that kept Dar pondering for half the day as they traveled.

Every so often Dar and Min had company— an emissary from Guma and the rest of the clan, sent back to make sure the two slower females were still on track, still moving along. Usually a younger male like Mabu or Yago, bringing an edible treat or marking an especially sweet pool of water. But the young ones never lasted long in the rear. Impatient and swift, for all their protests of reverence and respect they eventually left the two slow ones behind and disappeared into the undergrowth ahead.

Dar was young, too. But she just didn't have it in her to leave behind her friend and teacher. Without Dar's special Gift, her tingling sense of danger, she had a strong feeling that Grandmother Min would be dead by now. And as surely as she knew that every creature sooner or later has to grow heavy with fatigue and move slower and slower until she or he lies still on the ground, never to move again, she also knew that the chimpanzee clan still needed Min's experience and wisdom to face the uncertainties ahead.

Min? she asked, turning to peer back through the long shadows of afternoon, wondering suddenly how many steps ahead of the older chimp she was. But Min was nowhere in sight. Her heart suddenly a-flutter, she hurried back along her own tracks.

Min!

Still no answer. Now the sense of danger pulsed stronger and the fur began to rise along her spine. Through the trees she saw an opening she had passed through not long before, alive with slanting rays of light, tingling with the nearness of death. Death, which had been following them through the forest all day. Stumbling into the open place on all fours, she saw Min's dark motionless body sitting on the ground, facing back the way they'd come. Min's head turned, and Dar saw the familiar brown eyes looking back at her, weary of walking, weary of life.

And then, across the clearing, she saw the man. Advancing out of the shadow of the oncoming twilight, holding his rifle ready: a black spear aimed directly at Min's heart. He had not seen Dar yet, she was sure— but she stood stockstill, rigid and helpless, unable to move or cry out a warning. Even her Gift was paralyzed.

But why hadn't Min's own Gift warned her?

Perhaps it had. Giving Dar a haggard smile, Grandmother Min turned back toward the man. Without even a start of surprise she faced him calmly across the clearing. The man raised the gun to his shoulder and took one more step, as if totally sure of his—

Suddenly, with a deafening noise of limbs springing loose, inseparable from the twin explosions of the man's gun and his shout of dismay, the entire center of the clearing burst up into the air, raining a litter of dirt and leaves and twigs. The man hung tightly bundled in a stout net woven of ropes, swinging helplessly back and forth, suspended by a single rope from the flexible top of a tree. His arms were pinned to his body and his gun pointed up through the branches at the sky. As the tree finally quivered to stillness and the dust and leaves swirling in the air began to settle, Dar slowly realized that the man could not move. Not a single muscle.

"Son of a bitch!" the man's voice choked out. "Goddamn bastard sons of bitches!"

Dar had seen a snare like this before. Usually it was used by humans to catch large animals. But sometimes, she had heard, they used it to catch other humans. And this time, whoever they were, they had caught the man who had been tracking the clan for days now, who had fired his gun at Dar and Min back at the river. Dar spun in a circle, giddy with amazement and wonder and doubt, casting her Gift as far as she could. But the tingle of danger that had been haunting her was gone.

Come, Grandmother! Get up! We can't sleep here. But soon we will sleep.

Min looked up at Dar and smiled, as if she had known what was about to happen all the time. Slowly, with Dar's arm supporting and steadying her, Min climbed to her feet. Without a glance up at the snared poacher she stumbled on.

By the time the twilight had deepened into darkness, the two friends had both woven their nests and snuggled in to sleep. For the first time in days, they slept well.

Chapter 11

All One Gift

*

Jane woke up. She was a tall woman, like her mother, and the cramped back seat of her Subaru didn't allow anything approximating sleep. But this was the closest she'd come so far tonight, so finding herself suddenly wide awake was not a welcome development. Then she remembered Ralph, and sat up straight.

Duty calls.

She peered out through the Subaru's windshield over a wide expanse of moonlit parking lot and a trampled grassy field, both littered with broken shafts of wood and trampled protest signs. Everyone else had long since gone home. But Jane was a stubborn woman, like her mother, and she had started all of this. No matter what Mitchell Pauling claimed, it wasn't over yet.

The multitudes who had thronged the Boulevard Santa Fe had slowly evaporated after the celebrated trapeze partnership of Dale & Ralph came to its climactic end, though the long-awaited "special hometown show" had struggled on to its scheduled conclusion. Most of the circus spectators had stayed to the end, sheltered as they were inside the air-conditioned Big Top. But the three factions of demonstrators outside had begun fading early due to the heat of mid-afternoon and the lack of further action out on the boulevard.

Finally even the press had receded from the scene, after a heated final exchange of accusations between the Free Ralph! campaign and the circus management— both still claiming victory in the absence of *habeas corpus* evidence to the contrary.

The police, Jane noted, had not yet followed through on the threatened parking ticket— one small victory for the Free Ralph! campaign. But as she had emphasized repeatedly to the press, ticket or no ticket, she wasn't going home until she found out what had happened to little Ralph after he abandoned his trapeze act and attempted to escape the circus tent.

Of course nothing of the kind had occurred, according to Pauling. A certain Wilbur Trimble, widely associated with the Free Ralph! campaign, had disrupted the act in some unspecified way, causing Ralph's partner Dale to fall from the heights and Ralph himself to subsequently forget his years of training and act "confused."

No matter how many times Jane had emphatically denied that Wilbur Trimble was a representative of her campaign, the press could not seem to grasp that the man in the leopardskin loincloth and the pith helmet had acted entirely on his own— if in fact he had played any part in disrupting the trapeze performance at all. Pauling had been conspicuously unable to produce a single circus patron willing to say so. According to the dozen or so witnesses she had talked to, Trimble had simply left his seat, removed his clothes, and walked out in his loincloth.

Her one satisfaction in the chaotic round of media interviews that had followed the interrupted show was that she could challenge the circus to produce Ralph in person, show him to the press, prove that he still remained in its custody. The circus could not counter with a demand that she produce the mysterious Mr. Trimble, since she had repeatedly disavowed any connection with the so-called "Wild Man of Indiana." So it was not quite a draw.

But where was Trimble now? Unseen and unaccounted for, just like Ralph. The Wild Man's convenient disappearance lent weight to Jane's suspicion that he might have been a covert provocateur all along, planted by the circus to discredit her campaign. But something bothered her about that idea. Perhaps the reporter Sandra Reid's clear-eyed testimonial on his behalf. Miss Reid certainly appeared to be a real, rock-solid newspaper reporter. And Jane had to admit that Trimble's press conference on CNN the other night would have been difficult to fabricate.

The half moon was bright, but it was slowly setting in the western sky at last. In its surreal glare, through the Subaru's rear window, she could see men in uniform patrolling the circus grounds. If Ralph was still hiding out over there, he would stand a better chance of sneaking across to friendlier territory when the moon went down.

But given what Jane knew about chimp psychology, poor Ralph wouldn't have a clue where to go once he left the circus grounds. She was going to have to intercept him with the eight bunches of bananas stashed in her trunk. And that wouldn't necessarily be so difficult. After the long hot day, the bananas were making their presence known to anyone with a nose.

She shifted to her other side and curled up again on the cramped back seat.

*

Spring had just arrived in Florida, and already it was too hot to sleep. Kyle had spent most of the night walking.

The circus was over and the crowd outside almost gone when Rodolfo had extricated the long Rolls Royce from the narrow space between Ma's Subaru and the innocently bystanding palm tree, and ferried Gram home to Homestead with her righteous entourage—minus Kyle. He had promised Gram he would show up soon to pick up his trunk, and she had agreed, grudgingly, not to have it deposited on the curb for the garbagemen until "soon" had expired.

But having publicly announced that he'd had enough of Gram's condo and its Armageddon-themed hospitality, Kyle had found his plans suddenly foiled when his mother decided not to give up her strategic parking spot until Ralph the chimpanzee appeared in person, whether free or not.

At that point Sandra Reid, dedicated reporter that she was, had decided the chances of further developments out on the boulevard that night were too good to pass up. She had graciously offered Kyle the front seat of her rented Buick, which was parked in front of a shopping center down the street. But of course, Sandra herself would be occupying the back seat. Kyle couldn't think of a more excruciating form of torture than trying to lie down and sleep that close to Sandra Reid.

Not quite so graciously, his mother had matched Sandra's offer. But the Subaru was even smaller than Sandra's Buick, and the thought of sharing it with his mother brought back too many unpleasant memories. Besides, something in Ma's car stank of overripe bananas. Kyle had found himself wandering homeless between the two opposite but equally uninviting offers until long after midnight.

Homeless on the streets of Florida. Michael Ozawek's casual prediction had come true.

In his wanderings, he'd had ample time to do some wondering. Like whether he could ever break free of the Kyle Wilson he had been all his life to become the Kyle Wilson who could look Sandra in those deadly green eyes without flinching. Before tonight he'd never suspected such a person could exist. But now he knew for certain. Somewhere deep inside of him that other Kyle was lurking, waiting for a chance to elbow him aside and take over, like— like—

He blinked. Like Tanzar had lurked inside of Wilbur?

Leaning on the Subaru's front fender as the moon set behind the looming silhouette of the circus tent, Kyle eyed the security men patrolling the dark circus grounds across the street and they eyed him back.

Suddenly he lurched upright with an airless little gasp, blinking up into the empty vacuum beyond the moon. Every time he took a drink, he shoved that other Kyle deeper into the darkness inside. Was that the reason he kept drinking?

As he turned to walk the boulevard's palm-studded median toward Sandra's Buick once again, from the corner of his eye he saw something move: a low, crouching black shape that scuttled across the boulevard from the circus into the skinny shadow of a palm tree. Before he could blink and look again, something else caught his eye from the other direction: a tall, lanky black shape sprinting across the boulevard and diving behind another palm tree. Glancing back and forth, up and down the median, he saw first one silhouette, then the other darting toward him from palm to palm.

With any luck, the two shadowy shapes were friendly ones. Sandra had told him about the repeated death threats against his Ma. But since the threats had gone unfulfilled so far, it seemed unlikely that the circus was sending out assassins now that the campaign was over. At least that's what Kyle kept hoping. After the relative peace of the jungle, these urban perils unnerved him.

Whatever they were, in another minute the two silhouettes were going to converge where Kyle was standing beside his mother's car. Taking a deliberate breath to calm his rising alarm, he peered inside the Subaru, but Ma lay awkwardly doubled up on the back seat, asleep. He was still trying to decide whether to run or hide when a voice hissed out of the shadow of the nearest palm.

"Kyle Wilson! Thank goodness it's you."

To Kyle's relief, it was Wilbur. A moment later the second shadowy figure arrived— scampering down the tree and then leaping with startling precision onto Wilbur's shoulder. Wilbur swayed under its weight, but betrayed not a hint of surprise. His voice was as smoothly courteous and calm as ever.

"Kyle, I don't believe you've met young Kumbu."

Kyle stared. Then stuttered, "No, I— I guess I—"

He stopped. Young Kumbu was looking him intently in the eye and offering a slim, hairy paw. If Wilbur was right— if Wilbur wasn't hopelessly, irretrievably insane— the door between the species was opening at long last, and Kyle stood there in the spotlight of an all-but-vanished half moon, under inspection.

Still he hesitated. Something was extremely odd about this particular chimpanzee. Something about its bulbous red nose, the white smudge of its face. Wilbur seemed to be wearing a similar nose, and was smeared with white down to the waist. Kyle stared, tongue-tied and tingling, suspended between embarrassment and awe.

Finally recovering his merely human power of speech, he grasped Kumbu's dry leathery palm in his sweaty one. "Good to meet you, Mr. Kumbu, sir. I've . . . heard a lot about you."

Kumbu felt strange, very strange indeed. Across the boulevard he could see his whole world, his only life, disappearing with the last of the moonlight. At least the only life he'd known since he was a very small chimpanzee. It wasn't the biggest circus in the world, he knew, but until he'd made up his mind a few hours ago to run away— looking down from the platform as his first real audience applauded his first actual performance— it *was* the world in Kumbu's eyes.

Everything had changed in those few hours.

Hearing his true name called inside his head from somewhere

outside of him was what had made the difference. He still didn't know for sure where the disembodied, soundless voice had come from. But there was no denying who it was calling. Just hearing his name was enough to make him infinitely homesick.

When he had reached the maze of dressing rooms and offices and storerooms underneath the Big Top, he'd found the lights were out down there as well. That helped: Kumbu knew his way through the maze like he knew the way from his crib to the breakfast table in the little trailer he had left behind forever. Still trembling with amazement at his Daddy's furious fall and his own daring escape, his heart pounding in his chest, he'd crept into a random office and crawled under a desk to hide.

But not long after the lights blinked back on, two men had burst in, talking in panicky voices, each one trying to blame the other for something. Kumbu heard strange banging and grinding noises. When he peeked out, overcome by curiosity, he recognized Mr. Bragg and Mr. Wascoll, the lawyers. They were wearing their suits like they always did, no matter how hot it was outside. But their bored, serious expressions had vanished. They looked grim and scared as they searched through the drawers of a filing cabinet and stuffed papers into a machine. Shreds of paper foamed out of the other side of the machine, piling up in a frothy white mound on the floor.

They hadn't looked under the desk yet, and maybe they wouldn't. But their excited jabbering made Kumbu nervous, so he took a deep breath and dashed for the door. That was a mistake: right away someone spotted him and called out an alarm. In his haste he darted around the very next corner and found himself trapped in a dead-end passage. Then he realized the blank wall in front of him was the outer wall of the tent. Squeezing between the heavy canvas and the sandy dirt, Kumbu was free.

Once he had escaped the big tent, hiding was easy. He'd always wanted to climb a palm tree anyway. He just scrambled up the nearest one and sprang across to the roof of the tent. Peering over the edge, he'd watched little knots of men in blue uniforms hurrying here and there, poking their heads into all the sideshows and concessions, the ticket booths and carnival rides, even the restrooms.

Once or twice he'd thought he heard the strange voice in his head, coming from somewhere far below, but he was too frightened to leave his lofty hideout and go looking.

Beyond the tent's pointed peak, on both sides of the street and its narrow island of palms, he could see a huge crowd of people holding signs— many more than he'd ever seen out there before. But as the sun sank lower they began to break up and drift away, and Kumbu started to feel lonely. He missed his Mommy. He even missed his Daddy, a little. Had he done the right thing? Had the voice in his head been real after all, or had he only imagined it?

Then, late in the afternoon, the voice had spoken again.

Kumbu! This is your Uncle Tanzar. Wait until the moon sets. When it's good and dark, go halfway across the street and climb a palm tree. I'll find you there.

But Kumbu couldn't wait that long. After a while he heard the circus band play the jaunty tune that announced the end of the show. The crowd of spectators filed out onto the boardwalk and the cars pulled out of the parking lot one by one, leaving Kumbu feeling more and more lonesome. So soon after nightfall, he had sneaked back down the palm tree and started tracking the voice that called itself Uncle Tanzar.

The voice wasn't saying anything now. But without hesitating once, creeping from shadow to shadow, he'd followed it straight to the animal training barn, where he had learned his first simple games with Mommy long ago— then to the little room where the sacks of feed were stored. As he'd suspected, the voice belonged to the man in the loincloth and helmet, who lay sprawled across a pallet of feed sacks, sound asleep. While he waited for the man to wake up, he settled in and helped himself to a meal.

Slowly, as his eyes adjusted to the dimness, the man's thin sleeping face grew more and more familiar. Where had he seen Uncle Tanzar before? Then he remembered. It was in his dream yesterday morning. This was the man in khakis who had straddled a limb in the tree full of chimpanzees and listened without speaking even once— exactly the opposite of all the humans Kumbu had ever met. Curling up next to Uncle Tanzar, he immediately felt right at home.

Through the storeroom door he could hear the faint sounds of animals out in the barn: the horses snorting and shuffling, the pair of camels chewing steadily, an elephant clanking its chain. The family of llamas and the one lonely ostrich made no sound that he could hear, but he remembered how their solemn interested faces had watched him whenever he crossed the hay-strewn floor with his Mommy or Daddy, passing through the barn to someplace else.

The lions and tigers lived in cages in a separate room. The one time he had peeked in, they had looked at him through the bars with an interest keener than curiosity. Especially the lions: as if they recognized him from somewhere. It made all his fur stand up on end, as if he recognized them in turn. None of the big cats had so much as moved, lying there with a kind of lazy majesty on the hay. But Kumbu had backed hastily out of the doorway, bars or no bars. Suddenly he'd understood why the lions and tigers had their own room.

When the man stretched out beside him finally stirred and yawned, Kumbu sensed no surprise, no annoyance, no confusion.

Ah, you're here, Uncle Tanzar had said without a sound. *Let's give the moon another hour or so, and then we'll make our move.*

Kumbu had wondered distractedly how they would know the moon had gone down— and to his astonishment, without a sound Uncle Tanzar had answered.

I'll know, he said. *You'll know, too, if you close your eyes and pay attention.* He drew a little circle with one fingertip in the center of Kumbu's chest. *In here.*

As they snuggled together, Uncle Tanzar had told him stories of his family, far away in a place called Africa: his mother, Grandmother Min, his father, Guma, his Uncle Noko and the rest of the clan.

Until the time came to make their move. Though Uncle Tanzar was the first to stretch and stand up, what he had said was true: they both knew at the same moment. Kumbu held still while he whitened their faces, then his own sunburned torso, and fastened on two red noses. Then they'd crept out of their hiding place and split up to take opposite routes through the shadowy circus grounds out to the street.

Now, crouching on Uncle Tanzar's shoulder gazing across at the circus that had once been his home, Kumbu felt all those stories still seeping in, deeper and deeper. He didn't miss his human Mommy and Daddy so much any more, though his longago infant love came flooding back whenever he thought of them. But he could feel his connection to his relatives across the sea in Africa growing stronger and stronger, as it always did in the early morning when he had dreamed of the forest.

Suddenly he remembered the noises he'd heard from the animal barn while he hid in the dim storeroom. For the first time in his life, he found himself wondering why he'd always felt so distant from the other circus performers with fur. Wasn't he an animal too, as his Mommy and Daddy couldn't help reminding him? Hadn't he too been a captive until he made up his mind to escape? Wasn't his crib a kind of cage, even the stripes of sun and shadow on his bedroom wall a lot like bars?

Now he had the strange sensation that he could feel the other circus animals in the dark barn across the street, close by and aware of him as well, comforting and encouraging him on the day of his liberation.

"Ma?" He heard the young man named Kyle saying quietly. "Wake up, Ma. Kumbu is here to see you."

The electric jolt of hearing his true name spoken, even quietly, brought a fresh burst of memories every time. The taste of figs and termites and mushrooms and pure honeycomb. The smell of jungle flowers and the wet rush of jungle rain. No matter how many times the humans around him had called him "Ralph," those dreams of life in the forest had never let him forget who he really was.

"Ma, remember Ralph? His real name is Kumbu, and he wants to meet you. But first we've got to borrow your keys, so we can get out of here. There's still some security guys across the street who could spoil everything— Ma, wake up!"

"Kumbu?" came a groggy voice from the little car. "You mean . . . he's here?"

"Yes, Professor," said Wilbur. "But we need the key to your ignition. Quickly, before we attract any attention from across the way."

Kumbu climbed into the back seat as a dim shape groaned and sluggishly sat up. A woman blinked down at him, swaying sleepily. Even in the dark Kumbu recognized the silver streaks glistening in her rumpled hair. Grinning shyly up at her, all of a sudden he felt important. He was only seven, after all, still young even for a chimpanzee. But for the first time, thanks to Uncle Tanzar, he was meeting humans as their equal. And as a representative of his species, he felt obliged to meet them with a certain amount of dignity— which wasn't exactly easy when the lady he was meeting had not fully awakened. In either sense of the word. He grasped her smooth, naked hand.

"Ralph?" she murmured, still half asleep.

Ouch. Luckily, Uncle Tanzar was climbing in behind him.

"No, Professor. 'Ralph' was only a stage name, given to young Kumbu by his human captors. Yesterday afternoon— oh, I wish you could have been there to see it! Kumbu folded that name up along with his ridiculous little trained-animal outfit and claimed his true name, forever!"

"Ma," said Kyle from the front seat. "We need your keys, *now!*"

Across the street, two shadowy security men stood together under the circus's huge floodlit logo, staring across at the car. One of them was speaking into a radio. Kumbu heard the sound of running feet. The professor finally reached down and found her purse in the dark, groped inside for a set of keys and handed it forward. Kyle immediately dropped them on the floor.

"Whoa, here they come!" Uncle Tanzar called out.

Six or more uniformed men had congregated under the circus billboard, and now they came charging over the curb.

Suddenly a car came roaring up the boulevard from the direction of the freeway, headlights blazing, zigzagging and blowing its horn. The gang of security men scrambled hastily backward onto the curb.

Kyle and Uncle Tanzar slammed their doors together, and Kyle found the right key at last. Lurching into gear, the Subaru rolled off the median onto the street and they were moving— just in the nick of time. One of the pursuing security men reached out and slapped the trunk in frustration as they accelerated and took off.

"Who— what was that other car doing?" the professor gasped, wide awake now.

Heading down the boulevard as fast as the car could go, Kyle grinned into the rear-view mirror and cackled gleefully.

"You mean that little blue Buick? That was the independent press in action. Our good friend Sandra to the rescue!"

Kumbu could see the red taillights of the other car a few blocks ahead, speeding away. But little by little Kyle was gaining on them. And in a peculiar whispery voice that no one else seemed to hear, Kumbu heard him pleading:

Red! Red! Hey, all you traffic lights up ahead! Don't let me lose her now! Please, please, please turn red!

*

Wilbur awakened before dawn from a dream, remembering a vivid sunset painted across an unfamiliar range of jungle-green mountains— and a band of very familiar-looking chimpanzees relaxing in the branches of a new and even more magnificent Granddaddy Tree.

But where had he awakened? Neon flickered through drawn blinds and a truck rumbled noisily past outside. Someone was snoring beside him. Without his glasses he could not be sure, but it appeared to be Kyle. In the next bed, he recognized Sandra's red curls. And then he recalled the whole surreal, dreamlike day of Kumbu's aborted debut. The midnight getaway in Dr. van Pelt's little car. The stop at her apartment complex and the switch to Sandra's car. He'd been nearly asleep when they'd pulled into a rundown motel at the edge of town.

In comparison, the dream he'd just awakened from had seemed suspiciously real. He was not surprised when he closed his eyes again and found himself clinging to a forked limb at a dizzy height above the jungle. Sunset again.

Destroying oneself is one thing, Brother Tanzar, Guma was saying gravely. *But a highly evolved species, such as you humans claim to be, simply does not risk wiping out another species, accidentally or otherwise. And we know of many that no longer walk, fly, swim, or crawl among us due to human unintelligence.*

Wilbur was getting used to responding when the chimps called him "Tanzar," but he still thought of himself as plain old Wilbur. No matter how much he learned in these sunset sessions, he was still painfully aware how much "human unintelligence" he carried around in his head. Among his elders in the Granddaddy Tree, even the youngest, he still felt like an infant.

And when any one species is gone, Uncle Noko said, *the whole community of life around it is thrown out of balance. The creatures that species hunted for its livelihood continue to have young. Soon there are too many, and they begin to starve. Meanwhile, the creatures that hunted the missing species for their own livelihood also begin to starve, and their numbers decrease as well. And of course each declining population sends out ripples that affect other species in turn.*

Noko's gruff voice made the naked facts sound hard and bitter. But Guma's eyes were moist as he gazed out at the sunset.

With any luck, some other creature might eventually move in to fill the gap, he said. *But the whole intricate pattern of species that evolved together in that place has irrevocably shifted— which affects the balance of surrounding places, which slowly but inevitably affects the Whole. Surely by now your scientists understand how interconnected all of the world's living communities are?*

They were all looking at Wilbur. He nodded dumbly, swallowing.

Of course they do, said Grandmother Min. *Yet most humans seem blissfully unaware that they're part of any community at all— even their own. Each of them goes on living as if they exist all alone in the world. With all due respect to you, Brother Tanzar, can such a species hope to survive?*

I . . . I hope so . . . Wilbur blinked back the salty sting of tears.

Oh, I have no doubt that individual humans are capable of evolving, learning from their mistakes and correcting their behavior, said Uncle Noko. *The question is whether the humans as a species can evolve in time.*

I think they can, said Guma. *It's not just Brother Tanzar's extraordinary Gift that gives me hope. It's his real willingness to listen and change his outlook. I believe he must be one of these so-called "mutations" that catalyze an evolutionary leap.*

Pffft! Uncle Noko snorted. *Even among the chimpanzees, evolution is a slow, haphazard process, generation by generation. Why, in some clans the males still take the females by force! I'll accept that Tanzar's Gift is a mutation. But by himself he means nothing. Even if he survives long enough to reproduce— and at his age, he'd better do it soon— that's only one generation. He would have to find a faster way than that to influence the course of evolution. If I were you, Tanzar, I'd hurry back here to the jungle with little Kumbu as quick as you can. You're much safer with us. The human species is hopeless.*

Now, Noko, Guma answered evenly. *Surely Life has not sent Tanzar just to help us recover one lost young one. Tanzar has a mission here among us as well. I believe he's been sent to show us that evolution is alive and well, even among the humans, and Life has a plan. Life always has a plan.*

Yago had been scratching his back against the Granddaddy's trunk. Now he spoke up. *But the humans have always rebelled against Life's plan, haven't they?*

It's true, said Brapa. *I can think of many tales where humans played a part, and they always played the rebels.*

Oh, I don't think they mean to be rebellious, Min said. *They just don't seem to realize that every tiny little thing they do affects the rest of us, in so many tiny little ways— even something as small as throwing down an empty bottle because it happens to be a convenient way of getting rid of something you no longer need. Yet that springs from precisely the same attitude as spilling poison into a river because it's the most convenient way of getting rid of something you no longer need.*

It's odd, said Brapa, musing. *Because they see themselves as individuals rather than members of a community, they imagine themselves— each one individually— as all-important. Yet at the same time, for exactly the same reason, they seem to consider themselves— each one individually— as insignificant. So insignificant that their tiny little actions have no real impact.*

How very convenient! said Uncle Noko with a stern look at Wilbur. *While all the time their tiny little actions are adding up to a vast destructive force that is ravaging the entire world!*

Suddenly recognizing himself, Wilbur blinked and opened his mouth to reply. His friends waited politely. Then a tiny buzzing insect flew by, and he realized he'd better close his mouth until he thought of something to say.

For another minute Guma let the silence speak. Then he quietly interrupted it, so quietly that his voice seemed like merely the next thought to pass through Wilbur's head.

The world won't be destroyed, of course; don't worry about that. It's the human species that is at risk, along with any other species that can't or won't adapt to the ways the world itself will have to adapt. But if other humans can change, as you have— change their thinking and their habits, even a little bit— then in changing they can become a catalyst for others to change. It's how we all got here, after all.

Evolution! Wilbur exclaimed.

Evolution, came a reverent chorus from all around him.

Dr. Jane van Pelt, BA, MS, PhD, sat on her side of the bed in the Motel 777, staring at the carpet. This was not the triumphant conclusion to the Free Ralph! campaign she had envisioned. Far from it, indeed. On Sandra's expense account, they couldn't even afford separate rooms for the girls and the boys.

She didn't dare use her credit card after watching this morning's news report. Not only was Wilbur Trimble wanted for questioning in the wake of Ralph's disappearance, but so was the mastermind of the campaign herself. That nasty Mitchell Pauling must have some equally nasty connections in high places.

On the other hand, in spite of everything they had somehow managed to spirit away little Ralph— or rather, Kumbu. Just the sight of his innocent little face and wide, lopsided grin gave her courage for the infinitely greater challenges to come.

Luckily, she'd been able to reach Jim Rochdale during their brief stop at her apartment late last night, using Sandra's cell phone, and he had agreed to get out of bed and come right over to fetch Coo and Caw. It was too risky to wait for him there, but he knew where she hid her key.

"So what do we do now?" asked Kyle helpfully. "We rescued Kumbu with just enough cover of darkness left to grab Ma's toothbrush and pajamas from her apartment, and now all of a sudden we're fugitives."

Sandra stood by the window, keeping watch. The morning outside was overcast, like the mood in the room. Wilbur sat on the other bed, working on a crossword puzzle with Kumbu, a heap of banana peels on the crumpled bedspread between them. Oddly enough, it was the little chimp who wielded the pen, gripping it clumsily in his fist. But after two weeks of feverish activity and a second sleep-deprived night, Jane was too exhausted to be surprised.

"Only one of us has any money," Kyle went on. "Or rather, an expense account from an editor back in Indiana. At least as long as he thinks he's getting a decent story out of the deal."

Typical primate male, Jane sighed to herself. Still hoping to attract Sandra's attention with his keen analysis of their plight.

"Too bad it's not the kind of story he's expecting," said Sandra.

"You left out the car," Jane pointed out.

"Oh yeah— a rented Buick, which keeps us anonymous enough, and takes us where we need to go. But where the hell is that?"

"What's a seven-letter word that's the last name of a movie star?" asked Wilbur. "Starts with a J."

Kyle frowned over his shoulder at the interruption. "Dammit. Where was I?"

"You were wondering where we go from here," said Sandra. "Like all the rest of us."

"Blake Jameson!" said Wilbur. "Kumbu, you're not supposed to know anything about movie stars. But you're right, it fits!"

"You forget, Kumbu grew up watching over his human parents' shoulders," said Sandra. "He's old enough to remember Blake Jameson."

"Blake Jameson?" Kyle snorted. "He's getting a little grey these days. Why does he think he can still get away with playing the romantic lead?"

"Because he can," said Sandra. "You wouldn't understand."

"It's his integrity offscreen that I like," said Jane.

"Right," said Kyle. "Because he's big on the environment, you mean."

"There's no reason a man can't be a talented actor and at the same time care about the ongoing destruction of the planet," retorted Jane, annoyed. "In fact, Blake Jameson makes me wonder about the intelligence of some of the other golden glamor boys out in Hollywood."

"It doesn't hurt that he's rich, either," said Sandra.

"Which is precisely why Kumbu says he brought it up," said Wilbur. "After this crossword gave him the idea, I mean."

The four humans looked at each other. Kumbu bent over the crossword puzzle, painstakingly practicing his crude penmanship, the pink tip of his tongue showing at one corner of his mouth.

"Of course, he doesn't live in Hollywood any more," said Kyle. "Remember? He's got that resort in the Smokies."

"That's a lot closer, isn't it . . ." Wilbur mused.

Three pairs of eyes looked at Sandra. She stared out the window for a moment, stroking her freckled chin.

"I'd have to convince Sam it was part of the story," she said.

"Which it is," said Jane. "Except that the expense account he's offering you to cover it is the only source of funds for the fugitives to continue getting away with their crime."

Wilbur chuckled.

Kumbu snickered, almost in reply.

Kyle gave a loud guffaw, then flopped back on the bed next to Wilbur, sputtering.

Sandra giggled once, twice— then ignited the entire room with a howl.

Jane couldn't help joining in, gasping for breath between high-pitched shrieks of laughter.

They all stopped short when a sharp knock came at the door.

"You-all okay in there?"

"Yes!" Jane managed to stammer out, trying to hold back another burst of hilarity. "Yes, we'll be— we'll be fine, thanks!"

*

Solomon Purgis grimaced, swaying gently in the breeze, waiting. For the cramps to go away. For death to arrive. For whichever came first.

It hadn't been so bad for most of the night. The pain had alternated back and forth from one leg to the other as he swung helplessly beneath the young tree that held him aloft. But now both legs were cramping at once and it was agony. He shifted, relieving one leg temporarily, but shooting pains through the other that went far beyond the cramps. He shifted back.

His arms had a little space to move, so they were not cramping so severely. But they too were causing him steady discomfort. The leather bandolier cut into the side of his neck, and the tops of his boots dug into the flesh above his ankles. He could feel the netting of the snare imprinting its pattern into his skin wherever skin was exposed, and a few other places besides.

His only consolation was that the net he was caught in was definitely a snare, set here in this clearing by someone who might possibly remember setting it, and with any luck would return at some point to check it. And as soon as that unmentionable person showed up and cut Purgis free, the bullets that had been previously reserved for a pair of prize chimpanzees were going to be diverted to an even more deserving trophy.

He only hoped the snare-setter would come back before he passed out. His only timepiece was totally inaccessible, but by his subjective reckoning it had been roughly ten hours since the snare had sprung. The jungle dawn had slowly seeped into the clearing maybe an hour ago. Between the pain and the exhaustion and his constricted circulation, he didn't know how much longer he was going to last. As it was, he was running low on anger, close to empty on rage, and had only pure hatred to sustain him now.

Worst of all, he couldn't reach a single one of his weapons except his rifle, which pointed up uselessly into the sky.

"—don't know him," a voice was saying when he awoke. "You?"

"Go ahead and cut him down. I think I just might."

"Better watch him, though. All those weapons he's wearing, he must know how to use at least one or two."

He'd been out for a while then, Purgis realized; whether hours or only minutes he couldn't say. But it was still daylight, and three voices were now conversing underneath him as he swayed. None he recognized, just yet. But just give him a look at their faces. Just give him one look.

Slowly, the rope that held the net lowered it to the ground. Purgis toppled over and lay there with every muscle yelling bloody murder. Biting down hard on a section of netting, he managed to hold himself to a single unavoidable whimper. While he lay paralyzed, unable to unbend from the cramped position the netting had pinned him in, swift hands patted him down and emptied his pockets, pouches, compartments, holster and scabbards.

"Hey, look at that! I'll trade you my—"

"Forget it. You guys work for me, remember?"

Purgis's eyes rolled back under his eyelids, but he was doing his best to listen. Two were Africans, from the French colonies. One was definitely European. But not French. Not English. Not Portuguese. Afrikaans, maybe.

"Look at the belly on him. I don't know how much I can get for him on the plantations."

"White, though. Might have some useful education."

"They pay more at the mines. But it's a longer trek."

"And he do look dangerous, even without his weapons."

"They have ways of making them loyal down there, and keeping them that way."

"You know, this guy is starting to look a little familiar. Give him a shave, dress him up in uniform . . ."

With a start, Purgis recognized the voice.

"Waldo, you asshole," he groaned. "Do you know how long I've been hanging up there, waiting for you to show?"

Silence. Then the Afrikaans accent spoke, slow and reluctant.

"No! I can't believe it. Solomon Purgis, after all these years? Of all places, here? What happened to the fancy command with the mercenary brigade? Where's all your polished brass, your ribbons and decorations?"

"Von Rumbel, you goddamned bastard, you owe me! Remember?"

"No. The real Solomon Purgis would never miss the warning signs of such an obvious snare! One intended only to fool animals!"

"You've trapped plenty of two-legged animals, and you know it. Help me up off the ground, slug. Some brandy would do me a world of good. You owe me, and don't you dare forget it!"

"Help him up, boys. But first . . ."

Cold metal clamped around his wrists, his ankles; four strong latches snapped shut. The stout chain connecting them clanked softly. Manacled hand and foot! Something cold and metallic snapped around his heart as he realized how helpless he was. How little his old friend Waldo von Rumbel really owed him out here in the jungle. How little it would take to simply pull a trigger and leave him here for the buzzards and jackals. By now he had traveled far outside the bounds of Babarzark Game Park. Maybe even beyond the borders of Wanzanayi itself.

The two black boys heaved him upright and propped him against a tree: the very tree they had bent over to snare him. Breathing more easily now, he leaned there at the edge of the little clearing where he'd finally had his quarry in his sights, and lost it.

Von Rumbel puffed at a thin cigar, then let blue smoke trickle between his yellowing teeth as a wide grin spread across the narrow stubbled face. But Purgis saw no humor in the hard blue eyes. Nothing even remotely human. He wondered if his own eyes had ever looked that way.

"So! Solomon Purgis, the great mercenary, jungle tracker, trophy hunter, bounty killer— what have you been doing with yourself in these lean times, old friend?"

"If I was a friend you wouldn't feel the need for these, would you?" Purgis lifted his manacled wrists and rattled them in the air. "After your snare nearly did me in— who knows, maybe permanent damage to my circulation— I'd expect something a little more like hospitality. Come on, man. Cough up that key."

Von Rumbel dragged a pack over, sat down and drew a slim silver flask from his shirt pocket.

"Well, I don't know. Last time I saw you it was not exactly hospitality. It was more like hospitalization. I mean, sure, you got me started in the business. But I don't think I owe you anything after that last deal."

"Come on, kid. I explained it to you the very first time we part-
nered up. It's competition, pure and simple. Someone's got to lose on
every deal."

Von Rumbel grinned again. "Precisely my point! Pure and simple!
I knew you would understand. And you know, times are getting
tough. My bills are killing me! You know I got a kid at university,
down in Capetown? And the coppers these days are getting way too
smart. If they were to get a little more honest, business would absolutely crash."

"Tell me about it! I've been playing tour guide to the great white
hunters, just to make ends meet." Bringing up the last time they'd
met had been a mistake. If he could only lead Waldo away from the
memory . . .

"I really think I have no choice but to see how much you'll bring
on the brave, free market. I'm leaning toward the mines, even though
they're so much farther away. My boat is only a day's travel from
here. You know how it is, am I right, old friend?"

Purgis swallowed hard. "Waldo. I know I owe you an apology for
that last deal . . ."

"And for the deal before that?"

"Well—"

"No, Purgis. This time I think I've caught you fair and square.
You're going down the river, quite literally. And because I know how
dangerous you are, armed or not, you're going in manacles. It's a
time-honored tradition out here in the bush, as you know. Boys!"

From the corner of his eye, Purgis saw what Waldo's men were up
to. It was a pre-fab folding stretcher, lightweight, army issue— Aus-
trian or Hungarian, he was guessing— with a set of retractable wheels.
So at least they weren't going to make him walk. At least at first.
Once he was in shape to travel on his own two feet, maybe he would
get his chance. At worst, they were going to have to shoot him in his
manacles as he ran. Better than being sold to work off his remaining
years in a diamond mine.

"All right, Waldo, you miserable, dirt-eating asshole. But at least
grant me one small favor, for old times' sake. We did have some high
old times, you know. One drink of brandy. I know you never travel
without it."

Von Rumbel grinned, a yellow-toothed gash in his unshaven face, and held out the flask. A family heirloom, if Purgis remembered right. He took it gratefully and downed a couple of long swallows.

When he handed it back, he realized with a start that his face was wet. Damn. How humiliating. He was crying.

*

Orlando already, and it was Wilbur's turn to drive. The white dashes dividing the highway lanes ticked past on the blacktop and the rising moon hung low in his rear-view mirror.

As a reluctant concession to necessity, he was once more disguised in a shirt and long pants, courtesy of a thrift store down the street from the Motel 777. But underneath he could feel the comfortable crinkle of leopardskin. Kumbu lay curled against his side, fast asleep, and next to Kumbu sat the professor, staring out past the lights of Orlando into the dark. Kyle snored softly in the back seat; Sandra was busy on her laptop.

Wilbur was still a little dazed by the discovery that Jane and Kyle were mother and son, even though both seemed to regard the relationship as long since annulled. Yet here they were, riding together through the night. Kumbu, that sly little rascal, had done it again.

Driving itself was another concession Wilbur keenly regretted, given what Uncle Noko had told him about the cost of burning gasoline to the delicate balance of the world. But again, the others had convinced him it was the only way forward.

He was a little rusty at it, since in Cedartown his faithful old bicycle had been all he needed, and he never did acquire a car. But he recalled his mother's patience— not to mention bravery— as she'd sat beside him in the old Dodge Polaris, teaching him how to drive. And as that buried memory had surfaced his hands and feet immediately remembered what to do, almost as easily as they'd remembered how to climb a tree.

He'd never seen this country they would be passing through on their way north; that made him regret the further necessity of traveling only at night. But Kumbu's sensational vanishing act had made national news, and his furry little friend was more of a celebrity than ever. Anyone spotted traveling with a chimpanzee now would attract far too much attention.

Still, it had been a relief to see the last of Miami. To get moving after a day cooped up in that crowded little motel room. To do *something* at last, after hours of wondering what to do.

Suddenly Jane turned to look at him.

"You're more comfortable in that loincloth, aren't you, Wilbur, than in regular clothes."

He blinked at her in surprise, and she hastily went on.

"I'm sorry; it must seem like I'm saying that to be mean. I'm not. It's just that— a lot of things I've said and thought about you have been unkind, simply because I didn't understand. How genuine you are, I mean. Like wearing leopard. If I hadn't heard the story I wouldn't have understood, and even hearing it, well, it wouldn't matter how many times I heard it if I didn't understand that it actually happened just that way. You were really there, standing in that moment when the dead leopard's spirit spoke to you and told you to wear its skin. To anyone who's never stood in a moment that real, I can tell you, it seems positively unreal! And that's why I never— that's why I'm— right now, it's why I feel . . . I owe you an apology, Wilbur. Because it's just that real, this feeling that— oh, never mind. I can't get it honestly, properly out, the way I . . ." She trailed off. "You can't possibly . . ."

Wilbur smiled. "But I do."

She stared at him. "Now you're teasing me. You can't . . ."

"But I do. I understand exactly how you feel because, well, like you said: it's real. It's the nature of this Gift, you see. It can't grasp anything that isn't utterly, solidly real. So much of what you've said and thought I haven't understood. I've been waiting . . . for it to get this real."

She glanced down at the furry sleeping form between them. "And I've been jealous. Jealous of your Gift. I studied them for so many years, our primate relatives. And here you come along and spend a few days— a few days lost in the jungle— and come away with this amazing Gift, this Gift of perfect understanding—"

"Oh, no. Not perfect. A few days of practice couldn't do that. Kumbu teaches me every day. But he himself lacks teachers, real adult chimps who learned from teachers themselves, a full circle of teachers, as they do in the wild, learning from the whole extended family. We teach each other what we can. But both of us really need,

need and want to get back to the forest, where it's not just the other chimps but the whole circle of species, plants and animals and moon and sky, that teaches us."

He fell silent for a moment. When she didn't answer, he went on.

"I've been hoping, you know . . . I've been hoping you would come with us."

She stared again. "Do you— do you think I could learn . . . I mean I know you were born with it, this special Gift, but— do you think other people can ever learn . . ."

She stopped, tears glittering in her eyes, and he looked back at her for a long moment in the moonlight. The car sensibly kept itself on the road.

"Why else do you think I received this Gift?" he asked, and then finally looked back at the highway. "Surely not for myself alone?"

Again she didn't answer, but he could feel her deep, quiet joy, flooding up from wherever she kept it repressed, constrained, under constant pressure.

"Even Kyle can learn it," he added with a grin, and felt all her skepticism returning. "You know it's the only thing that can save us. Humanity's in real trouble, with the planet's ability to care for us declining so fast. Humanity needs the Gift. And that's our real mission. Now, at this very moment. Can't you feel how fortunate we are to be chosen?"

Kumbu let out a little bubble of gas right then and shifted in his sleep, leaning this time on Jane. Wilbur chuckled and glanced across at her with a tender smile— and saw her looking back with precisely the same smile. The tears were overflowing now, and not just Jane's.

She sighed and leaned experimentally toward Wilbur, past the vertical, past all of her rigidity and reluctance and resistance, all the way over until her cheek touched his shoulder. Then, little by little, he felt her allowing it to rest there.

Grandmother Min climbed slowly, but with an ease and assurance born of a lifetime of climbing trees. She felt lighter than she'd felt in months. Maybe years. Her Gift hummed with the feeling that something, somewhere, was perfectly all right. Even better— whatever it was, it had something to do with Kumbu.

The sun hung low in the west; it was almost time. And now that Kumbu's Gift was strong enough for him to join the Gathering of Gifts along with Brother Tanzar, the slowly gathering colors of the coming sunset gave her new strength for the long climb.

Looking up, she saw the faces of her friends and relatives smiling affectionately down from the upper branches where they waited for her. Here and there a pair of chimps groomed each other, searching through thick dark fur for savory snacks.

Just below Min, matching her handhold for handhold, foothold for foothold, her beloved spirit-daughter Dar climbed after her into the heights of the new Granddaddy Tree.

Two days ago the clan had reached the distant forest haven that Dar and Min had dreamed for them, deep in the mountains where they had their choice of towering Granddaddies whenever they wanted to talk things over. The forest around them was wise and old, so high in the mountain sky that the stars too perched in its branches to tell stories and discuss cosmological affairs with the moon.

Two youngers were joining their elders in the chosen Granddaddy Tree for the first time this evening, old enough at last to listen rather than talk: Kri, the daughter of Flor, and Kuk's son Molo. Min reached the branch where the two of them sat together, quiet and watchful, and kept climbing.

Mabu moved aside with a gesture of respect as Min approached the branch where he leaned against the Granddaddy's trunk. She touched him in the center of his back and kept on climbing.

Guma watched with a quizzical smile as she reached the crotch where he and Uncle Noko rested, the highest occupied point in the splendid old tree. She smiled at them each in turn and kept climbing.

Three branches higher she found a pair of limbs that were almost twins, allowing her to sit comfortably on one while leaning back on the other. She plucked a fern from the fork where the two limbs split, inserted it in her mouth and drew it out between her teeth, tossing the naked stem away and munching on the mouthful of delicate leaves it left behind.

Dar settled respectfully on a branch below Guma and Noko, gazing off down the mountain in the direction of their old home territory.

It had taken the clan six days to make the trek. After traveling hard for the first four days, for the last two they had moved at a leisurely pace, with many digressions to explore possible sources of food and water. Min and Dar had declared that the danger they'd been fleeing was no longer a threat, though many of the chimps refused to believe the outlandish story they told.

Why exactly they had made the journey at all was difficult to convey to some of the younger chimps, especially the mothers still suckling babies. But a gesture toward Min and Dar— seen together, more often than not— was all it took to quell their doubts. Dar preferred to maintain a dignified quiet, but Min, in the right mood, delighted in telling the whole tale of Kumbu, Brother Tanzar, and the paleskinned poacher who had taken it all too personally. The story came with a moral, of course, and she often told it when someone was acting "like a paleskin."

In time, she knew, it would be able to compete with any of the embroidered deeds and adventures of mythical ancestors passed down to Brapa by the long-gone storytellers of the clan. No one ever knew if she had simply made up the ending— how the snare-setter had returned and, instead of releasing the trapped poacher, had taken him away in chains to be sold as a slave— or if she had sat meditating in solitude until her Gift revealed it to her.

Even at this moment, Min knew, high in the branches of the Granddaddy Tree, the story was passing reverently from ear to ear in a whisper, lest she or Dar overhear.

What do you think, Noko? Guma said, elbowing Uncle Noko in the ribs. *Have we not led our beloved companions into an absolute paradise for chimpanzees? Has our wise leadership not once again proven beneficent, even providential, for these trusting young ones who gratefully followed us into the unknown? Do you not feel a deep gratification and satisfaction in the excellence of our seasoned wisdom and courage? Don't you—*

But his noble and eloquent speech was interrupted by a salvo of broken twigs from below, accompanied by hoots and jeers, quaking the entire treetop.

Throw the bums in the mud! Mabu called, climbing for a higher vantage point and breaking off more twigs to toss.

Dunk their heads in the waterfall, cried Flor, completely forgetting that her young one was listening.

Send them down to bring us some snacks, Yago snorted, scratching his back against his limb. *That will teach them a lesson!*

Start them out as Brapa's apprentices, snickered Tunga, *till they get their story straight!*

Grandmother Min! trilled Shan. *What should we do with these impertinent youngsters? Tell us!*

Yes, tell us! half a dozen voices cried.

Min, who was pretending to take a nap in her comfortable swaying seat, opened one eye and surveyed the general silliness below.

Grandmother, Guma pleaded. *Have mercy! I had no idea your majestic exaltedness was up there listening to my foolish babble. Please, be lenient with your humble inferior!*

I will consider it, Min answered quietly. *All right— I have considered it! From now on, I will expect you to bring each female in the clan a tasty flower every time you catch yourself imagining that you are better than they are, merely because you are bigger and stronger.*

A deafening burst of merriment rang out, gently bouncing her twin branches and nearly shaking her loose. Guma hung his head, but he was grinning like the rest.

Molo and Kri, the two youngers, looked at each other and giggled uncertainly. Neither one was sure exactly what was going on, but they wouldn't have missed it for anything. Both were secretly glad they didn't have to undergo their initiation into these complicated adult mysteries alone. They eagerly awaited their chance to discuss it later between themselves, and maybe approach their mothers for advice.

The Granddaddy Tree gradually stopped trembling with the laughter of chimpanzees, and the chimps started grooming one another again, waiting for sunset. One or two curled up in a nook so comfortable that they fell asleep.

Grandmother, young Kri ventured at length. *Please, what have you learned from the Gatherings of Gifts about our human brother and his mission so far? I try to reach to the west, holding Brother Tanzar's face in my mind, and I sense only confusion— mine, probably. I am not so advanced yet in the art of concentration.*

Min smiled down through the branches at the earnest young face. *All is well with Brother Tanzar,* she said. *He and Kumbu are together, and learning much from each other. And they have helpers— other humans who* have chosen to share Tanzar's mission. They still have obstacles to overcome, but I sense that these will not be so difficult, now that they are together.

Then she frowned. *No, that is not exactly what I mean. The more difficult these obstacles are to overcome, the stronger Kumbu and Tanzar will grow. Because through these obstacles they are learning to develop their Gifts. Learning that two can be infinitely stronger and wiser than one. Learning that their Gifts are in fact not separate at all, as they themselves appear to be.*

Uncle Noko bent his head to one side, almost touching his shoulder, stretching his neck. *This is something I knew*, he said. *But I have never heard it said quite like that.* Then he bent the other way.

I told you, Min said. *Kumbu and Tanzar are growing wise. Even at this distance, they are teaching me. When they return to us, we will all have much to learn. Just as it is our responsibility to teach our young to use their Gifts to learn, they have an equal responsibility to share with us in turn what they have learned. It is an exchange of Gifts.*

The whole universe is an exchange of Gifts! murmured Dar.

And the secret I am learning in my meditations, Min replied, *is that it is all one Gift. One Gift, given by Life to every species alike. A beautiful, intricate spiderweb of relationship that connects us all, whether we're aware of it or not.* Then she fell silent and, after a time, dozed off.

All one Gift. Molo and Kri pondered that as the sun sank lower and finally touched the western ridgecrest. *All one Gift.*

When their elders linked minds to initiate the Gathering of Gifts, the two youngers found it hard to concentrate deeply enough to keep up with the discussion. And what they were able to hear was even harder to understand. But even after the sun had disappeared behind the mountains, when they had followed their elders down the tree and woven their nests for the night, Grandmother Min's words kept coming back to them. *All one Gift.*

Both Molo and Kri woke up in the night remembering their first time up in the Granddaddy Tree with the elders of the clan. Those three simple, mysterious words still echoed inside them like a brand-new rhythm beaten on an old hollow log.

All one Gift.

THE END

How to Help the Chimpanzees

Chimpanzees are an Endangered Species, under constant threat from poachers and encroaching human development. The "Society for the Preservation of Wanzanayian Primate Habitat" is fictional, as is the country of Wanzanayi itself. But the following organizations are real and working hard to help the chimpanzees and other wild primates survive. Please support them.

International Primate Protection League: **www.ippl.org**
Jane Goodall Institute: **www.janegoodall.org**
People for the Ethical Treatment of Animals: **www.peta.org** ,
    www.circuses.com, **www.nomoremonkeybusiness.com**
Save the Chimps: **www.savethechimps.org**
Project Release & Restitution: **www.releasechimps.org**
Animal Legal Defense Fund: **www.aldf.org**
Animal Welfare Institute: **www.awionline.org**
Allied Effort to Save Other Primates: **www.aesop-project.org**
Animal Concerns: **www.animalconcerns.org**
Primate Conservation Inc.: **www.primate.org**
Species Survival Network: **www.ssn.org**
African Conservation Foundation: **www.africanconservation.com**
Ngamba Island Chimpanzee Sanctuary (Uganda):
    www.ngambaisland.org
Centre for Education, Research and Conservation of Primates and
    Nature (Nigeria): **www.cercopan.org**
Chimfunshi Wildlife Orphanage (Zambia): **www.chimfunshi.org.za**
Chimpanzee Rehabilitation Trust (Gambia): **www.chimprehab.com**
H.E.L.P. International (Congo Republic): **www.help-primates.org**
In Defense of Animals—Africa (Cameroon): **www.ida-africa.org**
Budongo Forest Project (Uganda): **www.budongo.org**
Limbe Wildlife Centre (Cameroon): **www.limbewildlife.org**
Wildlife Conservation Society (Congo Republic): **www.wcs-congo.org**
Center for Orangutan and Chimpanzee Conservation (Florida):
    www.prime-apes.org
Primarily Primates (Texas): **www.primarilyprimates.org**
Mindy's Memory Primate Sanctuary (Oklahoma):
    www.mindysmem.org
Primate Rescue Center (Kentucky): **www.primaterescue.org**
Chimpanzee Collaboratory: **www.chimpcollaboratory.org**

Author's Afterword

The main premise of *Free Ralph!*— that chimpanzees are capable of conscious evolution, and by extension, so are we— might make some readers uncomfortable. I can't blame them; the chimpanzees I read about in Jane Goodall's *In the Shadow of Man* showed no sign of the inner life I have imagined for mine.

But since Dr. Goodall's book was published in 1971, both chimpanzees and gorillas have been taught to communicate with humans using American Sign Language. A chimpanzee named Washoe first came to my attention when I read of a message she signed to a visitor: "Get me out of here!" A gorilla named Koko became famous after she asked in sign language for her own kitten. Photographs of her tenderly caring for her kitten appeared in a book called *Koko's Kitten*. And while working on *Free Ralph!*, I heard about new research with bonobo chimps at Iowa's Great Ape Trust, where they are learning to communicate with the aid of a touch-sensitive computer screen.

I also recently came across the intriguing story of some monkeys who have taken advantage of their protected status in Kenya to take over the food supply of the village of Nachu. They come at dawn to invade the village fields, devouring corn, beans, potatoes and other crops— and harassing and mocking the village women, who traditionally do the farming.

"When we come to chase the monkeys away, we are dressed in trousers and hats, so that we look like men," Lucy Njeri told B.B.C. News. "But the monkeys can tell the difference and they don't run away from us . . . They just ignore us and continue to steal the crops." According to the women, the monkeys add insult to injury by making "sexually explicit gestures" at them.

My imaginary reality might not be so far off, after all.

A steady stream of recent books has explored the topic of animal consciousness, written by scientists and researchers like Jeffrey Moussaieff Masson and Marc Bekoff as well as psychics and empaths. Though publicizing such books is one of the more enjoyable parts of my "day job," I confess that I have not read them. But any work that helps to change the current disastrous attitude of "dominion over nature" is a hopeful sign.

To me, the value of preserving all of Creation's species is as obvious as it was to Noah. The crisis which threatens the entire natural world needs our urgent attention before the chimpanzees and many more of our endangered relatives are lost forever— and we humans find ourselves next on the endangered list.

It's a hopeful sign that science is beginning to support this view. But I wonder if anything short of a divine revelation akin to Noah's can move us to change our short-sighted and self-centered ways. The will to preserve the wild beauty and integrity of nature springs naturally from a deep reverence for Creation, whether rooted in belief in a Creator or not. I pray *Free Ralph!* might play a small part in such an awakening. And I pray it comes in time.

To honor those who are already aware and doing their part, I am dedicating this book to my parents, Carol and Doug Wingeier. They exemplify to me the other kind of Christian: the kind who understand, unlike the ones in the story, that keeping Creation intact is far more important than any argument over its origins. Though I have taken a different spiritual path, through them I have come to appreciate how much human evolution owes to the Christianity of compassion rather than judgement.

I am also very much obliged to my friends and family members who read the story and helped it to "evolve," and most of all to my wife Dawn for her suggestions and support. Thank you all.

I owe a special thanks to Tom Brakefield, the renowned wildlife photographer, who graciously allowed me to use the image on the front cover. This young chimp has hung framed on my bedroom wall ever since Dawn clipped him from a calendar over a decade ago. Undoubtedly he played a subliminal role in my story's inspiration.

One final note: I have never visited central Africa, so the nation of Wanzanayi and its capital, Wanzani City, are wholly my invention. The characters and backdrops of the scenes that take place there are therefore bound to be inaccurate, but are not intended to be offensive. I apologize if any of my readers find them so.

On page 227 is a list of resources for helping the chimpanzees survive. Thank you for playing your part.

Stephen Wing

P.S. If you enjoyed the story, but wonder what happens next, stay tuned. A sequel is on the way.

About the Author

Stephen Wing gave up a 12-year career as a hitchhiker in 1990 when he met his wife, Dawn Aura, and settled in Atlanta. He now works as a newsletter editor and recycling coordinator at New Leaf Distributing Co., a wholesale distributor of metaphysical and holistic literature. He is a senior editor of New Leaf's magazine *Evolve!*

A lifelong writer, he is the author of *Four-Wheeler & Two-Legged: Poems* (Southeastern Front, 1992, now out of print) and *Crossing the Expressway: Poems from the Open Road*, a record of his travels by thumb (Dolphins & Orchids Publishing, 2001).

Other writings include *In the Presence of the Disappeared*, a chapbook-length poem about a visit with a peace delegation to Colombia, South America, and *Proof of the Miraculous: Campfire Poetry from the Rainbow Gatherings*, documenting 25 years of countercultural gatherings in the National Forests. An unfinished epic novel, *Last Testament: A Melodrama of the Post-Petroleum Era*, is unfolding in serial installments on his web site (www.StephenWing.com), where many of his poems, articles and essays may be found.

Wing has served a variety of causes as a writer, editor, and activist. Some current projects are "Earth Poetry with Stephen Wing," an ecologically-themed poetry presentation; Gaia-Love Graffiti, a collection of original bumper stickers (www.GaiaLoveGraffiti.com); and interfaith celebrations of the Solstices and Equinoxes in Atlanta.

In 2006, he became a cancer survivor and celebrated his fiftieth birthday.

About Wind Eagle Press

Wind Eagle Press was founded to educate people about the ecological crisis facing this planet and what we can do to turn it around. If you enjoyed *Free Ralph!*, please pass the word to others who might be interested. Among other benefits, your assistance will help to ensure that we'll be able to publish the story's sequel when the time comes. You can order more copies by using the order form on the next page, or by visiting our web site, www.WindEaglePress.com. If you maintain an email network, please feel free to spread our web address around. Other ways to help are listed below the order form. Thanks for your support!

About the paper

The forests of planet Earth—an irreplaceable source of fresh air, fresh water and fresh topsoil—are disappearing rapidly due to shortsighted over-harvesting, mostly for paper. Though recycled paper is making strides, and tree-free papers like kenaf and hemp are coming along, paper made from tree-pulp is still the norm in publishing. Wind Eagle Press is committed to preserving our forests by using paper with the highest post-consumer recycled content we can afford. Your purchase of this book helps to support the recycled paper industry. We (and the trees) appreciate it.

About the typeface

Prospera, the font used for the body text of this book, is a digital typeface initially developed in 1986 by Peter Fraterdeus (www.fraterdeus.com) with the assistance of a grant from the National Endowment for the Arts. It was one of the first original type designs to be produced in its entirety on a personal computer, in this case an Apple Macintosh. Its first appearance in a printed book was Stephen Wing's first book, *Four-Wheeler & Two-Legged*. Updated and revised in the early 1990s, Prospera is available as a PostScript for Macintosh and Windows font from Alphabets Fonts (www.alphabets. com) and other quality font sources.

ORDER FORM

Please send _____ copies of *Free Ralph!*

Name: _____

Address: _____

City: _____ **State:** _____ **Zip:** _____

Telephone: _____

Email address: _____

Price: $14.99 (U.S.) per book, plus:

Sales tax: 7% for books shipped to addresses in Georgia

Shipping: $3.00 for one book, $1.00 each for additional copies

Mail orders to: Wind Eagle Press
P.O. Box 5379
Atlanta GA 31107

Online orders: via PayPal at www.WindEaglePress.com

Optional: Please tell us how *Free Ralph!* came to your attention:

WIND EAGLE PRESS

APPRECIATES YOUR BUSINESS!

IF YOU ENJOYED THIS BOOK, PLEASE HELP SPREAD
THE WORD TO OTHERS WHO MIGHT BE INTERESTED.
OUR READERS ARE OUR ONLY SALES FORCE!

✷ REQUEST IT AT YOUR LOCAL LIBRARY
✷ BUY EXTRA COPIES AS GIFTS
✷ WRITE AN ONLINE REVIEW
✷ LINK TO US ON YOUR WEB SITE OR BLOG
✷ EMAIL A LINK TO YOUR NETWORK
✷ YOUR IDEA HERE!